RED TURBAN WHITE HORSE

My Sister's Hurricane Wedding

Published by Scholastic India Pvt. Ltd.
A subsidiary of Scholastic Inc., New York, 10012 (USA).
Publishers since 1920, with international operations in Canada,
Australia, New Zealand, the United Kingdom, India, and Hong Kong.

For information regarding permission, write to:
Scholastic India Pvt. Ltd.
A-27, Ground Floor, Bharti Sigma Centre
Infocity -1, Sector 34, Gurgaon 122001 (India)

First edition: May 2013

ISBN-13: 978-93-5103-003-4

Printed at: MicroPrint India, New Delhi-110020

NANDINI BAJPAI

Red Turban
White Horse

My Sister's Hurricane Wedding

SCHOLASTIC
New York Toronto London Auckland
Sydney New Delhi Hong Kong

For my mother, Pushpa Raman Chauhan, and my daughter, Anika.

I'm lucky to be the link between you two.

Treasure—in Ink and Gold

'You'd like to open your safety deposit box?' The bank teller looked perplexed at my request—it wasn't every day a teenager asked for access to the bank vault. 'Do you have your key, Ms Kapoor?'

Our tiny bank branch in Westbury, Massachusetts was as far from Diagon Alley as you could get, but this reminded me of the Gringotts scene in Harry Potter. Except the teller didn't have pointy ears and needle teeth. A hysterical laugh formed in my chest.

Does Mr Harry Potter have his key?

'Right here.' I dug up the simple key—not goblin made, alas—from my newly acquired Kate Spade handbag. 'Please call me Mini.'

The teller came around the counter. 'This way, Mini,' she said.

I followed, shortening my stride to stay behind her, and watched as she unlocked two massive doors—one with steel bars, the other studded with gears and bolts—then followed her into the strongroom. It was insanely solid. Dementors would have had trouble breaking in.

'What number?' she asked.

She found the matching key in a metallic drawer, and read the numbers off of the deposit boxes until she found mine. Both keys had to be inserted and turned simultaneously for the box to open. She pulled the box—long, metallic, coffin-like—out of the locker and handed it to me.

'You can open it in there.' The door she pointed to led into a tiny closet-sized room.

I shut the narrow door, deposit box clutched tight—and took a deep, deep breath in the tiny space. Probably exhausting its entire oxygen supply, for I was suddenly breathless.

I lifted the lid.

Oh. My. Three hundred and thirty million gods.

Jewelry boxes with clear lids stared back at me, the brilliant yellow of Indian gold gleaming richly through them.

Vinnie was never going to believe this!

Yashasvini, my older sister, was the reason I was standing in that bank vault. Always the steady, serious type, Vinnie had recently lost her head, fallen in love, and was getting married in sixty days. Also, she had just graduated medical school and was starting residency—which meant she had no time to plan her wedding.

Add to this the fact that our dad, still in shock over the

whole thing, said he was not paying for any of it. His five-year fiscal plan involved frugal living and aggressive saving in the year between Vinnie's graduation and me going off to college; spending lavishly on a wedding did not enter into it in any way, shape, or form.

But getting married she was, and whatever the budget, I was going to make sure that my sister looked fabulous—Indian style.

The only problem? There's one thing an Indian bride can't do without—gold. Twenty-two karat gold. And a couple of ounces of that stuff probably cost more than my second-hand car.

Not to worry, Dad said—evidently Mom had left us some jewelry, information no one bothered to share with *me* before—just take the safety deposit box key, and check it out. Which brings me back to our friendly neighborhood Gringotts.

I untied the strings of a velvet pouch and emptied its glittering contents onto the table. More jewelry. I *knew* this stuff. Some of it was heirloom old—passed down from my nani. Some of it was new. Kind of. Mom had it made for Vinnie and me.

I opened a box. A note in Mom's neat handwriting was tucked under the necklace. I touched the familiar, well-loved pen strokes with one finger. I could pick out Mom's note from a million scraps of paper. The inky cursive—written, I was sure, with Mom's ancient Sheaffer pen—was an unexpected treasure.

The necklace with it was beautiful too—a dainty kundan piece with an old-fashioned tassel clasp. Mom's design. The date was seven years ago. Only two months before Mom ... my throat was suddenly tight.

That's for your wedding, Mini.

For something so delicate it felt heavy. The price of gold back then was not astronomical apparently. Talk about return on investment. Well played, Mom, well played. What with the recession sinking the stock market, you probably beat the FTSE, the NASDAQ and the Dow Jones combined.

I opened another box. Earrings with missing pairs. Broken chains. All gold though. The note in it said matter-of-factly: *Junk—sell it if you girls ever need money.* I had to smile. Mom was nothing if not practical.

I closed the lid on the broken jewelry and picked up the necklace Mom had designed for Vinnie. What would Mom think of a simple civil ceremony with twenty guests? The answer to that was staring back at me. She didn't save and scrape for such kick-ass jewelry if she didn't want a proper Punjabi wedding. That's what she would have liked. Lots of family, food, flowers, music. Vinnie in a gorgeous lehenga. Her groom in a red turban on a white horse.

No way was that going to happen, the way things were.

I closed the lid on the necklace with the peacock pendant. Maybe ...

I bundled the jewelry into my messenger bag, and

zipped it up carefully. Stepping out of the tiny room, I knocked on the glass pane between the teller station and the vault and gestured that I was done.

The younger teller, clearly Indian and recently married—going by her glass bangles and the red sindoor powder in her neat, straight-down-the-center parting—sized me up in one glance. Tall, by Indian standards—thanks to Dad's genes. Lean—thanks to cross-country running and the fact that Beeji, my grandmother, who never cooked anything I didn't immediately want to eat, had left the country four years ago. Long, dark hair, olive skin, brown eyes—pretty, I've been told. I've been mistaken for South American/North African/Middle Eastern, but *not* by other Indians.

I smiled back, and wondered if she'd bring up region, caste, or marital prospects.

'You're Gujrati?' she asked. There it was.

'Punjabi,' I said, apologetically.

'Oh!' she said. 'In senior year?'

'Starting in fall,' I acknowledged. Good guess.

'You're Mr Kapoor's daughter!' She was happy to have placed me. 'Your sister is called Winnie, right?' she said. 'She's doing medical, I heard?'

'She just graduated in May,' I said.

'Very good! You must be a good student too, like Winnie?' She looked to me for confirmation.

I resisted the urge to tell her that it was Vinnie with a V, like My Cousin Vinnie, not Winnie with a W, like Winnie the

9

Pooh. 'I'm OK, I guess.' Something made me add, 'She's getting married. In two months!'

'That's great,' she said, genuinely happy. 'Is she marrying an Indian boy?'

'South Indian,' I said.

She nodded in sympathy. Gujratis and Punjabis, though different, are at least both not *South* Indian. 'Well, it's better than you know ...' her spread hands encompassed the plethora of humanity that is not Indian at all. 'He's a doctor too?' she asked, and smiled her approval when I nodded.

That is almost as good as being Gujrati!

'It would have made your mummy happy,' she said. Apparently nothing is a secret from bank tellers at the intersection of Route 30 and 27. 'If there's anything I can do, only ask,' she added, awkward yet sincere. 'OK?'

'OK,' I promised, but automatically stuck her offer in the forget-about-it-zone of my brain.

They always meant well, the people who wanted to help because they knew about Mom—but they just totally embarrassed me instead. The extra weight in my handbag weighed down more than my shoulder as I walked to the car park, but my mood lifted as I caught sight of what was waiting there—my one-week-old pride and joy on wheels—my Mini Cooper Hardtop S.

Six-speed, four cylinders, hyper blue metallic color, black panther interior, white roof, white side mirrors, and two white racing stripes on the hood. And ridiculous amounts of insurance.

One week old for me, that was. The Mini Cooper was really

a 2005 model, but it totally rocked.

***

'She was always so level-headed, you know?' Dad said. He was still grappling with the notion that Vinnie was getting married—whether he liked it or not. 'No dating in high school or anything. I never expected her to rush into something like this. She should be thinking of her career. She's much too young to get married!'

He looked like his hair had gained some extra greys since Vinnie announced her engagement. That and the worry lines on his brow were the only physical changes in him in the last decade.

'Dad, she's twenty-five!' I said. It was hard work being a Vinnie apologist.

Given that my parents' loving marriage of twenty years was a match made in the Times of India matrimonial section, I didn't expect Dad to understand about dating. Mom was a pretty and popular good girl type, who only crushed on guys from afar. And Dad was seriously uncool in high school. I mean, dork-glasses, skinny-frame, peach-fuzz-mustache uncool. Let's face it. They needed the help. Vinnie did not.

But from sophomore year all Vinnie thought about was grades—and Mom. There was no time for dating when Mom, in the final stages of cancer, was fading away before her eyes. That was also the reason she didn't want to waste time now.

'I tried to explain it to her. And you know what she said?' Dad was still going on. 'She said there will never be a good time. First she had seven years of medical school, now there's three years of residency, and then she'll have her oncology fellowship. She said if she's old enough to help deliver a baby she's old enough to get married.'

'She's kind of right,' I pointed out.

'I don't know …' He scowled at the picture of Vinnie and Manish that I had framed and set on the mantel—Vinnie in her graduation gown, and Manish in a suit and tie with his arm around her—both glowing with happiness. 'He's from *Bangalore* …,' he paused, 'they're … you know.'

'What?' I asked, and watched with amusement as he tried to articulate his misgivings without coming off as insufferably North Indian.

'They're …' he spluttered, 'they're just …'

'Not Punjabi,' I said. Yeah, that was it.

Dad nodded, worry lines etching deeper.

'She doesn't care about that,' I said. 'It's not like we live in Punjab or something.'

'She got into the Honors program in Medical Education at Northwestern,' Dad said, changing tactics. It was true. My sister, the genius, got accepted into the seven-year, straight-from-high-school medical program for gifted students—Mom had known before she passed away that Vinnie would be a doctor. 'And he went to state college.'

'*Dad!*' I said. 'It's not like he isn't super smart—he got into Feinberg, didn't he? The same school as Vinnie!'

They had met at medical school. Manish was a year ahead of Vinnie, and they clicked because they were both from the Boston

12

area. Their first date was an MLB baseball game where they were the only two people in Wrigley Stadium rooting for the Red Sox. I heard about him from Vinnie off and on, of course, but I had no idea how serious they were. When Dad and I went to Chicago for her graduation and Vinnie told us they were engaged, it was a seismic-level shock to our family—but I could see Manish made her happy, and that was good enough for me. Dad, meanwhile, was still struggling to comprehend our new reality.

'She's putting him before everything,' Dad said. 'She was going to come back here, and now …'

We had always expected that Vinnie would come back to Boston for her residency—there are so many good hospitals here. But when she placed at University of Chicago Medical Center on match day, the same place that Manish was a second-year resident, it was clear that things had changed.

'Dad, it's natural, isn't it?' I said.

'And he's allergic to dogs.' Dad played the trump card.

I sighed, my hand going instinctively to the furry head planted on my knee. Our dog Yogi was never more than five feet from me when I was home.

'Who knows what else runs in the family,' Dad mumbled ominously.

'We're the ones with the dodgy genes,' I said. 'And Manish doesn't care.'

'Well I'm not paying for an expensive wedding out of *your* college fund,' Dad said.

'It doesn't have to be expensive,' I said. 'But we have to do *something* special—it's Vinnie's wedding!'

'It's not just the money,' Dad said. 'She doesn't have time to plan it. I don't have the bandwidth to do it either—you know how things are at work!'

'I have time!' I said. 'I could do it.' It was true. I had over two months of summer vacation.

'Nonsense,' he said. 'You have SAT prep, and Math tutoring, and college visits, and college essays. And you're not responsible enough to plan a whole wedding—you're seventeen!'

I bristled at the words but it was no use arguing with him right now.

'Let's see what Vinnie says,' I said, very calm. I would be a model of responsibility and he would see sense. 'I've got Kumon, and then I've got to walk the dog.'

Mystery Guy

'I am not interested in doing my math.'

The kid's solemn eyes could have melted the iceberg that sank the Titanic. For a five-year-old she articulated every word ridiculously well. But what could you expect from a preschooler who knows multiplication?

'Come on, Kalie, it'll be fun,' I wheedled, but she darted out from behind her desk and made for the door. I chased her down, tackled her and carried her back to her worksheet.

Where's her nanny? I mouthed at Sona. She was checking algebra worksheets for a bunch of pimply middle-schoolers.

Sona shrugged. Nannies that dumped their kids at math tutoring and took off for a coffee next door were not new to her.

I didn't sign up to be summer camp counselor like half my friends because I didn't want to wrangle teeny kids. Who knew that math tutoring would be full of them? More than half the kids who went to our Kumon were elementary age or under, and Asian kids—Indian, Chinese, and any country in between were heavily represented. I felt bad for them, doomed to daily math torture for all of summer vacation. At least I got paid for it. It paid surprisingly well to spoon-feed math to overscheduled tykes.

My sister Vinnie and I are nothing alike, but we do have math in common. Vinnie is small, springy, and athletic, and I totally suck at team sports. In high school she played every sport she could fit around her course load—field hockey, soccer, volleyball. I stuck to cross country, art, and drama club—painting sets, designing costumes, and putting make-up on oompa-loompas, munchkins, and the lost boys of Peter Pan. But we're both math whizzes. She always was, and I became one because Dad would have been crushed if I wasn't, so I tried extra hard.

But I don't have the same nerd gene they do, the kind which makes them drop everything to watch Nova specials with total attention. I'd rather watch reruns of Project Runway instead.

Kalie slaved through her multiplication tables, to both our relief.

'Gimme five,' I said, and turned her sad-faced Kumon logo into a smiley face. She slapped her dimpled hand into mine and ran over to the corkboard that said 'Today's Good Job!' and pinned her worksheet to it.

'Hi Mini Kapoor,' said an apple-cheeked seven-year-old. Wide hazel eyes gazed into mine, pools of unquestioning trust.

'Hi Rahul Singh,' I said. Rahul, my favorite student, had no problem in doing his math. His mom told me he had trouble relating to his teachers at school, due to his Asperger's, but Rahul and I got along just fine—probably because Math was

16

his favorite subject. No surprise; Rahul breezed through his worksheet wicked fast, and sat smiling at me as I marked his sheet—he had gotten everything correct.

'Is this getting a little too easy, Rahul?' I asked.

'Yes,' he nodded solemnly. He tapped his digital wristwatch. 'Only took three minutes and forty-two seconds for twenty-four problems.'

'That is fast!' I said. It was definitely time to move him up to something more challenging. I walked over to the huddle of moms and nannies in the waiting area and searched for Rahul's mom. Some of the Indian moms were in the middle of an animated discussion about the merits of the latest Bollywood blockbuster, starring Koyal Khanna, the newest sensation to hit the silver screen.

'But have you seen her dancing in that song 'Meri Jawani'? Supeeerb, I tell you!'

'They should pair her with Shahrukh in her next movie.'

'What are you saying? Shahrukh will look like her grandfather!'

'Uh, uh!' I cleared my throat, not wanting to interrupt their conversation.

'Is everything OK?' Preet asked. Preet Singh was cheerful and dedicated, and completely unfazed by her son's special needs.

'Oh, yes, super,' I said. 'I was actually wondering if we could skip ahead, move him up a notch. Rahul is ready I think. He can do this without even trying.'

'Oh!' she beamed. 'Yes, if you think he's ready, then I've no problem.'

'Yes, he's ready,' I said. What a lovely hand-embroidered shirt she had on, I thought, and the woman beside her too. Gujrati mirror work, if I wasn't mistaken. I hadn't seen so many Indian outfits since my mother's one-year memorial.

So many Indian outfits! I looked around the waiting room—moms in jeans, moms in salwars, moms with ipods and books, moms with babies and toddlers—but they were all South Asian! If someone here didn't know everything about desi wedding vendors I don't know who would.

Meanwhile, Rahul had grabbed his mom by the hand and was tugging her towards the door.

'Preet!' I said. 'I had a question …'

She looked at me inquiringly.

'My sister is getting married in two months,' I blurted out. 'I have to help her organize everything and my dad … he's not much help. I don't even know where to start. Do you know how to find a good wedding decorator, or DJ, or caterer?'

'Your mom will take care of it, no?' she asked.

'She …' I squared my shoulders. 'She passed away. Years ago.'

Suddenly all the chatter around me hushed. Crap. What a dumb idea this was. Great way to identify myself as the clueless, motherless ABCD freakshow. I wanted their help, I didn't want their pity.

The first one to speak was not one of the Indian moms but

my boss Sona Saxena.

'Mini,' she said. 'I'm so sorry. But don't worry, ya? We'll help you.'

The moms unfroze into a chorus of me-toos. It was hard to make sense of all the excited chatter since everyone was talking at once, but apparently Preet's uncle owned a restaurant and catered at very reasonable prices, Pinky's sister had a bridal boutique in Cambridge, and the Srinivases' niece got married last month and they knew all the best wedding vendors.

Wow, they were more useful than two days of Googling. I grabbed a handful of Kumon of Westbury visiting cards from Sona's desk and wrote my email address on each one. 'Please email me any leads. Thank you!' I said, handing them out.

'I know a lighting guy, honey,' Kalie's nanny piped up unexpectedly. I promptly gave her a card too.

Time to get back to work. When I left work an hour later, no-nonsense Sona Saxena gave me a hug. 'I don't want you to stress,' she said. 'If you need time off work, just tell me. And if you're not sure of anything, just ask. We'll help you.' I walked off to my precious Mini. I'd look into their leads, of course. Their quick offer of help had nearly downed my automatic defenses. Nearly.

***

Yogi pounced on me when I got home—all licks and wagging tail. From the reception I got you'd think he'd been locked up all day instead of having been walked once already, and had Dad for company all day long.

'Alright, alright,' I told the beast. 'At least let me get changed.'

I got out of my responsible math tutor outfit—dark wash Seven for All Mankind jeans, dip-dyed t-shirt from Forever 21, teal Converse lace-ups—and changed into my new Lululemon capris and crop top. Over that I threw on a ripped t-shirt made by my friend Jackie—she had dyed a regular cotton tee, shredded its sides into strips and knotted them to fit me perfectly. If I had to walk the creature in that heat wave and get all sweaty, I planned to do it feeling comfortable and looking fine. Good thing my math tutoring, Etsy shop, and job at Amy's brought in enough cash to support my fashion habits. God knows Dad didn't give me enough of an allowance to buy anything decent.

The capris were a weathered purple. Mom would have called it *baighani*, and the top was a soft vintage tea-washed pink— Jackie is a genius with color. Both set off my honey brown skin tone nicely. I slathered on the moisturizer, the sunscreen, and the bug spray and added a slick of lip gloss, just in case.

The whimpering had turned into deafening barking. Yogi was clearly losing his mind.

'Let's go, Yogi,' I said, and a blur of white fur streaked off for the car.

A towel covered the front seat—my lame attempt at keeping the car fur-free. In spite of this, stray bits of white hair stuck to the mat on the floor. I'd have to vacuum them. Again. It wasn't easy to love a living shedding machine.

I backed out carefully into the street and headed for the campus. When I got my license Dad and I negotiated the places where I could go dog-walking. Dad shook a bunch of news reports (about girls who tragically vanished in the woods while walking their dog) under my nose, and threatened to impound the car if I didn't comply. It wasn't fair that he never put restrictions on Vinnie. To be fair, she has a black belt in Kempo while I only made it to a junior yellow with a stripe.

The town we live in is Westbury, not to be confused with Weston, or Sudbury, or any other of the extremely expensive towns in metro west Boston. No, Westbury is a middle-class enclave, best known in years past for the first Bible written in a Native American script, and in the current era for having the biggest and most upmarket mall in the Northeast, where the residents of the surrounding affluent towns could shop without fighting traffic gridlock in their own streets. Point being, except for the town woods there weren't many options for walking Yogi off-leash in Westbury.

But one of the spots Yogi and I loved was Lake Waban in our neighboring town of Fellsway. Half of it lay on the campus of Fellsway College and the rest of it in the upmarket burg of South Fellsway. Given that the exclusive Fellsway student body is 99% female, though it's not called a women's college anymore, Dad felt better about my safety there than in the town woods. Even when school was out there was no one there but the moms of South Fellsway with their family-friendly dogs.

I parked the Mini in a safe place with open parking spots

on both sides, and the shade of a tree to keep its paint from sun damage.

Unleashed, Yogi took off up the track, fur bristling with happiness. I followed at a slower run, knowing he'd come back to me if I called.

A shoal of sporty girls in saggy sweats jogged by. The Fellsway College track team. In-training even though school was out. My kind of athletes. I might not be able to hit a ball with anything to save my life—tennis racket, softball bat, my fist, or my foot—but I could run.

Yogi and a brown and brindle Catahoula dog circled each other for a friendly sniff before passing on. I stripped off my top layer. I waited till five to take the dog out and it was still hot. If it wasn't for my dog you couldn't have paid me to be out with so much UVB bouncing around destroying my epidermis. But it was worth it. Yogi leapt up a hill like a mountain goat, struck a gallant pose at the top, and grinned down, radiating happiness. I smiled back. Anything for Yogi.

When Mom and I picked out Yogi he was a gangly puppy, all legs and floppy ears and whipping white tail. She knew by then that she didn't have much time, but when they leveled with her about her prognosis she went straight to the animal shelter. Did she know that with her gone, Vinnie in college, and Dad's long hours, I would need someone waiting for me at home? That I'd need something upbeat to talk about when everyone acted awkward around me? Other people would have gone all hyper clean and germ-o-phobic but Mom got a not-yet-housebroken puppy instead.

Dad and Vinnie took Mom to the hospital for her surgery, chemotherapy, radiation, physical therapy. Mom and I took Yogi to PetSmart for obedience training. The nurses taught Vinnie to give Mom shots of painkillers, and how to operate the oxygen machine. Mom and I taught Yogi to fetch, sit, and stay. OK, he never really got 'stay', but we tried. They brought the hospital bed into Mom's bedroom. Mom brought the dog crate into my bedroom. Every morning when Yogi was let out of his crate he ran to Mom's room, jumped onto her hospital bed via the futon Dad camped out on, and spent an hour curled next to her. Until the sound of a can being opened said breakfast. But one day I emptied his puppy food into his bowl and he didn't come. I walked into Mom's room and found him by her, not moving an inch. Just curled tight with his nose in his tail looking at me with sad, sad eyes. Mom's hand lay on his back, cold and still, her gold bangle gleaming against his snow-white coat.

I sank onto the futon. And screamed. I could hear footsteps in the hallway as Dad, Vinnie and the Hospice nurse ran to us. Yogi stayed still, his floppy puppy ears tucked back. He didn't flinch or bark. If I'm brave enough to think back that far I can still feel his warm tongue licking my face.

I blinked away tears behind my sunglasses. Why did that memory surface just then? What was even the point of going there? Yogi was seven years old now. We had all moved on.

A huge black dog bounded out of the undergrowth. There was no owner in sight. Not again! If you think poodles are little lapdogs you've never seen a standard poodle in a bad mood. We had run into this particular critter before, and for some reason she had it out for Yogi.

'Yogi, come.' I didn't like the poodle's body language one bit. Yogi turned to me with cautious sideways steps, his eyes never leaving the dog.

He was nearly right up to me when the poodle launched on him with a savage snarl. Yogi dived behind me. 'Hey, hey,' I said, keeping my voice gruff, and my stance wide. 'Cut that out!'

The poodle's white teeth snapped less than an inch from my ankle.

This was so not going to end well!

'Shadow!'

It was the owner.

'Get over here,' she said to the dog. 'She's not like that usually,' she said to me.

Sure, lady. That's what you said last time. 'Come on, Yogi,' I said as calmly as I could. 'Let's go.'

The magic words unfroze Yogi from cowering behind me and we took off up the dirt path. The poodle and her person headed in the opposite direction.

I pulled out my cellphone with shaking hands—another reason Dad insisted that I only walk here is because there's cellphone coverage right around the lake. Trust me, he checked.

'Hello.'

'Jackie,' I said, relieved to have someone to unburden this on. 'A dog just jumped Yogi.'

'No way!' Jackie said. 'Are you OK?'

'I'm fine,' I said.

'What kind of dog?' Jackie asked.

'A poodle,' I said. Was that laughing at the other end? 'It's not funny, Jackie!'

Meanwhile Yogi decided to run through the trees and assume the I'm-about-to-take-a-dump position on a manicured lawn with a series of signs nailed to the tree above it.

KEEP OFF THE GRASS

DOGS MUST BE LEASHED

NO TRESPASSING

'Wait, Yogi! Yogi, STOP!' I yelled.

'What's up?' Jackie said. 'Is the poodle back?'

'Got to go,' I said and herded Yogi off the grass. The lawn was unsullied by Yogi doo-doo. Whew.

'Go. Potty. In. The. Woods,' I explained carefully. I think I may have made helpful hand gestures to emphasize the point.

'Good advice.' There was a laugh hidden in that deep voice, even though it was trying to be deadpan.

'Thank you.' I nodded civilly at the runner who tossed that at me as he jogged past.

But when he vanished from view I was like: Face. Palm.

Really, Universe, really?

Did *that guy* have to go by just as I was scolding Yogi about his shitting habits?

This was even worse than our first meeting—and *that* is saying something!

I first saw Mystery Guy three weeks ago. I had taken Yogi

out early that day, around 7:30 am—it was that freakishly hot week in June when the temperature got into the eighties by nine. So, there we were having a nice cool early morning run along the lake, with the sun just coming up, when what should we see but a cat—a large grey Main Coon cat, just sitting in our path like it owned the place.

Now, Yogi is a sweet, friendly dog—he even gets along with cats if they're introduced to each other indoors—but he is a *dog*. And when a dog sees an unknown cat, he is morally obligated to chase it.

Next thing I knew Yogi had bolted after the cat. The cat had morphed into a yowling, bushytailed, puffball that sounded like it was being skinned alive. I chased Yogi, who chased the cat, and suddenly there was this great big guy looming over us all. And then the cat jumped into his arms and magically calmed down.

I had grabbed Yogi's collar and was fumbling around trying to get his leash on, so I didn't at first get a good look at him. Then I straightened up, fully apologetic about my dog's antics, and realized that the guy was wearing plaid pajamas (Who knew that the classic Burberry check looked this good in PJs?), and a Dr Who t-shirt, and that he was barefoot, slightly stubbly, and, even with a bad case of bedhead, utterly gorgeous. I got a weird feeling in the pit of my stomach, like at the bank when I recognized Mom's handwriting. Which is ridiculous, right?

'I'm *so* sorry,' I said. 'Is the kitty OK?'

The cat had attached itself firmly to his shoulder and was lashing its tail.

'He's in one piece, I guess,' he said. What was that accent—British?

At this point my hair burst free and exploded over my shoulders.

He smiled. It crinkled the whole of his face, even the apples of his cheek. I didn't bother looking for my hair tie. 'Come on, Yogi,' I said, red-faced, and dragged the dog away from the scene of the crime. I was suddenly aware that my spandex yoga shorts and racerback tank top were both on the skimpy side. Thankfully my now loose hair covered up at least some of the skin.

So, there you have it—our first meeting—wherein my out of control mongrel dog chased down his pedigreed cat, forcing him to come to its defense barefoot, in his designer pajamas, and me to trespass on private property to retrieve said dog before beating a hasty and disheveled retreat.

Not exactly a proper introduction, huh?

After that I saw him 3.5 times (the .5 was a day when I saw him, but he didn't see me) and each time we simply nodded and smiled as we ran past in opposite directions. And now this. Not much of an improvement, frankly.

'It's all your fault, Yogi,' I said. 'Again!' And it was. But Yogi pricked his ears and cocked his head so trustingly that I couldn't stay mad. Time to call it a day—it had been a long one. I trekked back to the car park, feeling hot and sticky and cranky, and felt for my car keys.

Only, they weren't there.

Whaaat?

They weren't there!

The dog whined, waiting for me to open the car door, and I had nothing. I wracked my brains. I must have dropped them when the poodle incident happened.

Oh, crud.

Lost Keys, Fast Cars

'It was right here!' I wailed, cellphone clutched to my ear. 'Jackie, I swear!'

'I believe you, OK?' she said. 'But I can't ditch my camp kids and help you search. Just ... keep looking.'

'Will you give me and Yogi a ride back?' I begged. 'I have a spare key at home I can try to find. If Dad realizes I lost the key he's never going to believe I'm responsible enough to plan anything.'

'I'll come get you, I promise,' Jackie said. 'Got to go.'

I stuck my cellphone into my pocket and started over, slow-walking from the beach where the poodle had jumped Yogi, all the way to the lawn, eyes scanning the ground, searching for any glint of metal.

Straight into a sweaty chest. One that I would have seen if my eyes had not been glued to the ground.

I sprang back. 'Excuse me!'

Way to go, Mini. Looking dorky twice in an hour to the same guy was a record even for me.

'You've lost something,' Mystery Guy said. The deep voice

was matter-of-fact, and yes, the accent was definitely British. 'These maybe?'

He was holding up my Mini Cooper car keys.

Oh yay! I was not in trouble. I didn't need to call AAA. Or tow the thing back to the house and pay for a new pair of keys. Dad didn't even have to know! I could kiss the guy. Well, he was pretty kiss-worthy anyway, as you may have gathered, but I digress.

'My keys!' I said. 'Thank you! I didn't think I'd ever find them.'

'Hey, no worries,' he said, dropping them into my grateful hands.

'We've met before,' he said. 'Your dog chased my cat, right?'

Shoot, he remembered.

He held out his hand. 'I'm Vir, and you?'

Okaaay. Who shakes *hands* when they introduce themselves? And Vir—that was Indian, wasn't it?

'I'm Mini,' I said.

'What kind of dog is Yogi?' I could tell by the way he said 'dog' that he knew perfectly well that Yogi was a mutt.

'He's a rescue,' I said. 'A Sato, from Puerto Rico.'

'What are they?' he raised an eyebrow. 'A designer breed?'

'Sato means 'street dog',' I said. 'There are too many strays in San Juan so they fly them here. The dogs have a better chance of getting adopted.'

'Makes sense,' he said. I realized that he'd fallen into step with me and seemed to be headed the same way as me, back to the car park. 'You know what he looks like?'

'What?' I asked.

'A coyote,' he said. 'No—a dingo!'

'Dingos are usually brown, aren't they?' I said.

'He looks like a dingo that's been dipped in bleach,' Vir said.

I laughed. Yogi was as white as a vampire, mostly. He even sparkled in the sun.

'But his ears are brown,' I said.

'He looks like a dingo that's been dipped in bleach and pulled out by his ears,' he said.

'OK—stop! That's just ...' I spotted the amusement in his eyes. 'Wait, you really think Yogi's awesome, don't you?'

'Who wouldn't?' he said. 'He reminds me of street dogs in India too, by the way. Street dogs that have been ...'

'... dipped in bleach, I get it,' I said. 'Are you Indian?'

He nodded. 'And you?'

'Yeah,' I said. 'It's Mini Kapoor.'

He still didn't crack a smile but his shoulders were shaking with silent laughter. 'You own a Mini Cooper,' he said, pointing to the logo on my keychain, 'and your name is Mini Kapoor?'

Didn't miss a thing, did he?

'My dad's into British cars,' I said. 'And if that's what you've been handed, you may as well own it, right? It would be silly not to.'

He tilted his head, as if conceding a point. 'You sure he didn't name you after the car?'

'My name is PADmini,' I said. 'Mini is just short for it.'

'Nice name,' he said. 'And the car fits you and that umm … dog, Padmini Kapoor.'

'Thanks,' I said. I could tell by the way he pronounced my name—he did it better than I could—that he had spent way more time in India than I had.

'Did you drive a long way to get here?' he asked.

'I live over the town line,' I said. 'In Westbury. And you?'

'There,' he waved over his shoulder to the graceful old house on whose manicured lawn Yogi had nearly done his business.

'There?' I asked. 'Wow, that's some house. I love the architecture! It's a Georgian Revival, isn't it? What is it—hundred and fifty, two hundred years old?'

He shrugged. 'We only live there because my mum works at the college.'

I stared at him with dawning realization. 'Is she the dean?'

'Yes she is,' he said.

'You're Gulshan Chabra's son?' I asked. 'She's amazing. The first Asian American woman to be dean of Fellsway. The youngest woman to be provost at Harvard. I thought she was …'

'Single?' He finished the sentence for me. "She is." No hint of a smile this time.

Uh-oh. But by now we had reached the parking lot.

'Oh crap!' I spotted a splat of bird poop on the windshield.

'Crap it is,' Vir confirmed.

I couldn't have that blocking my view! I unzipped a tiny pocket in my capris and extracted a wet towelette sachet I kept for emergencies.

'Could you please hold Yogi?' I handed Vir the leash, and wiped off the icky stuff carefully. Done! I dropped the wipe in the garbage bin by the car.

Vir had been watching the proceedings with interest, Yogi's leash firmly in hand.

'If you have a pocket in those pants,' he enquired, 'why don't you put your *keys* in it?'

Because the towelette fitted flat and didn't look like I'd grown a lump, that's why.

'The keys don't fit,' I explained.

'Really?' he leaned over to stare at the pocket, which, unfortunately, was located on my butt. 'That material looks pretty stretchy.'

I snapped straight, turning that part of my anatomy away. 'I could stuff it in, but it would look like I've grown a lump or something,' I said. 'Look, it doesn't matter.'

'Does your dad have other British cars?' he said, changing the subject smoothly. The silent laugh was back in his voice.

'A 1991 Lotus Esprit,' I said.

'Sweet,' Vir said. 'Bond car, right?'

'Yeah,' I said. 'Most people don't know that, actually.'

'But it's legendary!' he said. 'In *The Spy Who Loved Me* it turned into a submarine! And took out a helicopter with a surface-to-air missile while *submerged*.'

'I can see you know your cars,' I said.

'As do you,' he said.

'Didn't have a choice,' I said. 'I've been forced to watch Top

Gear since I was a kid. And I got dragged to all the car shows—you know, at the Larz Anderson Auto Museum. German Car Show, the Tutto Italiano, but especially the British Car Show—Jaguars, Rolls Royces, Aston Martins, they have everything. But I liked the Mini Coopers best.'

'They suit you,' he said. 'The pocket rocket.'

Was that a crack about my size, about the pocket, or something else? 'I'm not exactly small,' I said, standing tall. He was still a head above me. Dang.

'That's what they call the car,' he said.

'I know!' I said. It was way past time to end this conversation. 'Listen, thanks for finding my keys,' I said. 'You've no idea how much trouble I'd be in if I lost them.'

'Anytime,' he said. 'See you around the lake?'

'Sure.'

***

'Dude,' Jackie said. 'Who was that guy?'

'What guy?' I asked. My cellphone had lit up five minutes after I left the car park.

'The guy hanging out with you in the car park,' Jackie said. 'Holding Yogi's leash and staring at your butt.'

'You saw him?' I asked, mortified.

'I came by to pick you up,' Jackie said. 'Like I promised. But you were standing there with the keys in your hand talking to him.'

'Why didn't you come over?' I asked.

'Didn't want to break up the cozy chat you were having,' Jackie said. 'God knows you don't talk to many guys.'

'He found my keys,' I said. 'That's all. He wasn't, like, chatting me up or anything.'

'Sure he wasn't,' Jackie said.

Jackie and I had met in kindergarten, and we've been close since sixth grade. Back then we took Yogi for a walk every day after Dad got home from work. I rode ahead on my purple bike with the blue and silver handlebar streamers, and Dad and Yogi followed on the sidewalk. That was my favorite part of day, way better than school where people stared and walked on eggshells around me (Her mom, like, *died*! It's *so* sad!), and more fun than the quiet dinner and homework that came later.

Jackie's mom, Sue Chartier, always waved to us on our walks, which led to us stopping to chat, which led to invitations to cookouts at their house. The Siegels were usually there too. Jackie, Rachel and I rode razor scooters in the driveway while Dad tried to cope with stilted conversation that tiptoed around Mom's passing. I found out later that Sue's niece had died of cancer. All the people in our unofficial support group had been affected directly or indirectly by the disease. Jackie's cousin, Rachel's grandmother. Even Dad's friend Uncle Ernie was a cancer survivor. They understood.

Anyhow, that's why Jackie knew me well.

'I mean it,' I said. 'He's not my type.'

But I don't think I convinced her.

'Look, I'm home now,' Jackie said. 'Come over—I want details!'

'Fine,' I said.

Namaskar, NPR

I dropped Yogi home before going to Jackie's. Who was in full-on interrogation mode.

'So he has a cat?' she asked. A Camp Woodtrail headband held her dark springy hair out of her pretty green eyes—the better to quiz me with.

'Uh huh,' I said.

'And his mom's a dean, and he's into cars?' she said.

'Yeah,' I said.

'Hmmm,' Jackie analyzed the available information with care. 'So, he's probably smart—because of Mom, kind—since he likes animals, he's athletic, he's cute ... but is he seeing someone, or not?'

We both agreed that he must have a girlfriend. He hadn't made the slightest attempt to ask for my number. We also agreed that he had a James Franco vibe. James Franco in *Freaks and Geeks*—not *now*. Except he was browner and brawnier, and Brit—the first two were improvements on Franco, at least.

'Well, at least you've talked,' Jackie strategized. 'So *next* time you can …'

'No!' I said. 'I've too much to do for Vinnie's wedding. I'm not getting involved.'

'But you finally found someone you LIKE,' Jackie said. 'It's like a miracle!'

'What's a miracle?' Sue, Jackie's mom popped into the room and we dropped the subject. Sue, an avid quilter, was my sewing guru. And she wanted to know all about what Vinnie was planning to wear to her wedding.

'Come home with Jackie after you watch the parade,' Sue said before I left. 'We're having a cookout.'

Our small town fourth of July hoopla was no Macy's Thanksgiving parade but it was fun to watch the fire trucks, school kids, and marching bands anyway.

Back at the house all was quiet.

No dog at the front door. No Dad either. But Dad had to be home because the minivan was sitting in the garage—he'd probably taken Yogi for his evening walk.

I checked in the garage, just in case. God, Dad really *had* to clean the garage before the wedding! It was full of junk—car tires, garden tools, old files, computers. Even if he did, I'd still have to park my car outside. The Lotus was too delicate, and there was no question of putting the minivan out in the cold. The Japanese Mazda MPV with the American Ford V6 engine outranked both our Brit cars for one simple reason—it had belonged to Mom.

I looked at my key bunch. Did I still have a key to the minivan? Yeah, I did.

On impulse I opened the door and turned the engine on. Familiar scents cocooned me. But it didn't feel right to be sitting in the driver's seat. I left the minivan on park and climbed over the armrest into the second row.

The thing was a time machine, I swear. If I closed my eyes I could go back to being ten years old. I could almost imagine Mom sitting in the driver's seat ...

My eyes snapped open. No, the radio channel was wrong. I leaned over the armrest, turned off Dad's talkshow channel, and put on National Public Radio. A measured voice filled the van, talking about the senate race. Yeah, that was right. I smiled remembering the time when Mom called the number and got on air. It was amazing that she could be right there in the car, driving me home from karate, and people all over Boston could hear her on their radios.

In here, I could admit it. I was terrified that Vinnie was getting married. I was ten when she went away to college. That first summer ... I wouldn't have made it without her. When she left for college, the house felt so empty with just Dad and me and Yogi. I always thought that when she finished med school I'd get her back. Then she met Manish, and now she was getting married—soon she'd be gone forever.

'Hey.' Dad knocked on the window.

I rolled the window down sheepishly. 'Hey,' I said. 'I made sure the garage door was open so I wouldn't die from fumes.'

38

'Good. But do you have to sit there with the engine idling?' he asked. 'I thought you cared about global warming.'

He knew very well why I camped in there once in a while. When Vinnie left, he sold his other car and made the minivan his daily driver. This is a man whose other car was a Lotus Esprit.

'I do,' I said. 'Just need a minute in the van.'

He nodded. 'I'm going in,' he said. 'Don't stay out here too long.'

I turned the window up and went back to listening to NPR.

'Our guest tonight is Sudha Moorty of Namaskar,' the voice on the radio said. 'Sudha, thanks for joining us today.'

'My pleasure.' The husky voice had a clipped New Delhi accent.

No way. That sounded just like Mom and Masi. What the heck was Namaskar?

'So what brought you into the wedding planning business, Sudha?' the host asked. 'And why only Indian weddings? Is there even enough business there to keep you afloat?'

'Enough business?' The rich laugh sounded familiar too. 'We're so busy, David, that I have to turn away events. I'm booked out months in advance.'

'Really?' David asked, sounding intrigued. 'I had no idea that Indian weddings were so big in New England.'

'Indians like to spend on two things, David,' she said with confidence. 'Education and weddings. They may cut corners on everything else, but you won't find them taking out student loans or having a Vegas Wedding. Indian weddings are big business.'

'How do you spell Namaskar?' David asked.

'N, A, M, A, S, K, A, R, Namaskar,' said Sudha. 'You can find us at www.namaskarweddings.com.'

I slid open the door, turned the engine off unceremoniously and zipped into the house.

'Dad, pen!' I said. 'Write this down.'

'What?' he asked.

'N, A, M, A, S, K, A, R, Namaskar,' I chanted.

'No need to shout,' he said. 'I know how to spell namaskar.'

He typed the address onto the ipad screen. 'Here it is.'

I grabbed the tablet from him and stared at the webpage he brought up. It had a tasteful design with mango leaves, gold drapes, and a white horse wearing red wedding livery. I smiled at the image of the horse. 'Jackpot.'

'What are we looking at?' Dad asked.

'Wedding planner,' I said. 'I found one.'

Dad snorted. 'It's going to cost us.'

Us? That was a change! I looked at him questioningly. Could it be that he had finally seen sense?

'I guess we've got to do this right,' he said gruffly.

'We do,' I said.

'I used to know a Sudha Moorty,' he said. 'When we lived in Brookline.'

'Good,' I said. 'Because we need her to fit Vinnie into her booked-out-for-months schedule.'

'We have nearly two months,' he said.

'Not enough,' I said. 'Not even close to enough.'

'Speaking of Brookline,' Dad said. 'They're having the British Car Show this weekend. Do you want to go?'

'Do I *want* to go?' I said. 'Do Louboutins have bright red soles?'

'Do they?' Dad asked.

I rolled my eyes at him.

'Yes, they do.'

Namaskar Event Planners

Wedding Decorators

ABOUT NAMASKAR EVENT PLANNERS

Namaskar is the Boston area's premier wedding consultant for South Asian Weddings. We have been in business for twenty-five years. Our warehouse has the finest selection of Mandaps, Aisle Decorations, Dolis, Ceremonial Arches, Chairs, Drapes, Brassware—everything needed for a truly memorable wedding or event. Our decorator Sudha Moorty will work with you and create an event to perfectly suit your taste and style. We also specialize in inter-faith weddings and have full knowledge of Hindu, Jewish, Christian, Muslim, and Parsi customs. Nothing is impossible with NAMASKAR by your side.

CONTACT US

Call us for a free consultation!

'Thanks for bringing Bollywood to Boston for our wedding.'

'Thanks for your beautiful decorations. They were spectacular.'

'The Miss South Asia pageant was a huge success, thanks to Namaskar. You were wonderful, as usual!'

Read More

Vinnie's Take

I clutched the phone.

It was time to stop staring at the computer screen and actually, like, *call* the number that was up on it, but I was nervous.

The average budget for a wedding in Massachusetts was thirty-five thousand dollars, as per Sudha Moorty on NPR, and the typical desi wedding, she said, was probably triple that. But our budget was half the standard amount. How was she going to take that?

Worst case, she'd blow us off.

I had a notepad and pencil out on the coffee table. The dog had been walked and fed and given a bone to chew. I picked up the phone and dialed. Someone immediately answered.

'Sudha Moorty here,' the voice at the other end said.

'Hi,' I said, my voice a bit shaky. I cleared my throat. 'I'm calling about a wedding in August,' I said. 'We need a quote for decorations.' Could she tell it was a teenager at the other end?

Apparently not.

'What's the date?' Sudha said briskly.

'August 21,' I said. 'Tentatively ...' They hadn't picked a date yet but I had to give her something.

'I'm sorry, I'm booked for that day,' she said. Great, the conversation hadn't lasted even a minute and she had already panned me. 'Can't do the 27th of August either, that's the Patel-Bernstein wedding,' she added. 'How about August 28? I've had a cancellation.'

'Sure!' I said. 'August 28 would be great!'

'What's the venue?' she asked. Was she taking notes?

'We have some places in mind,' I said, fibbing freely, 'but we haven't booked a place yet.'

'Sure, sure,' she said. 'Are you the bride?'

'No, the bride's sister,' I said. Seemed like my grown-up act was going down pretty well.

'And your name?' she asked.

'Mini, umm ... Padmini Kapoor,' I said.

There was a pause at the other end. When she spoke her voice had lost its impersonal businesslike tone. 'You're not Megha Kapoor's daughter, are you?' she asked.

'Um, yes,' I said. Guess Dad was right about knowing her. 'Dad said you were our neighbor in Brookline, but I wasn't sure you'd remember.' I was glad she had made the connection.

'Of course I remember!' The warmth in her voice sounded genuine. 'So it's Vinnie who's getting married? Why isn't *she* calling?' She remembered her name too.

'Vinnie is in Chicago,' I said. 'She can't really get time off her residency to come here. So Dad and I have to.'

'But you're just in high school, no?' she said.

'I am,' I said, trying not to sound defensive. 'But there's no one else.'

'What about your grandmother?' she asked.

'Beeji and Bauji moved back to India,' I told her. 'The winter was getting too much for them.'

'Are they coming for the wedding?' she said.

'Well,' I said, 'they don't know about it yet. It was all kind of sudden.'

'Who's the boy?' she asked. 'He's Indian, isn't he?'

Guess the number one reason not to tell the grandparents about a wedding is that the boy or girl isn't Indian.

'Manish Iyer,' I told her, settling her suspicions on that score. 'He grew up in Needham.'

'Oh, Manish!' she said. 'I've known him since he was little. Very nice family. They're from my community—Tamils, you know.'

'Great!' I said. 'I don't know that much about Tamil weddings—or Punjabi weddings either!'

'Yes, yes, they're quite different,' she said. 'Have you talked to his parents?'

'No,' I said. 'We've only met once.'

'His sister got married last year,' Sudha said. 'I decorated for them, of course. It was at the Hyatt in Boston. Very big wedding.'

'We really don't have that kind of budget,' I said.

'Oh,' she said. 'Well I can work with any budget—it just reduces the options. Just tell me what you want to spend and I'll work with that.'

'Dad just founded a new technology start-up with two of his friends,' I backpedaled, trying to set low expectations so she wouldn't be shocked. 'He's the CTO, and he's putting money into it right now, not the other way around. If things work out he may start paying himself, but for now …'

'All these techie start-up types,' she sighed. 'Wasn't Vinod with some big corporation?'

'He was. But this start-up was made for him. So he locked down my college fund before investing in the company,' I said. 'That's why, for the wedding, it isn't going to be more than twenty to twenty five thousand total.' Better let her know how little she was dealing with!

She whistled. 'That's going to be hard,' she said. 'But we can do something, beta. Listen, why don't you come to my office and we'll run some numbers, OK?'

At least we were on board with one of the top wedding decorators in New England. And she knew Mom. Vinnie would be so impressed with how well I was doing.

***

'Sorry, Sona!'

I was late for work again.

Ten hours a week of part time work isn't a lot really, but it felt like I hardly had time for it anymore. What with SAT prep, trying to get my art portfolio done (without letting on to Dad how much painting I was doing) and trying to research the wedding for Vinnie.

46

'It's OK,' Sona said. 'Just call me next time you're late. What's new with the wedding?'

'I've found a decorator!' I said. 'An Indian one!'

'Namaskar, or Ayojan?' Sona asked, without lifting her eyes from her paperwork.

'Namaskar,' I said. 'I didn't know about the other one.'

'Oh, there are more than two!' Sona said. 'But Sudha Moorty has been around the longest. She does the Miss South Asia Pageant, you know? And she was the Desi New England Woman of the year—twice.'

'Yeah, and she knows my dad apparently,' I said.

'She knows everyone!' Sona said.

Rahul ran in and took a place at a desk. He was early today; the center had just opened.

'So sorry we're early,' Preet said, following him in. 'We have to go to my cousin's daughter's birthday party in the evening. I'm going to tell him about the wedding, Mini. Did you call him?'

'Um, no,' I said. 'Not yet.'

'Call him,' Preet said. 'Sher-e-Punjab on Route Nine. I know it doesn't sound like much, Mini, but trust me. Bhai makes the best food outside Punjab. And he will give you the family rate.'

Rahul fixed his eyes on me and said, 'Rajinder Singh makes the best samosas in the USA.' I smiled. That child spoke only the truth, this I knew.

'If you're recommending him Rahul, then I'll definitely call,' I said. 'I promise.'

***

My second job—not a proper job actually—was at my friend Rachel's mom's shop, a fashion consignment store called Amy's Attic. I worked there on weekends sorting and evaluating clothes and accessories. It was pretty high-end for a second-hand shop—we only took in new or lightly used designer wear from the past two seasons. I could basically set my hours because it was hard for Amy to find people who know top brands like I did.

I didn't get paid—but I got dibs on new stock and a 50% staff discount! It wasn't easy to find things in my dress size, but I'd scored a ton of cool accessories. In May I got 'paid' through a *serious* discount on an almost new Kate Spade handbag—*every* girl should have one quality accessory with a kickass bow. My Kate Spade was the 'Bow Bridge Kennedy'—spearmint green, bow bedecked, and totally awesome. And a pair of bright red Tory Burch Reva ballet flats. All for a grand total of $15. Total win!

I missed Rachel though. Of my two friends, Jackie was more like Vinnie—there were some things she'd try with her look, but mostly she played it safe. But Rachel was an experimenter—she took *risks* with style. Sadly, she was in Israel for the summer with her pals from Camp Micah. It wasn't half as much fun finding a gem of fashion in Amy's Attic without her around.

I still liked going though. Amy, with her soft curls, pretty freckles, and warm hugs, was comforting to be around. She always had fresh flowers and lit candles and bowls of candy at her store. It was so nice that people liked to come in just for a browse and a chat with Amy—she knew everyone. She also stocked hand-crafted jewelry from local artists, and vintage items—my staff discount applied to those as well. All my Potter trinkets were locally made—Golden Snitch earrings, Deathly Hallows bracelet, Time Turner pendant—you get the drift. Though I was *really* getting too old to wear them!

Today was my day to go in and help Amy, but I had to skip it—I had a Skype session planned with Vinnie.

***

Vinnie *still* hadn't seen the jewelry.

She had been so busy lately she hadn't even found time to Skype. She was packing up her old apartment and moving in with her friend Shinu, also a first-year resident, until the wedding. Shinu was closer to the hospital and to Manish's apartment.

I turned the laptop on and waited.

She was in shorts and a cami; behind her I glimpsed a room crammed with packing boxes. I grinned—it was good to see her!

'Hey Vinnie,' I said.

'Hey,' she said. 'Awww, Yooogi!' She made kissing sounds as I pointed the laptop webcam at the dog. He whined, because he had no clue how Vinnie's voice was magically coming out of my computer.

I put the computer back on the table.

'How was the parade?' Vinnie asked.

'Awesome,' I said.

'And how did it go at the bank?' she asked.

'Great!' I said. 'Wait a sec and I'll show you.' I ran to my bedroom and grabbed the jewelry boxes which had been lying on my SAT prep papers. 'Here, look!' I carefully unwrapped the beautiful necklace tagged with Vinnie's name, and held it up to the webcam.

'Wow!' she said. 'Hold it closer, Mini. Turn it a bit? Oh, I remember that necklace so well! And the bangles and the earrings!'

'Me too,' I said.

'But you were so little ...' she said.

'I still remember,' I said. 'And Mom left notes in each of the boxes. Look at this ...' I clicked open another jewelry case and unfolded the note inside. 'You won't believe it girls, but this necklace is actually one of your nani's anklets,' I read from it. 'She turned them into necklaces for Malika and me. Anklets are usually silver. You're not allowed to wear gold on your feet—unless you're nobility.'

'That's so cool!' Vinnie said.

'She says I can have it,' I said. 'Your necklace is a fancier version of it. See how the pattern repeats all the way around, just like an anklet? And it has tiny bells!'

'It's so pretty!' Vinnie said. She didn't usually get excited about jewelry like I did, but this was different.

I modeled all the heirloom jewelry like a kid with a Disney Princess Dress Up box, and read out Mom's notes to Vinnie.

'Where are you keeping these, Mini?' she asked suddenly. 'What if the house gets burgled?'

'Don't worry,' I grinned. 'I used Beeji's trick.'

Beeji sealed her jewelry in a ziplock bag and buried it at the bottom of the Basmati rice bin—I wasn't her granddaughter for nothing.

I put the jewelry away—it was time for business.

'Listen, I talked to a wedding planner and her rates are pretty reasonable. But we need to get her a date and a venue and a headcount, ASAP. Have you figured out what day works for you and Manish?'

If the 28th didn't work for her we were sunk.

'It'll have to be a weekend at the end of August,' she said.

'How about August 28th?' I asked. 'It's a Sunday.'

'I don't know …' Vinnie said. 'I have to ask Manish.'

'Text him now!' I said.

'Bossy!' Vinnie observed, tapping away. 'What happened to my quiet little sister?'

'Someone's got to step up,' I said. 'What does he say?'

'Nothing yet,' Vinnie said, glancing at her cellphone.

'So, what about the guest list?' I asked. 'You want to make sure that your must-have guests can make it.'

'We're working on it,' she said.

'How about Beeji and Bauji, and Nanaji, and Mallu Masi?' I asked. 'Dad hasn't called them, you know.'

'I'll talk to them,' Vinnie said. 'Masi already knows …'

'You talked to her?' I was amazed that she had told Masi before our grandparents.

'Yeah,' she said. 'Hey, we should send out a hold-the-date card.'

'I've got it,' I said, making a note on my sketchpad. 'Aaaand, the venue! Sudha said Manish's sister got married at the Hyatt on Memorial Drive—would you like that? Or do you want me to scout other places?'

'It's a nice hotel, I guess,' Vinnie hesitated. 'But it's so beautiful in Boston in summer—I wish we could have an outdoor wedding. I've no idea where, though. And I don't want to make more work for Dad ...'

'I'll ask around,' I said. 'And see what's available. But we have to move fast, Vinnie. These things are usually booked out months in advance.'

'Sounds like you're doing everything,' she said. 'Is Dad going to help?'

'He will,' I said. 'It's just that he's busy. And he's still coming to grips with it, you know. It was kind of a shock.'

'Yeah,' she said. I could see by the unhappy shadow that had come over her face that this was troubling her.

'What about a wedding outfit?' I asked, changing the subject. 'Will you wear a lehenga?'

She hesitated. 'I thought we could ask Mallu Masi ...' she said. 'She does work in fashion after all.'

'Really?' I said. Mallu Masi was Mom's flaky sister. The one who didn't even show up for Mom's funeral. I knew Vinnie spent a lot more time with her than I did but, '*Really*?'

'Look, you don't remember her much,' Vinnie said, 'but I do. All those vacations in Delhi, when she was just starting her business, she was so fond of both of us. She always said she's the one who should have had the girls, not Mom.'

'She hasn't bothered remembering us since you went to college,' I said.

'She's never forgotten my birthday,' Vinnie said.

'She's never remembered mine,' I said. It was true. She was O for six on getting it right.

'But I can't call her, Mini,' she said. 'I'll be at orientation during daylight hours in India all week.' She gave me the look. 'Maybe you could talk to her?'

Me? I cringed at the thought. But there was no one else who could get us a wedding lehenga from India, except Beeji. And I didn't trust Beeji to pick out anything remotely suitable. Mallu Masi was our only choice.

'Look,' I said. 'I'll talk to her—for you. But FYI, there isn't enough money in the budget for a Mallu Masi dress.'

'Oh! I was thinking,' Vinnie said, tucking a hank of hair away from her face, 'that I might even fit into Mom's!'

'Mom's wedding lehenga?' I asked.

She nodded. 'Can you get it out of the attic?'

'You're sure it's in the attic?' I asked. It could be anywhere. It could even be gone—Dad had given away boxes and boxes of old clothes to Goodwill recently.

'I remember Mom had Dad put it up there,' Vinnie said. 'Just check it out. It's worth a shot.'

'OK, I'll look,' I said. I didn't want to put a damper on Vinnie's idea, by telling her about Goodwill. 'Vinnie, put your hair down!' I said, on an impulse. She had it up in a scraggy ponytail, as she usually did.

'Why?' she said.

'Just do it!' I said. 'I want to see how much it's grown.'

She dragged the tie out of her ponytail and her thick hair

sprang out, framing her face. My practical, no-nonsense sister had actually let it grow!

'I know, it's a mess!' she said, snaking a hand through it self-consciously—her nails blunt and unpolished. I had to book her a manicure before the wedding. 'I haven't got around to cutting it for months.'

'If you DARE snip an inch of it I will personally fly to Chicago to murder you,' I threatened her. 'Don't you touch it until after the wedding.'

'OK, OK!' she said. 'Jeez!'

Her phone buzzed. 'It's Manish,' she said, glancing at it. 'He checked at the hospital for both of us—28th is fine!'

'Yay!' I said. I never told her that the 28th was our only option. Because—why spread the stress? 'If you get that guest list to me I'll send out hold-the-date cards. Then start on everything else.'

'And just talk to Mallu Masi,' Vinnie said. 'I'd do it, Mini, but honestly I have no time!'

'Yeah, yeah. Fine!' I squared my shoulders. 'I'll talk to her.'

My Loving Masi

I hate her. I totally hate her!

I paced up and down the immaculately vacuumed carpet, and then threw myself on the couch. It was not going to be easy, but I had promised Vinnie.

How ironic! There was a time I couldn't wait to see Masi, when I hung on her every word. But that changed the winter after Vinnie left for college.

I flipped open my battered MacBook and adjusted the computer screen. I had spent the whole morning obsessively cleaning the house, as if someone was actually coming over. I'd even washed and waxed my car—washed the dog too, since I had the garden hose out. But it was only a virtual visit—she was going to see my face and shoulders, and approximately ten square foot of wall behind me, total. I put my bottle of Poland Springs down by the laptop, clicked my Skype window open, and waited for the ring.

I couldn't even exchange ten words with the woman, and now, for Vinnie, I had to beg her for handouts.

The singsong tone rang loudly, making me choke on my gulp of spring water.

The Skype window popped open. 'Answer with video?' it asked politely, and I clicked 'OK'.

I expanded the video window to full screen and waited for the screen to refresh.

'Mini? Are you there?' a familiar voice said. It killed how much she sounded like Mom, when no two women were ever less alike. 'I can't see, beta.'

'Just give it a minute, Mallu Masi!' I said. 'It'll come up soon.'

And there she was. Dark shoulder-length hair with classy caramel highlights, her finely featured face a younger feminine version of Nanaji. She had a huge pair of very stylish glasses perched on her nose. Hello? Who wears sunglasses indoors?

She pulled them off to reveal wide brown eyes, just like Mom's—and mine. Like the boy-who-lived I had my mother's eyes. I noticed Masi's had a few more lines around than I remembered.

'There you are! Mini!' she smiled. The office behind her was tastefully decorated. Was that a real M.F. Husain hanging on the wall? For all I knew, the master artist used to be a personal friend of hers or something. She certainly didn't have to spend an hour vacuuming and mopping and picking up, like I did. No, Mallu Masi had a live-in housekeeper, a driver, a cook, a gardener for her penthouse terrace garden, a massage lady (I kid you not), and sundry other specialized servants.

I nudged the wet mop gently away with my toe so it wasn't visible leaning against the ten square feet of wall behind me.

'You look great, Mini,' she pronounced. If I didn't know better I'd have said that her cheerfulness sounded a bit forced, just like mine. I wiped the sulky look off my face, and tried a genuine smile. It wouldn't do to look rebellious if I was trying to get something out of her.

'Thanks Masi,' I said. 'So Vinnie's wedding is most probably going to be on August 28.' No point beating about the bush. 'And she really needs a wedding lehenga. I know it takes months to custom-embroider one—but is it possible to get one off the shelf?'

She ignored me completely, and asked a question instead. 'Who is this boy Vinnie is marrying? Why didn't anyone tell me about him?'

'*We* didn't know about him either, Masi,' I forced myself not to sound impatient. Vinnie had been over this with her, surely. 'Vinnie kind of sprang it on us, you know.' I tried to steer the conversation back to the lehenga. 'Um, Vinnie is going to be home next week. Could we pick a few options for her to look at? And did you get my email with her measurements?'

'Yes, yes.' She waved one bejeweled hand. 'I got the email. Don't worry, we'll fix Vinnie up. And we can look at everything I have in stock next week—whatever she wants. But what about the boy? Is he … nice?'

'Yes, he's nice.' I didn't know Manish well enough to give him a ringing endorsement, so I went over his basic resume instead. 'He's a doctor. He's 27 years old. He was one year ahead of Vinnie in med school. He's an attending physician now, at the same hospital where Vinnie is doing her residency.'

'But where is the family from?' she prodded. 'Has anyone checked them out?'

She called Vinnie exactly once a year, and now she wanted to 'check out' the family of the guy she was marrying. What next? Was she going to arrange a marriage for me?

'They're from Newton, Masi,' I said. 'Newton, Massachusetts.'

'No, no, where are they from *in India*?' Masi said.

Oh, that.

'They're … uh … Tamil?' I said, trying to remember what Sudha Moorty had said. 'His name is Manish Iyer.'

'Iyer!' she said, her face clearing. 'Yes, they're Tamil. TamBrahms.'

I probably looked confused because she added, 'It's short for Tamil Brahmins.'

'OK,' I said. Not that I cared about caste or anything, but it felt oddly nice that someone had a clue about where Manish's folks were from, geographically speaking. Apart from Newton, Massachusetts, that is.

'They'll probably want her to wear a kanjivaram sari for the wedding,' she said.

'What's a kanjivaram?' I asked. I was always interested in fabrics, and though I knew a lot about saris I hadn't heard that one before.

'They're very rich handwoven silk saris,' she said. 'Like a South Indian version of Benarasis. You know what those are, right?'

I did. Mom had some. One of them even had real gold thread woven into the border.

'Aren't they kind of heavy?' I asked.

'They are,' she said. 'I'm not sure Vinnie can handle that. She should wear a lehenga—one of mine—I can make it as light as she wants. The wedding customs should be from the bride's side of the family, no? After all, we're hosting.'

'About that,' I said. 'Mallu Masi, how much would the lehenga cost? Or that sari you're talking about. We can't really afford an expensive lehenga, you know.'

'Cost?' Mallu Masi said. 'You think I'm going to charge my own niece for her lehenga? It hasn't come to that yet!'

I had been hoping she'd say that. But it was a relief nonetheless.

'Thanks … Mallu Masi,' I said.

'No problem, Mini,' she said. 'Just tell me when you need it. Did you look at the link to the 2011 bridal line I sent you? Which one does Vinnie like?'

'She hasn't seen it yet, but I'll send you a short list of lehengas to pull,' I said. 'I'd love to see her in the A-line lehenga on page four. She doesn't usually like gold, but she'd look totally hot in it, if you ask me.' I stopped for a second—no point getting all excited in front of her.

'She will,' Masi concurred. 'Good choice, beta.'

Funny that we were sympatico on this when I couldn't remember ever having a grown-up conversation with her—about anything.

'Then her bridesmaids could wear saris too, in a complimentary color—it'll look so nice in all the pictures,' I said.

'Aren't you the bridesmaid?' Masi asked.

'Yes,' I said, 'but you can have multiple bridesmaids here. People do—all the time. She has friends from high school that she wants to include.'

'American girls?' Mallu Masi said. 'You sure they'll wear saris? Who's going to tie it for them?'

I suppressed a flash of annoyance. 'I will,' I said.

'You know how to tie a sari?' she asked.

'It's not that hard,' I said, feeling defensive. 'I was nine when Mom taught my whole girl scout troop how to tie a sari. I'm pretty good actually.'

'Oh!' she said. 'And Vinnie?'

'Vinnie never learnt,' I said. 'She was too busy with sports and studies to do girl scouts.'

'One time I came to visit,' Masi said, 'and your house was full of cookie boxes. Hundreds of them. They've even more calories than your Beeji's cooking.'

'I remember, Masi,' I said with a tight smile. 'So, can we talk next week?'

The last time I'd seen Masi was four years ago. I was in the middle of my chubby phase fueled by Beeji's lovingly made Punjabi cooking. Masi had been furious at her for 'feeding my depression'.

Beeji and Masi had never gotten along, before or since.

'Of course we can. But you know, Mini,' she said, 'the best thing would be if she came down here for a fitting. That's the right way to get a custom fit.'

'She can't do it, Masi,' I said. 'But don't worry, I've taken the measurements very carefully. And if something needs fixing we can get it altered here. But we need it here in good time to do that.'

'OK,' she said. Someone appeared at her elbow and put down a tea set. The kind in period dramas, with a kettle in a tea cozy, and fine bone china teacups and saucers. And a creamer and sugar pot. 'One sugar,' she said absentmindedly to the unidentifiable person next to her; I could only see their headless middle.

'What about you, Mini?' she said. 'What will you wear for the wedding?'

'I haven't thought about it, Masi,' I said. There wouldn't be enough money left for a pair of shoes after we were done, to be honest. Forget about a full wedding-worthy outfit.

'I can pick something out for you,' she said. 'Something that will complement Vinnie's look but not overshadow it.' Her face brightened up. 'In fact, I have just the thing for you, Mini.'

'No, really, it's OK,' I said. The whole thing was awkward. What if she picked out something hideous and I was stuck wearing it? 'You don't need to bother.'

'No, no,' she said. 'What size are you? Same as Vinnie?'

'No, I'm five inches—' I said. Her cellphone rang.

'Five inches bigger—got it,' she cut in, glancing at her cellphone. 'I have to go, beta. Sooo sorry, but I can't miss this meeting.'

The screen flickered off.

'Five inches *taller*,' I finished to the empty screen.

I felt drained. I flipped down the lid of my laptop and punched the air. Arrgh! Why did she get under my skin? Why was she so … Both my hands formed into fists.

Who knows what old junk she was going to send me? She did have good taste, though, however irritating and neglectful she was. Truthfully, I was a teeny bit excited to see what she could possibly think was perfect for me.

***

The day of the British Car Show dawned sunny and clear.

Dad was relieved because he didn't like to take the Lotus out in the rain. We headed out to Brookline right after breakfast. Yogi and I stuck our heads out of the window as we flew down Route Nine—our hair (or fur in his case) flapping in the wind.

The Larz Anderson Auto Museum has the feel of a castle on a hill. It is a stone building overlooking a vast green park with an outstanding view of the Boston skyline. I'd been to these car shows many, many times with Dad, but it was always fun to ride over to the showground in Dad's Lotus even with Yogi stuffed with me into the passenger seat. You're ridiculously close to the ground and the engine (even with only four cylinders) has enough oomph to launch you into orbit. OK, not really, but that's how it felt.

Once there, Dad parked the Lotus in a carefully selected shady spot, and we walked around and looked at all the cars, and the people, and the dogs. Personally I liked the dogs almost as much as the cars. There were always lots of them at the car show.

Dad went back to check on the car and I wandered off with Yogi to get myself some guilty treats—warm honey-roasted nuts, and a stick of cotton candy. Something that shade of neon pink couldn't possibly be good for you, but it tasted wonderful!

I was busy licking the cotton candy or I would have seen Dad talking to that guy. Because it was him … you know … from Fellsway.

'Hi Mini,' he said. He looked great in cargo shorts, a North Face t-shirt, and Teva sandals. I wasn't surprised. A guy who looked good in pajamas could look good in anything.

In my defense, even someone who gives a damn about personal style doesn't dress up when they're going out with their *Dad*. I wore well-worn cut-off denim shorts, a Red Sox t-shirt, one dollar flip-flops from Old Navy, and had my hair up in a goddamn *ponytail*. In other words, I looked like a well-scrubbed twelve-year-old, and I carried, as you might recall, a bright stick of cotton candy that was just then probably the same color as my face.

'It's Vir, right?' Apparently I could still talk while in shock, and remember stuff.

'Yogi's behaving well, I see,' Vir said.

'Thanks,' I said. 'He's been here every year since I was ten, so he knows the rules. And he does behave well most of the time—you just haven't seen him at his best.'

'I was just talking to your Dad,' he said, 'about his car.'

He leaned in a little and smiled, causing momentary confusion and tongue-tiedness in me.

'Are those snitches?' he asked. 'Like in Quidditch and *Harry Potter*?'

Great, now I looked even more juvenile. I was so going to bury these earrings at the bottom of the basmati rice bin—forever.

'Yes,' I said briefly. 'I'm sure my Dad liked talking about his car.' I sneaked a look around to scope if Vir was here with anyone. No girlfriend in evidence as far as I could see.

'He did,' Vir said. 'Actually, I had one more thing to ask him.'

He walked back to Dad and the Lotus. I stood there for a moment—undecided, then went off to get some lunch instead of following him. Yogi whined as I pulled him away.

'You'll like a hotdog better than him,' I told the dog, and got a sizzling hot one for him and Dad. By the time I got back to the car Vir had vanished.

Dad took the hotdog from me.

'I just met the nicest boy, Mini,' he said. 'He knew more about cars than most kids these days. Remembered the Esprit from *The Spy Who Loved Me* and everything.'

I'm sure he did, Dad. I'm sure he did.

Scouting Venues

It was the farthest I had driven on my own—ever.

Since I could pretty much stay on Route 27 all the way to Sudha Moorty's office, Dad said it was OK for me to go by myself. I even put on the radio instead of driving in total silence, fists clamped around the steering wheel, the way I used to the year before.

It was easy to find the little office strip—it said 20 Washington Street on a large address plaque next to the parking lot, with all the businesses in the complex listed beneath. There was a real estate agent, a dental office, and a florist on the bottom level. Namaskar was in a suite on the first floor. I smoothed my hair down nervously and rang the bell. 'Coming!' Yes, that was Sudha Moorty's voice all right.

She opened the door. She was very tall. Her kohl-rimmed eyes had hanks of spiky hair falling into them. Yoga pants, sweatshirt. Lots and lots of gold chains. Barefoot. Huh! I mean, I hadn't expected her to be wearing a sari or anything, but this was not what I had visualized either.

'Come in, come in, Mini,' she said. 'You have Vinod's height, but you look just like your mama.'

'Really?' It was a compliment—we both knew it. 'Thanks for saying that.'

'Your sister takes after your dad,' she said, 'athletic and smart and all.'

'Hey, I'm smart,' I said.

'Yeah,' she said. 'But,' she gave me the once over, 'you have style. Like I said … you're like your mom.'

Couldn't argue with that.

'Masala chai?' she asked

'Sure,' I said, looking around the large sunny space.

She padded off to a kitchenette.

Her office was hung with giant pictures of wedding mandaps. They looked like Bollywood sets, glitzy and *completely* over the top. No way Vinnie would get married in something like that.

'So, Vinod doesn't want to pay for Vinnie's wedding?' she said. 'I should call him and straighten him out.'

'You have Dad's number?' I was shocked.

'*If* it hasn't changed,' she said. 'It's been years though. How's he doing? Since Megha passed, he's not been in touch with anyone.'

I guessed that by anyone she meant anyone Indian. 'I know,' I said. 'He didn't really feel like going to, you know, Indian get-togethers, for the longest time. Dad doesn't cook, for one thing.'

'Or return phone calls,' she said. 'No, I understand. It's always the women, beta, that keep the social circle going.'

'Vinnie kept in touch with some of her Indian friends,' I said, a bit defensive. Vinnie had grown up in and out of all these Indian people's homes because Mom was around for practically her whole childhood. It was me who was stuck with Dad and his lack of desi social skills. After Dad stopped going to the gatherings Mom used to take us to, and hosting any of his own, we gradually stopped seeing any Indian people at all.

Vinnie kept in touch with her friends via emails and Facebook and she made a lot of Indian friends in med school—they're well represented there—but my friends gradually became school friends and neighborhood friends. It didn't help that I dropped Indian dance too. Without Mom or Vinnie to ferry me there after school, and no one close enough to carpool with, it was too hard to stay in the class.

Dad still feels bad about that, I think, since that was another one of the things Mom and I shared.

'Never mind, beta,' she said. 'At least she found an Indian boy. That's more than so many of our girls are doing now.'

'I guess,' I said. Though what was wrong with a non-Indian boy I couldn't fathom.

'So where are you thinking of booking?' she asked, handing me a cup of steaming masala chai that she had conjured out of her kitchenette. 'Does she want to be closer to Newton or Westbury? There's the Newton Marriott, or the Crowne Plaza, and the Westborough Doubletree has really reasonable rates.'

But Vinnie wanted an outdoor wedding. The picture she had sent me that morning of her and Manish on a hiking trail at sunrise, flashed before my eyes. Vinnie was *so* not a cookie-cutter, five-star hotel ballroom wedding kind of girl.

'I don't think a hotel will work for her,' I said. 'Some place natural and green, and outdoors. All this,' I gestured, somewhat apologetically at the walls of glitzy Bollywood sets, 'this really isn't her style.'

If she wasn't willing to offer anything other than the mandaps on display I would try making one. A basic bamboo structure and a ton of fresh flowers ought to do it. Rachel's aunt had a homemade canopy for her wedding—I think the Jewish name for it was 'huppah'. We could probably even rent one from a temple, come to think of it.

But to my surprise Sudha Moorty didn't look at all offended. 'I give them what they want,' she said. 'Most people want what they see in the movies. All gold-shold, and tamasha.' She shrugged. 'What to do? It isn't my job to judge.'

'Really?' I said.

'Yeah. And don't rule out hotels, beta,' she said. 'Most outdoor locations don't have wait staff, or linens, china, and silverware—you have to truck everything in. Some insist on their preferred caterers, so you can't have Indian food. But hotels usually allow Indian caterers, and some have gardens available for the ceremony. That can work out really well.'

'Do you have a list of hotels I can research?' I asked. 'Dad and I can shortlist them for Vinnie, and she can finalize it.'

'Sure, I'll email you a list. What's this?' She pointed at my sketchbook. She had a good eye, that woman.

'I have some ideas about mandaps, Aunty. Can I call you Sudha Aunty?'

Her eyes twinkled merrily. 'How about Didi?'

She had to be kidding! 'Um,' I said, not sure how to respond.

She waved a hand graciously. 'Aunty is fine.'

I opened my little folder and pulled out a sketch or two. 'These are some of my ideas. This one is a basic bamboo structure draped with sheer tasseled silk drapes. And another idea is to have four real trees be the basic structure of the mandap and have flower garlands to connect them together.'

'Hmm,' she said. 'I could do the first one really easily. I have a simple mandap that we could cover with silk. I have the sheer drapes in old gold and I'd add a cranberry red fabric for a pop of color. Can I keep this picture?'

'Sure!' I said. I was thrilled that she was open to trying it.

'How much would it …' I gulped, dreading the price tag, '… how much would it cost?'

She tilted her head and considered. 'For the mandap, and the wedding garlands, I have them flown in fresh from India, and some table centerpieces, and a guestbook.' Would she just get to the point?

She looked me in the eye and named an amount.

I was frozen to the spot because it was a lot less than I'd expected. She must have given us a huge discount. 'OK, I'll let Dad and Vinnie know.'

***

It was hard to start narrowing down venues when I didn't have a final guest list—but I had to make a start somewhere. From the list of hotels Sudha Moorty sent I marked off three venues that fit Vinnie and Manish's requirements:

Reasonable cost.

Close to Westbury and/or Newton.

Catering by an outside vendor (Indian) allowed.

Outdoor garden or patio for the wedding ceremony.

This last one was the hardest. Most hotels didn't have a garden large enough for a mandap and all the guests. The ones that did tended to be in Cape Cod or western Massachusetts—too far to work for us—but after a dozen phone calls and massive amounts of Googling I found three that looked promising. I set up appointments for us; Dad was supposed to come check them out with me—but of course he canceled.

So there I was at the Newton Marriott, looking grown-up and organized (I hoped) in a sleek blowout, cute wrap dress, and sensible pumps.

I clutched my Vera Bradley folder nervously and approached the front desk at the Newton Marriott hotel. I had taken ten pictures of the car park and the lobby. Evidently Ragini Aunty, Manish's mom, liked the Newton Marriott, and it was halfway between Westbury and Newton, so at least it worked location-wise. But how much would it cost?

'I have an appointment with the event manager,' I told the receptionist.

'Mini Kapoor?' she asked, and I nodded. 'She'll be right down.'

The event manager showed up—blond hair pulled back, pant-suited, early twenties. I felt intimidated for about a minute before I spied her KS 'Plan Adventure' idiom bracelet—she was a kindred spirit.

'Hi! Mini?' She took me under her wing. 'I love your bracelet!' I was wearing a blue 'Take the Plunge' bangle in honor of this appointment. 'Let's start at the ballroom, shall we?' And soon we were examining the ballroom which could accommodate between 200 to 500 guests, and yes, the linens, silverware and wait staff were included in the price. We could book hotel rooms for out-of-town guests at discounted prices, and they would throw in a room for the bride and groom for free. My head was spinning with the details she tossed out—how on earth did she have everything memorized?

'Where is the garden?' I asked. The garden would make or break the deal.

'Come right this way,' she said.

A small neatly mowed strip of grass rolled gently down towards the river. There were pretty azalea bushes and tall pines overhead, and the water of the Charles lapping the end of the lawn, but when you turned away from the river the hotel loomed over everything. I clicked a bunch of photographs, angling the shots away from the building.

'You'll definitely want to bring bug spray,' she said apologetically.

I so got that. Two mosquitoes had bitten me in the ankle in the five minutes we'd been standing there.

'Right!' I said. 'Thanks so much—we'll let you know!'

***

That's what you get for assuming your way and not bring directions, or a GPS, or a Mapquest printout!

I took the wrong turn at the intersection with Route 128 and ended up on the highway—it was confusing, OK? Next thing I knew, cars were speeding alongside me at warp speed and I was either going to have to speed up or get run over. I shifted into fourth gear and caught up with the rest of the roaring traffic. I looked for the next exit, but I was in the wrong lane and there was a huge tractor trailer in the next lane blocking it. Dang! I kept going. How far could it be to the next exit?

I stepped on the gas and suddenly I was enjoying myself. I liked the feeling of zipping along in my Mini. I turned up the volume on the radio. That thing could go!

But the gas gauge was *way* less than a quarter tank of gas, even though my reserve light had not turned on—yet. I had to get off the highway. And get some gas. And call Dad so he wouldn't freak. And also break it to my boss that I wasn't going to get to Kumon on time.

I managed to get into the rightmost lane, in position for the next exit. The reserve tank light was now on—blinking red on the dashboard. Great, now I had less than a gallon of gas left!

I pulled off onto Route 2. Where was that—Lexington? I grabbed the cellphone—no bars, no service whatsoever!

I kept driving, and a street sign went by that looked familiar. Wasn't Ernie Uncle's garage somewhere here? Sure enough there was the sign for AUTOBAHN AUTOMOTIVE—the place where I learned to change oil and a flat tire and helped Dad fix the radio on the Mini. The red neon sign that said 'OPEN' was like a homing beacon.

I pulled in, parked and got out on shaky legs.

'Ernie Uncle?' I wandered onto the shop floor—a couple of cars were up on the lifts getting some work done—and opened the door to the office. 'Anyone there?'

'Heeey, Mini.' It was Ernie Uncle, wearing neat blue overalls, his broad face lit up in surprise. 'What's up?' He did a double take when he saw my fancy outfit. 'Whoa! You look so grown-up! Car doing OK?'

He had no idea how happy I was to see him.

'Car's fine, but it could do with some gas,' I confessed. 'It's running on fumes!'

'Minnnni!' he said reproachfully.

'Look, I'll be more careful in the future, OK?' I said. 'And, my cell is dead. Can I use your phone?'

'Sure you can.' he said.

'Thanks!' I dipped a hand into the candy jar he always kept on the check-in counter, feeling like a kid again.

'Dad?' I said, when he picked up. 'Dad, don't get mad! I'm at Ernie's. I took a wrong turn onto the highway by accident … No, I'm fine. I just want to let you know because I'll be late and I didn't want you to worry … No, he's filling up my gas; will

73

you pay him next time you are here? … Yes, I know how to get home from here!'

I called Sona too, who was far more understanding than I deserved, then left the office to find Ernie Uncle.

He was all excited about some Indian car he'd just been working on.

'It was an Indian SUV,' Ernie Uncle said. 'The Mirchandani Stinger. Am I saying it right?'

I shrugged. 'Don't ask me!' I said. 'I've heard Dad talk about them, though. They use them in the army, I think. The Indian army.'

'Neat little thing,' Ernie Uncle said. 'It's no Hummer, of course, but it's well built. I guess this Mirchandani company got the contract to make US Jeeps in India during World War II, and they've been in business ever since. Anyway, what I want to tell *you* about is the guy!'

I raised my eyebrows. 'What guy?'

'The guy who brought it in. His dad owns Mirchandani Motors—how about that?' Ernie Uncle said. 'Good-looking kid—can't be much older than you. He's coming back on Saturday.' He rocked back on his heels looking proud of himself. 'Want me to introduce you?'

'No way!' I said. If his dad owned a motor company he was probably some rich, overbearing brat. 'Will you stop acting like Beeji? She wanted to set me up too—with Chintu Patel.'

Ernie Uncle waved off Chintu Patel impatiently.

'This kid, he's nice, and good-looking, and rich,' Ernie Uncle said.

'Which means he's totally out of my league,' I said. 'I really appreciate the thought though!'

'Fine,' Ernie Uncle said, resigned to my indifference. 'Hey, do you need any help with the wedding? Anything we can do?'

'No, we're good,' I said.

He nodded. 'You're all set with the car. Give me a call when you get home, OK?'

'Thanks,' I said. 'I will!'

I could see them grinning in my rearview mirror as I turned back onto the street. I had to add three more names to the guest list—Uncle Ernie, his wife and daughter. That made one hundred and eighty three. Yikes!

Venue Found!

'Well?' I waited for Vinnie's reaction.

I had just uploaded two hundred pictures of the Marriott on Facebook for her to see. 'Do you think it'll work?'

I didn't mention the mosquitos, yet.

'It's nice,' Vinnie didn't sound too thrilled. 'It would be really convenient, and the price isn't bad …'

'But …?' I said. I could tell there was a 'but'.

'But it's not really atmospheric,' Vinnie said. 'You know?'

I sighed. 'I know,' I said. 'Onwards, I guess.'

'But it is such a good rate,' Vinnie said, with forced cheerfulness. 'Maybe we should just book it anyway?'

'Not yet,' I said. 'Let me check out the other options.'

'But it's taking up all your time,' Vinnie said.

'So?' I said. 'We're not booking anything until we find the perfect place, OK?'

'OK,' Vinnie said, and that was that.

I Googled venue options until I was cross-eyed, and fell asleep exhausted. This was so much harder than I thought it would be.

In another week things were no better.

The Westborough Doubletree had the most delicious chocolate walnut cookies on the planet, and a really cute patio, but though it had some pretty flowerbeds, it was completely bricked over. It also had a fabulous view—of the car park!

The Four Seasons and the Boston Taj were just too far from Westbury, and too expensive. The Hyatt was where Manish's sister gotten married a year ago and though I loved driving down Memorial Drive to look it over—I even took Yogi for a run along the Charles afterwards—it didn't have a garden option, so it wasn't for Manish and Vinnie.

By the time I had been through five hotels and their event managers I was feeling like a pro.

But still no deal.

***

It was thanks to Yogi that we cracked the venue in the end.

I came home from yet another venue-scouting trip to find Yogi looking all hangdog and miserable. Usually he jumped up and fawned all over me, but today he barely lifted his head. Guess he thought I was going to ignore him again.

'Aww,' I stroked his soft ears. He gave me a look of utter resignation. That settled it. I was exhausted, but I couldn't let him down again.

'Just give me a minute!' I dragged myself off to my bedroom and changed into shorts, a tee, and running shoes. I slapped together a sandwich in the kitchen and wolfed it down with a glass of cold milk, and grabbed Yogi's leash. He leapt off the couch, ears up, tail lashing. Now he got it. He could smell honest intent a mile away.

'Where to?' I asked, as we set off. 'Fellsway College or River Bend?'

We hadn't been to River Bend in a while, what with work, wedding research, and SAT prep. Jackie probably thought I'd abandoned her for the summer.

I cut through the scenic but narrow Pond Street and turned into the River Bend reservation—the home of the Massachusetts Botanical Society.

The place was beautiful and peaceful—usually. Not that day though. Camp Woodtrail was in full swing and the grounds overrun by kids, kids, and more kids. I slowed down to ten miles an hour so they could see me coming.

'We. Are. TI-GERS!' chanted a bunch of ten-year-olds. 'Mighty, mighty TI-GERS!' I peeked around the crowd of kids and spied Jackie leading them on, along with a couple of other camp counselors. She was yelling louder than the rest of them, her face red with the heat and the effort.

I slowed to a stop, turned down the window, and waved at her frantically. 'Jackie!' I said. 'Here!'

She jogged over to the Mini. 'Where've you been?' she said. 'I haven't seen you in days!'

'Wedding stuff,' I said apologetically. 'It's driving me nuts!'

'You brought Yogi-wan-Kenobi!' she said. 'Want to walk with us? Wanna go walkies with Jackie Aunty?'

'With all of you?' I scanned the kids milling around her. 'Is that a good idea?'

'Sure!' she said. 'The more the merrier.'

I parked the car and Yogi bounded out, grinning like a wolf. A couple of kids looked alarmed. 'He's friendly, see?' I put Yogi in a sit and let them pet him. He was really patient, putting up with ten hands patting his fur at a time.

When we got to the wooded trail along the river I let him off the leash. He bounded off and raised his leg at a large pine tree. A couple of kids broke ranks to chase after him. 'Timmy,' Jackie yelled, 'get back here. Stay with the group.'

Yogi quickly figured out that staying a hundred feet ahead of us meant he'd be unmolested by the kids, and promptly took the lead.

'So, tell me what's up,' Jackie said. 'You've nailed everything down yet?'

'We. Are. TI-GERS!' the kids kept up the refrain as they marched.

'Nailed down?' I wailed, yelling above our background noise. 'Are you kidding? I don't even have a venue yet.'

'I thought you looked up tons of places,' Jackie said. 'Is Vinnie being fussy?'

'Not really,' I said. 'She wants an outdoor wedding, that's all, and all the places in our budget have the lamest gardens.' I shook my head. 'Or they're on Cape Cod or Western Mass or something. Nothing close!'

'What about here?' Jackie asked.

'Here?' I asked. 'What do you mean?'

Jackie crossed her arms and stared me down. 'I mean River Bend!'

I stared at her stupidly. 'What?' I said.

'River Bend!' Jackie repeated. 'Don't you know they do weddings?'

'NO WAY!' I said. 'I did NOT know that! How come it doesn't show up on any of the wedding sites?'

'Because it's members-only,' Jackie said. 'But membership at the Massachusetts Botanical Society is only ninety bucks a year. Not bad, huh? And they have different options—you can put up a tent in the gardens, or have it in the Italian Garden by the manor house. You know, the one with the big fountain? I've seen five weddings here since camp started!'

My heart was suddenly hammering.

Yes! That felt right.

River Bend was where Vinnie spent half her school years, playing soccer and field hockey and what not. Mom even came here for one of Vinnie's big games. She had the biggest smile on her face as Vinnie pushed her wheelchair around the field for a lap of honor.

She had on her brand new wig, a pageboy style made of thick beautiful hair—Vinnie's hair. If you didn't know that Mom had had chemotherapy, you'd never have guessed it was a wig. Vinnie looked strangely grown up in her new bob—she had always had hair halfway down her back before then. Afterwards, she never ever grew it long again.

Some Hindu men shave their head in mourning for close family members. It was almost like Vinnie kept her hair short in mourning for Mom. That's why I was so determined not to let her trim her hair again. She had to grow it out—thick, long and beautiful—in time for her wedding. Mom would have wanted her to.

'Do they have an indoor space?' I asked. 'In case of rain?'

'I think they use the carriage house,' Jackie said. 'You know, the one where they have the Christmas Tree festival.'

I remembered the space. It was a huge hall with really tall vaulted ceilings. With some draping and lighting and decorations, it could be epic.

'Jacqueline Chartier, you've nailed it!' I said. 'I'm going over there, right now!'

'You're welcome!' Jackie said.

I called for Yogi and took off down the trail in a run. Behind me I could hear the chant of the kids fade away. 'Mighty, mighty TI-GERS!'

You'd think she might have seen it in all those years she played soccer at River Bend, but no. It was so well hidden by the tall hedgerows on either side, that unless you knew the way in, you'd never even guess it was there.

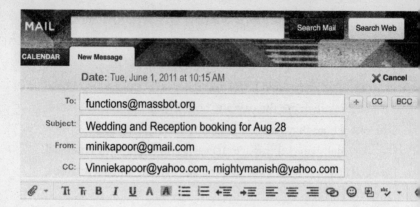

MAIL   Search Mail   Search Web

CALENDAR   New Message

Date: Tue, June 1, 2011 at 10:15 AM   ✕ Cancel

To: functions@massbot.org   +   CC   BCC

Subject: Wedding and Reception booking for Aug 28

From: minikapoor@gmail.com

CC: Vinniekapoor@yahoo.com, mightymanish@yahoo.com

Dear Caroline,

Thank you so much for showing me the gardens and carriage house at River Bend last Friday. I shared the pictures I took with the couple and they've decided on River Bend for their wedding. I'm including the contact information and address you requested (below). Please email the contract to me and we'll complete it and return it with the downpayment.

Thanks again!
Mini

Contact information
Bride:
Yashasvini Kapoor
Vinniekapoor@gmail.com

Bride's father:
Vinod Kapoor
vkapoor@gmail.com

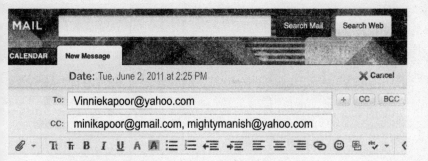

From: functions@massBot.org

Dear Yashasvini & Manish,

Thank you so much for choosing the Massachusetts Botanical Society at River Bend for your special event needs. The rental agreement for your wedding, which will be held at the Massachusetts Botanical Society located at River Bend Reservation on Sunday, August 28, 2011 is attached. We have reserved the use of the Carriage House and Grounds for your special day.

Please return the signed contract, with your deposit. We accept checks and all major credit cards. Once we have received a deposit we will forward your updated invoice.

If you have any questions, please do not hesitate to call me or email me at functions@massbot.org. I will be happy to help you with anything that you need.

I look forward to working with you both and your families, and creating a heartwarming and memorable wedding day for you and your guests.

Warmest regards,

Caroline Kelly

Functions Manager

Massachusetts Botanical Society

River Bend Botanical Center

900 Washington Street, Fellsway MA

Attachment: Kapoor-Iyer_Wedding_August_28. doc

Food Fight

Venue finalized. It was time to move on to other vendors.

I had been trying to get a response from Vinnie's preferred caterer, Curry Cuisine, for over a week. Sondhi Jr, the dude I kept reaching wouldn't give me a quote without Dad's input, and Dad seemed too busy to write up quotes.

Vinnie wanted them mainly because Manish's mom recommended them. They had catered Manish's sister's wedding. So, if I could get them to return my calls, we would probably go with them—even though Sher-e-Punjab, the guy that Preet told me about, was much more reasonable.

But since Curry Cuisine was still dragging their feet, even after five messages, I decided to go over to Sher-e-Punjab. Just in case.

I knew where it was, of course. It's the kind of place you passed before stopping at the next fancy new restaurant that had popped up on Route 9. Those fancy restaurants vanished as quickly as they appeared, but Sher-e-Punjab never changed its signage, or paint, or decor, and yet stuck around year after year after year. It was a mystery really, how it stayed in business.

I mean, it was a tiny modified diner by the side of Route 9. No parking space. And yet, I've seen Indian people slam the brakes on their Toyota Corollas to pull in there. Not me though. Yet there I was.

I was surprised. It was bright and cheerful inside, in spite of the plastic flowers on the tables and the backlit Golden Temple poster on the wall—or maybe because of them. Gurbani music played in the kitchen and I could hear voices chatting in Punjabi. The buffet was well stocked with glistening aromatic curries, warm crusty garlic naans, fragrant rice, and heaps of red tandoori chicken. It smelled wonderful—as good as my Beeji's kitchen, and that's saying something.

'Hello?' I called out.

The curtain parted and a middle-aged man with a beard, a handlebar mustache, and a prosperous belly appeared behind the counter. He wore a Sikh turban in a delicate shade of sky blue. So the picture of the Golden Temple wasn't only for decoration. I hadn't realized that Preet was Sikh because Rahul's hair was short and he didn't wear a turban.

'Yaas?' he asked, his accent as thick and earthy as *makke di roti* made of the finest Punjabi corn.

'I wanted to get a quote on a catering order?' I said.

'OK,' he said. 'What would you like?'

'You have a catering menu?' I asked.

'No,' he said. 'We've been meaning to get one, but,' he shrugged helplessly, 'it's very hard to do everything.'

'I can tell you what I'd like,' I said. 'We'd like to have a vegetarian meal. Rice, naan …'

He cut me off. 'For how many people?' he asked.

'About one hundred and eighty,' I said, after some mental calculations. 'Give or take thirty or forty people.'

He raised his eyebrows. 'I'll have a firmer count soon,' I promised. 'We're working on it.'

'It's OK,' he said. 'No problem. You can check what you'd like on this menu.'

I grabbed the piece of paper and looked it over.

'*Aap* Rahul *di* teacher *hein na*?' he asked in Punjabi, surprising me.

'*Haanji*,' I said, automatically before switching back to English. 'Rahul's mom said you have the best Indian food in Boston.' How did he know that Preet had sent me?

He chuckled. 'Maybe not the best Indian food,' he said modestly. 'But the best Punjabi food, we have it, yes.'

Not so self-deprecating after all.

'Preet said so many times you would come,' he added. '*Unne appko* describe *kiya si*, that's why I could recognize you. She's our sister, cousin sister. We give you the best food, and the best rate. Family rate.'

'Oh, thank you.' I was floored by his warmth after getting the runaround for days on end by that snooty Curry Cuisine. 'I'm sorry I can't order from you for the wedding but I need catering for the mehendi also.'

I was going to give Sondhi Sr one more day. If I didn't hear back from him in twenty-four hours we were booking with Sher-e-Punjab.

***

Dear Mr Sondhi,

I've been trying to contact you to get a catering quote for an August wedding, but haven't heard back. I thought I'd try email in case it's easier for you to communicate this way. We need catering for a wedding reception at River Bend Reservation in Fellsway. They have enough tables and chairs but we will need wait staff, silverware, china, and linens. We are expecting about 150 people.

The menu we'd like (this can be changed, if need be) is listed below. We're particularly interested in balancing the Punjabi dishes with some Tamil dishes—aviyal, kootu, poriyal, sambhar, rasam, payasam, etc. We'd also like to line the dinner plates with banana leaf. Based on this, could you provide me with a ballpark estimate? If you need any other information, please feel free to contact me at mini.kapoor@gmail.com, or by phone.

Thanks!

Mini Kapoor

MAIL   Search Mail   Search Web

CALENDAR   New Message

Date: Tue, June10, 2011 at 7:18 PM   ✕ Cancel

From   mini.kapoor@gmail.com   +   CC   BCC

Subject   Total cost for catering

To   Vinnie.kapoor@gmail.com; mightymanish@gmail.com

Vinnie,

Check out his quote, it's very reasonable. And he can do the Tamil dishes Manish likes. He suggests having a live dosa station to add a bit of pizzazz—it'll be extra for that. $28 per hr for 5 wait staff, 12% gratuity + 25% for china. Add it up. HOORAY!

To: Mini.Kapoor@gmail.com
Cc: DevSondhi@currycuisine.com

Hello Mini

Sorry about the communication problem. Please find attached our proposal based on your email. I also recommend having a live dosa station—it adds flair to the dinner experience. Please review and get back to me with your comments/questions.

Thanks

Sunny Sondhi

Vinnie was swamped what with her orientation at the hospital. Dad had a conference call from Intel Capital (It's really important, Mini!) so I finally ended up totaling it myself.

If I included the cost per person, the wait staff, the dosa chef, the china and linen charge, and the gratuity, we were still under $10,000. It was another $1500 if we brought the guest list up to 180 people—which was the maximum number of people the Carriage House at River Bend could hold for the wedding reception.

Dad and Vinnie would just hire whatever vendor I recommended. They were just too busy to do any of the organizing themselves. I was tempted to have them check out Sher-e-Punjab. Thanks to Preet, the rate they were giving us was out of this world! Curry Cuisine could do the TamBrahm food that Manish loved—but was it worth the extra money? It was a lot to think about.

DJ Vir

The best place for me to think was out walking with Yogi.

I grabbed a notepad and the leash and whistled for the dog.

Just turning into the parking lot by the athletic field and seeing all the tall pine trees in the distance made me feel better.

I unclipped Yogi and he ran off ahead of me. We both knew the path well by now. First there was the gentle uphill, then a steep descent with a spectacular view of Lake Waban. Then a wooden boardwalk over the wetlands, filled with rushes, ducks, and wetland birds, followed by a long level stretch along the south side of the lake. After that we entered 'Private Property' where the 'No Trespassing', 'Dogs must be on a Leash' signs were nailed to a gazillion trees.

I didn't want to have to bother with holding on to Yogi so I veered off, up a hill track, away from the lake. After a steep incline it went along the spine of the hills surrounding the lake. Great view, cool breeze, no bugs, and Yogi could run free—what could be better?

I found a cool shaded rock to sit on. Yogi was still unleashed but he never wandered too far from me.

I pulled out my notebook and pencil and started to make a list.

Date : Sunday, August 28th

Venue: River Bend/ Mass Bot

Wedding decorator: Sudha Moorty of Namaskar

Guest list: Finalize numbers, get addresses.

Hold-the-date cards: Designed and ordered. Mail ASAP when cards arrive.

Invitation cards: Have Vinnie approve design.

Food: Curry Cuisine for wedding, Sher-e-Punjab for mehendi

Wedding Cake: Check out the bakery recommended by Amy.

Wedding lehenga: Masi

Priest: Krishna Ji, Ashland Temple?

DJ/Lighting: ???

Photography: ???

Hotel rooms & transport to Mass Bot for out-of-town guests: Westford Marriott

Bartending: ???

Licenses: Wedding license, Alcoholic beverage license, etc.

I went back to chewing the end of my pencil. Time to pencil in some numbers. Next to item number 3 (Wedding decorator: Sudha Moorty of Namaskar) I put $5000. Next to item number

1 (Mass Bot/River Bend Venue) I put $7000. Next to Wedding lehenga I put FREE. Next to Curry Cuisine I put $10,000. I had three quotes, and two contracts signed and ready.

'Hey.' The warm voice was just next to my ear.

I dropped my notepad. I knew that voice, that accent. It was Vir.

'Hey,' I said.

'What's that?' he said, looking over my shoulder.

'It's private,' I said, clutching the notepad to me.

He held up both hands. 'OK!' he said, heading back to the walking trail.

Oh—he was going away!

'I'm just sketching actually.' I turned the page hurriedly to a sketch of Yogi I had done the other day. It was kind of good. I was thinking of doing a version of that for my portfolio. And, if that turned out well, maybe doing a large one as a wedding gift for Vinnie.

'Wow!' he said, examining the page closely. 'That's amazing. You're really talented!'

'Thanks,' I said.

'Are you in art school or something?' he asked.

'I wish!' I said. 'I'd like to apply to design school, but I have to convince my dad it's not for deadbeats first.'

'It's your life,' he said. 'You should apply. Totally!'

'He's paying for college,' I said. 'He wants to make sure I manage to get skills I can earn a living with.'

'Like what?' Vir asked.

'You know—engineering, medicine, law.' I counted them off on my fingers. 'The usual things you're allowed to do if you're Indian.'

Vir laughed. 'But you've clearly got talent.' He turned a page to another sketch. 'That's awesome!' He flipped another page. 'What's that?'

I snatched back the notepad. 'Nothing!'

'It said "Wedding checklist"!' What did he have—a photographic memory or something?

'It means that it's a checklist for a wedding,' I explained.

'Aren't you a bit young for that?' he said.

'Vinnie's wedding,' I said. 'My sister?'

'Your sister's wedding!' he said. 'Of course. How come she isn't planning it herself?'

'She's starting residency on July 1st,' I told him. 'In Chicago. And her fiancé is an attending physician. They don't have the time to plan it, so I'm helping out.'

'So big sis got into medicine, huh?' he said. 'Is that why you're not applying to design school?'

'I never said I'm not applying,' I said. 'I still have a few months to decide.'

'You'll be a high school senior in fall?' he asked. 'Where do you go?'

'Westbury High,' I said. 'And you?'

'Nowhere,' he said. What? I must have looked confused because he added. 'I took a gap year. After being stuck on a boarding school campus in the Thar desert it was nice to have a break, you know?'

94

'Cool,' I said. 'What did you do?'

'Worked in Mumbai for ten months,' he said. 'And traveled—Australia, Singapore, the UK ...'

'That explains the British accent,' I nodded wisely.

'Very funny!' he said. 'The British accent is from living in England. I grew up there. Lived in other places since, but it kind of stuck. Sorry.'

'So, are you going to school in the US?' I asked. If not, he'd be leaving soon ...

'Yes,' he said. 'Starting in fall.'

'At Fellsway?' I asked.

'Yeah, right!' he said. 'No way I'd go there!'

'It's officially co-ed!' I said. 'I've read their prospectus.'

'Any college where my mum is dean is not for me,' he said. 'Ever!'

'Where *are* you going?' I asked.

'MIT,' he said.

'Impressive,' I said. 'So after telling me not to stick to the doctor/lawyer/engineer mantra, you want to be an engineer?'

'Why not?' he said. 'It *is* what I want. That's what matters.'

Jackie was right about him being smart. He had that casual aura of self-assurance that comes from having it all—brains and brawn.

'That's great!' I said. 'It's really hard to get into MIT.'

'Where are you applying?' he asked. I swallowed.

'Fellsway, for one,' I said. 'Put in a good word for me with your mom, will you?'

'Fellsway doesn't have a design program,' he said. 'You should be applying to Parsons, or FIT, or Rhode Island Institute of Design, or ...'

'I know what the good design schools are,' I said. 'But Fellsway is close to home, so I can still see Yogi, my dog, you know, and my Dad too. Why are you dissing the school anyway, when your mom runs it? Jeez!'

'None of my business, I know,' he said. 'But you have talent, clearly. Don't sell yourself short.'

'It's not like I haven't thought about it,' I said. 'I'll get a portfolio together and apply. And if I get in, I'll see how I feel then.'

'Good plan,' Vir said.

'You must have been to some Indian weddings,' I said, changing the subject. 'Any tips for me?'

He pulled such a horrible face that it made me laugh.

'Like weddings that much, huh?' I said.

'I didn't mind so much when I was a kid, but now ...' Vir said. 'Hey, why aren't your parents planning it?'

I rolled my eyes. 'Dad's hopeless,' I said. 'And Mom's not around.'

'Oh,' he didn't ask for details. 'I'm sorry.'

'It's OK,' I said.

'Divorce isn't easy,' he said. So, that's why he didn't want to talk about his dad.

'It isn't that,' I explained. 'She passed away.' I had a lot of practice saying this, and it had gotten easier to say. 'It's been seven years.'

'Your father didn't remarry?' he asked.

'Nah,' I said. 'Mom was the love of his life, evidently.'

'He's lucky to have had her,' he said. 'It must have been hard.'

'It was years ago,' I said. 'It's fine now. We're over it.'

'Uh huh.' He wasn't buying my we're-fine line, I could tell.

'OK, so maybe we're not,' I said, surprising myself. Weren't we? 'I mean, how do you get over something like that?'

He said nothing, just tapped my list. 'You still need a DJ?' he asked. 'Hire me.'

'You're a DJ?' I said. 'What do you charge for a gig?'

'Charge?' he looked blank. 'Oh, I'll give you a discount on whatever's the going rate. I just haven't had a chance to, you know, cost it out.'

I raised an eyebrow. 'You have references?'

'Not in Boston,' he said. 'Like I said, I'm trying to get the business started.'

'You're making this up, aren't you?' I said. 'What kind of DJ are you that you don't even know what to charge?'

'The cut-rate kind,' he said. 'The kind people pay with free dinner.'

I didn't know if he was being serious or not. 'I'll think about it,' I said.

He grabbed my notepad and penned 'Vir' and a phone number next to the DJ line.

'I'll do a good job, I promise,' he said. 'Try me.'

Talk about being unbelievably pushy! 'You're not shy, are you?' I said.

'No,' he said, before running off down the trail. 'I'm a good DJ though.'

I stared at his retreating back, flabbergasted. (It was also nice to look at, let's be honest.) How on earth did I just spend an *hour* talking to some guy I'd just met about my mom, and my college applications, and my sister's wedding? I'm really not the kind of person who spills everything about their life to strangers. What was happening to me?

***

'Spill!' Jackie ordered over the cellphone. 'You can't just say you're thinking of hiring that guy to DJ Vinnie's wedding without a proper explanation. I want to hear everything.'

'Well,' I dithered. 'I was making a checklist for the wedding. By the lake, you know.'

'Very romantic,' Jackie said, encouragingly.

'Shut up!' I said. 'Or I'm hanging up.'

'Fine, fine—continue,' Jackie said.

'And he happened to run by, and he saw me and stopped to chat, and then it came up,' I said. 'So he mentioned that that's what he does, and he's starting up here and he'll give me a discount. That's all.'

'But he's starting at MIT in September!' Jackie said. 'You don't launch a DJ business the year you're going to MIT!'

'Maybe he DJ'd over his gap year. To help pay for college tuition or something!' I suggested. 'Not everyone taking a year off goes backpacking you know. Jackie, he gave me his number— should I call him, or not?'

'You should definitely call him. But I think he's offering to help because ...' Jackie said.

'No. I don't want to hear it!' I said.

'... he likes you,' Jackie said, fulfilling her need to have the final say, however delusional her conclusions.

***

So, I went down to the Indian grocery store to pick up some supplies—a crate of mangoes from New Jersey, creamy Indian style yogurt, cilantro, ginger, lentils, a few boxes of KDH Spices, and freshly fried samosas from the little kitchen café they had in the back of the store. And I picked up a bright flyer for wedding horses. For, apparently, it's possible to hire a decorated wedding horse for weddings in the fine state of Massachusetts.

BAARAT WEDDING HORSES
by Springmeadow Farms.
We provide white decorated horses for your weddings.
We serve Massachusetts, New Hampshire, Maine and Vermont.
Our horses are well mannered and gentle.
Our staff is experienced, courteous, and professional.
We have provided horses and carriages for many Baraat/ Hindu weddings & matrimonial events.
Safe, fun and memorable.
Fully insured.
Please contact us for more information, quotes on our low prices, or for reservations.
To see more pictures of our horses visit our website.

'It sounds legit,' I said to Jackie after reading it to her over the phone.

'It sounds nuts!' Jackie said.

'Wait, there's more,' I said. 'It says here: Elephants available on request.'

'Elephants??' Jackie said, and I pictured her eyes turning round like Ritz crackers.

'Elephants,' I confirmed. 'They have pictures.'

'Get out of here,' Jackie said.

The elephant was out, of course, because a) Vinnie and Manish weren't nuts, and b) as per the rates on the pamphlet, it cost a shitload of money to rent one.

But the decorated white horse—that might actually fit in the budget.

Because, why not?!

***

'Hello,' the deep voice with the British accent was Vir alright. He sounded distracted.

I nearly panicked and hung up.

'It's Mini,' I said. 'Mini Kapoor. We met by Lake Waban?'

'Mini!' he said. 'What's up?'

'I'm calling about my sister's wedding,' I said. 'You said you could DJ for it?'

'Sure can,' Vir said. 'If you give me the date I'll put it on my calendar, right away. And if you like, we should probably meet to go over the music, and the lights, and the schedule of events—that kind of stuff.'

He said SHED-ule instead of SKEJ-ule—it sounded sweet.

'Umm, we're having a meeting at the venue on Tuesday with some of the vendors. Could you come to it?' I said. 'My sister will be there too. We could go over everything then.'

'Where is it?' Vir asked.

'The River Bend reservation. You know, Mass Bot,' I said.

'I don't,' he said. 'But I'm guessing that Massbot is not, as it sounds, a robot of some sort.'

'What?' I said. 'No! It stands for Massachusetts Botanical Society. It's right by Fellsway College.'

I gave him the time when Vinnie and I were meeting with Sudha Aunty, Sondhi Sr of Curry Cuisine, and Jan Courtney of Mass Bot.

'Okay then,' he said. 'I'll see you Tuesday!'

I was smiling as I hung up. Massbot indeed!

Homecoming

My sister was finally coming home!

I hummed a happy tune that sunny morning as I drove off to get her. Yes, me—all by myself, all the way to Logan Airport. And why was I even allowed to do this after my last driving debacle you ask? Because Dad was in meetings all day long, and unless he wanted her to take the Logan Express Bus Service to Framingham, or pay for a taxi, there was no one to get her but moi.

Only, this time Dad had made sure I was prepared. Gas tank? Full. GPS? Functioning. Cellphone? Charged. Mass Pike Fastpass? Velcroed to my windscreen. I was good to go.

I didn't feel guilty about leaving Yogi at home either, because he'd be psyched when I got home with Vinnie. Not that we were planning on hanging out at home for too long. After tonight, we had to hit the ground running—there was a ton of wedding stuff to cover in the two days she was there. The best part would be taking her back to River Bend—I couldn't wait to show Vinnie the gorgeous carriage house!

I made it to Logan without screwing up, and also reverse-parked in a supertight spot in central parking without incident—huzzah! Vinnie was waiting by the baggage carousel, even though she had no baggage.

'Mini!!!' She grabbed me in a bear hug. 'I'm getting married!'

'Vinnie!!!' I hugged back as we hopped in excitement, arms locked. 'I know!'

People were staring at us, but I didn't really care and neither did Vinnie. We didn't have to wait for bags—she just had a carry-on—so we were out of the airport in no time.

Sadly, she didn't seem to share Dad's confidence in my driving abilities.

'Slow. Down,' she said. 'I want to live to see my wedding day. And have babies and stuff.'

'Hey, I drive well,' I protested.

'You drive way too fast,' she said. 'Now, slow the hell down. Or stop and let me drive.'

'Okay!' I eased off the gas. 'Relax, I'm doing the legal, promise!'

She unclutched her fingers from around the seat armrest.

'So what are we doing today?' she asked.

'We're talking to Masi when we get home, to pick out your wedding outfit,' I started. Might as well get the worst over. 'Then tomorrow we have an appointment with the caterer, the wedding decorator, and the DJ/lighting dude at River Bend. And the town fire marshal is coming too.'

She didn't know about Vir being the DJ/lighting guy. She didn't know about Vir, period. What would she think of him?

'Why is the fire marshal coming?' she said.

'Because there's a fire at the wedding ceremony,' I reminded her. 'The fire department has to OK it. Also, we need to check about the dosa station—it has an open flame.'

'What else?' Vinnie asked.

'On day two and three we have to meet the mehendi lady, the bridal make-up lady,' I said.

'On day three we're meeting the Iyers,' she said.

'Manish's parents?' I said. 'I didn't know we were seeing them.'

'They invited us to dinner,' she said. 'It's time we all met properly.'

'OK,' I said. 'You should have warned me so I could have prepared Dad.'

'He'll just have to deal with it,' she said. 'Hey, how's Yogi?'

'See for yourself,' I said, because we were pulling into our driveway and there was a frantic, crazy dog at the front door, who knew via some finely honed canine instinct that the second most important girl in his world was home.

***

It was mid-morning in Massachusetts and evening in Mumbai. The pink glow of the sunset over the Arabian Sea lit up Mallu Masi's office windows, even on our computer screen. She must have a kickass webcam on her computer because Skype was never that clear. Mallu Masi herself was dressed in linen capris and a

104

kurti shirt in pale green, and looked as cool as a cucumber. She was also smiling a lot more today because Vinnie, her favorite, was here to chat with her.

'Vinnie, beta, congratulations!' she said. 'You're ready to see the lehengas we pulled?' Why did she always talk so loudly? Like she thought the webcam wasn't picking up her voice or something.

'Yes!' Vinnie said, all excited. 'Thanks, Masi!'

'I've an assistant, Ria, who's about your size—Mini sent me your measurements. The models were all too tall,' Masi said. 'Ria is going to try the lehengas on so you can see how they look worn.'

'That's awesome!' Vinnie said. 'Let's go; I can't wait!'

'OK, here's lehenga number one,' Masi muttered at someone off camera and the webcam was expertly trained on the model, I mean, the assistant.

The lehenga was brilliant, and I don't use that word loosely. Among the people that can afford to buy this stuff, Masi is known for her gossamer laces and light-as-air lehengas and saris. She has workshops full of craftsmen working on them—some of them months ahead of time. She doesn't sell anything readymade, every single piece is custom-tailored to her wealthy clientele's needs. Seriously, they're all loaded, and she's booked out a whole season in advance. Unless you're lucky enough to be her niece. This lehenga was classic Mallu Masi—which meant it was awesome, but not necessarily perfect for Vinnie. It was a subtle moss green silk contrasted with rich red velvet, traditional wedding colors, but it would look too Christmassy on Vinnie, I thought.

'Ooh,' Vinnie said. 'It's beautiful!'

The girl walked around and did a slow turn then spread the chunni out to show the intricate embroidery on it. After we'd examined every bit of the outfit, thanks to Masi's camera assistant, we moved on to the next one. And the next. They were all gorgeous but not quite Vinnie.

'It's really nice, Masi,' I said after checking out the newest lehenga Ria had modeled, which had to be the understatement of the decade. 'But I think the A-line lehenga will look spectacular on her. The one with the antique gold lace?' I consulted the catalogue in my folder. 'It's on page four. Remember we talked about it?'

'Yes,' Masi said. 'Ria, can you change into this one?' She pulled out the gold lehenga from the stack of garments on the table.

'Masi, Manish's parents have invited us for dinner tomorrow,' Vinnie said. 'Do we have to bring them gifts or anything? I don't know what the etiquette is …'

'You've already had an engagement, right?' she asked.

'Manish gave me a ring and we took our friends out to dinner, and his friend Kristan took engagement pictures for us,' Vinnie said. 'That's about it. Mini and Dad and his parents and sister weren't there.'

'What I don't understand is why you kids don't do anything properly!' Masi wasn't impressed by Vinnie's short and sweet engagement. 'You live in America, not in a jungle. You're supposed to have a shagan, when the boy's family comes with gifts and formally accepts the proposal. And then your dad and uncles and brothers go with gifts to the groom's house for the tilak ceremony.'

'That's ridiculous!' I said. 'They're getting married, not the parents!'

'I'm not saying it makes sense,' Mallu Masi said. 'I'm just saying that's how it's done.'

'Not in his family!' Vinnie volunteered. 'They have this thing called a janvasam at the temple. The girl's father announces the wedding date to everyone there. And then they parade around the temple with the groom in a decorated car and invite everyone they see to the wedding.'

'Good luck dragging Dad into a temple,' I snorted. 'Have you leveled with Manish about us? He should know he's marrying into a family of skeptics.'

'Of course I have. And Manish isn't really religious or anything,' Vinnie said. 'I don't really know about his parents though.'

'Hmmm,' I said. This was going to be a disaster, I could feel it.

'Here she is!' Masi said, and Ria the assistant sashayed into the room in the antique gold lehenga. It was so so incredible and so perfect for Vinnie that I felt like standing up and applauding.

'Wow!' Vinnie was speechless. 'What do you think, Mini?' Masi may have been a big noise in fashion but I was practically

Vinnie's designated stylist—when she listened to me.

'It's outstanding.' I gave her two thumbs up. 'I just *knew* that was it!'

'Will it look like that on me?' Vinnie asked. I leaned over and whispered in her ear, so I wouldn't offend the helpful Ria. 'It'll look better on you, I promise. Your arms and shoulders are so much more toned and tanned than that skinny Ria's. That old gold color always looks amazing on you. And it's made to go with Mom's jewelry.'

'Really?' Vinnie's eyes were shining.

I gave her a squeeze. 'Really.'

'What are you girls whispering about?' Masi demanded. 'D'you like it or what?'

'I LOVE it, Masi,' Vinnie said. 'That's the one—I'm sure. Could I please, please, have it?'

'Of course you can, darling,' Masi smiled magnanimously. 'Get this one altered to the measurements I gave you,' she ordered some poor off-camera underling. 'It has to be couriered to this address. Jaldi se, OK? They need it NOW.'

***

'Vinnie, read this!' I clicked on a bookmark in my web browser. 'We can order your wedding garlands from India via fancyflowers. com.'

Apparently, a florist exists that ships flowers straight from India to Canada and the US every week. Vinnie could choose from tens of wedding garland designs. Who would have known?

'Niiiice!' Vinnie said. 'But I hate this one!' The garland Vinnie hated was made with banknotes as well as flowers! 'And what is this one?' Another garland, this time with 24-karat gold-plated beads threaded in with the flowers.

'We can order jasmine strings for the mehendi!' I said, inspired by the gorgeous flowers and reasonable prices (for non-OTT items).

'We're having a mehendi?' Vinnie asked.

'We most certainly are!' I said. 'How can you have a Punjabi wedding without a mehendi and sangeet?'

'How can you have an American wedding without a bachelorette party?' Vinnie countered.

'We're combining them both,' I said. 'And having it at home! Unless you think your girlfriends won't want to do the mehendi?'

'Oh they will!' Vinnie said. 'But won't it be expensive?'

'Sher-e-Punjab is giving us a great rate,' I said. 'And the mehendi lady's rate isn't bad either.'

'We can't fit everyone into the house!' Vinnie said.

'I'll get tables and chairs from Taylor Rental. There's plenty of room if we set them up outdoors,' I said. We had an acre yard, much of it level enough for tables.

'TamBrahms don't do mehendi,' Vinnie said.

'We do!' I said, and set my jaw stubbornly. I was not budging on this one—there was no way we were skipping it.

'OK, fine, let's do it,' Vinnie said. 'If you think it'll fit in Dad's budget. By the way, who's coming to River Bend? Is it just the decorator and the caterer?'

'And Vir ...' I added. 'I mean, the sound and light guy. I haven't hired him yet, but he said he had to take a look at the venue to give me a proper quote on the lighting and all.'

'Alright,' Vinnie said. It's a testament to how distracted she was that she didn't pick up on how awkward I sounded when I mentioned Vir.

'I don't even know if I should hire him, but he's really, really cheap,' I said, in a burst of guilt.

'Mini, is he cute or something?' Vinnie asked, finally clueing in.

'No!' I said, but my face was flaming red.

'Really?' Vinnie said.

The sound of the garage door opening signaled that Dad was home! Yogi, Vinnie and I all ran out to ambush him with a big Kapoor group hug.

Meet the Iyers

The Iyers—Dr Ragini Iyer, PhD, and Dr Manoj Iyer, JD, PhD—lived on a tree-lined street in Needham in a pretty little colonial house with well maintained rose bushes, books stacked in every available bit of space, and musical instruments—both Indian and Western—scattered throughout the house. The instruments looked well used—seemed like anyone in that family could pick up any of those and play at a pro level.

'Come in, come in.' Mrs Iyer was the tiniest woman I'd ever met. Vinnie at least didn't tower over her, but Dad and I definitely did. 'Sooo nice to see Yashasvini's family.' I hunched down automatically—Dad did not.

Mr Iyer stepped out from behind her. 'Welcome, welcome,' he said, beaming. Awww. He had the sweetest face. Manish obviously got his charm from him.

Dad was trying not to scowl, or step on an instrument or book or something. He looked like a bull in a china shop. Along with the instruments there were also brass statues of Ganesh, and Laxmi, and various other deities. They were adorned with fresh flowers and kumkum. Dad's scowl deepened.

'Heyyy!' There was Manish. He put an arm around each of his parents. I had thought he was of medium height but he was clearly the tallest person in this family.

'We got you some flowers.' Vinnie looked lovely in the salwar kameez I'd fitted for her. It was a gift from Mallu Masi for me at the peak of my chubby phase. But after I chopped off swaths of material it fitted Vinnie's petite frame perfectly. It wasn't one of Masi's couture pieces, just something sweet and summery that she had specially made for me when she still bothered doing such things.

'Yashasvini, you look so pretty!' Mrs Iyer said. 'I've never seen you in Indian clothes. You should wear them more often— they suit you!'

'Thank you,' Vinnie said. 'Can I help with something?'

'No, no,' Mrs Iyer said. 'I want to tell you, Mr Kapoor— Vinod, isn't it?' She looked at Dad for confirmation.

'Yes,' he said.

'I want to tell you, Vinod, that we're so glad these two found each other,' she said. 'We've had so many proposals for Manish ...'

'*Mooom*,' Manish said.

'It's true,' she said. 'So many people had sent proposals, from our community you know, but he had decided long back that it was Yashasvini and no one else for him.'

Dad cleared his throat. 'I think they're going a little fast myself,' Dad said. 'I tried to talk some sense into them. Why not wait and finish with their residencies before getting married?'

'Very correct,' Mr Iyer said, in brotherly solidarity. 'I was thinking that also.'

'Nonsense,' said Mrs Iyer, giving her husband a look. And it was suddenly crystal clear who was boss. 'There is never a good time to get married. This way they can start a family when they're done with residency.'

Dad looked like he was about to explode. 'Yeah, yeah,' Manish said. He didn't seem all that upset about his mom's comment. 'We'll decide that, OK, Mom? Let's just take it one step at a time.'

'Ragini Aunty,' I said. 'We've booked the River Bend Reservation for the wedding.'

'Yes, Manish told me,' she said. 'It sounds very nice.'

'We're thinking of booking Curry Cuisine to cater.'

'Curry Cuisine is exccccellent,' Mrs Iyer said, brightening up. 'They catered for our daughter's wedding. Sunny Sondhi makes the best payasam—so delicious. They did a great job for Mohini's wedding.'

Her enthusiasm made me smile. Would Mom have been that stoked about Vinnie's wedding?

'We're getting Sudha Moorty to do the wedding decorations,' I added, when she paused for breath.

'Sudha is my *verrrry* old friend,' Ragini Aunty said. I wondered how Sudha 'Didi' would react to being called a '*verrrry* old' anything. 'We've known her so long, since when Manish was a baby. Manish is like a son to her. She did the decorations for my daughter's wedding—for Mohini's wedding too.'

'Aunty, we were thinking of having Krishna Ji from the Sri Laxmi temple to perform the ceremony,' I said.

'Krishna Ji is wonderful of course, but how about Sundaraman?' Ragini Aunty asked. 'Manish really likes him. He always said to Manish that he would be the one to marry him.'

'We've known Krishna Ji a long time,' Vinnie said, quietly.

It was true. Granted we had not seen him for years, but he had visited Mom throughout her illness. Even Dad tolerated him because it was clear that whatever he believed or did not believe, he brought Mom comfort.

'But he's Iyengar, you see,' Ragini Aunty said. 'Sundaraman is Iyer. Of course it's up to you, but it's better if Sundaraman does the wedding.'

It clearly meant a lot to her.

'Sure,' I said.

'What is your family?' Ragini Aunty asked, her face shining with anticipation.

'Actually, we're ath …' Dad stopped short as I stomped without mercy on his foot.

'Arya Samaj,' I said. 'We're, umm … Arya Samaji.' It was a semi truth—my Beeji had been a leading light of the New England Arya Samaj scene when she lived here. I smiled brightly before continuing.

'There was a lady priest my grandmother liked very much, Pandita Gayatri Vohra, but we've lost touch with her.'

Beeji would have preferred that the Pandita visit with Mom

114

too, but since Gayatri Ji had a full-time job as well as her other priestly duties, we had to turn to Krishna Ji instead.

Meanwhile Ragini Aunty was looking rather stunned. Too late I realized that Arya Samaj was scandalously liberal, by their lights.

But at least I had prevented Dad from blurting out the even more shocking truth—that after Mom passed away, Dad, Vinnie and I had been nothing but your simple garden-variety Massachusetts atheists. Manish knew, I assumed.

'Well you could get Krishna Ji to be your family priest, even though he's Iyengar, and Sundaraman could be ours,' Ragini Aunty said. Evidently even Krishna Ji, the Iyengar, was better than a Punjabi lady priest.

'How many priests does it take to marry two people?' Dad said. 'Let's just go with your guy!'

'How many ...?' Ragini Aunty said. 'Oh, that's funny, Vinod! How many priests! Your father is a real jokester, Yashasvini!'

Thank heavens Ragini Aunty took everything in such good humor! Vinnie probably looked OK to everyone else, but she was inwardly cringing, I was sure.

'I'll go help Uncle,' she said. In the time we'd been talking Mr Iyer had made tea for everyone and was carrying in a tray of snacks that looked bigger than him. What a sweetheart! I hoped he had brought up Manish to be as caring as himself.

'We're going to do what Vinnie likes, Mom,' Manish said. 'She likes to keep it simple.'

'Do you have pictures of Mohini's wedding, Aunty?' I asked.

'Yes, yes, of course!' Ragini Aunty said. 'Would you like to see?'

'No,' said Manish, Mr Iyer and Dad simultaneously.

'You stay with them, Yashasvini,' Ragini Aunty said. 'I'll show Padmini the pictures.'

***

'The clothes, the flowers, the food!' I said. My mind was blown, clearly. 'The GOLD!'

I was still trying to digest the pictures that Ragini Aunty had shown me. 'And the *veshtis*, Vinnie!' Wearing veshtis with a scarf instead of a shirt was common practice at Tamil weddings—which looked great on fit guys and not so great on the rest.

'Maybe we could buy him an outfit,' Vinnie said. 'I'm not having him show up shirtless!'

'The groom's clothes are supposed to come from your mother's brother's house,' Dad said with an air of authority. I had no idea if we could trust that piece of information, given that it came from Dad.

'*Now* you want to buy him stuff,' I said to Dad.

Dad had the grace to look embarrassed. He had vetoed all my attempts to buy gifts for the Iyers, saying it smacked of tacit dowry demands. *As if!*

When Ragini Aunty presented gorgeous kanjivaram saris to both Vinnie and me, and a thick gold bracelet to Dad, he felt awful. Luckily I had fitted in a trip to our local Indian jewelers—Kay Jee Jewelers—and traded in Mom's broken and mismatched gold for a gold chain for Manish.

'Mom didn't have a brother,' I said. 'But Masi is Mom's sister. That's close enough, isn't it? We should pick his outfit! Then we can make sure that he'll complement your lehenga. And be as covered up as Vinnie wants. OK, done! Let's get his measurements and send them to Masi.'

***

Forty minutes of driving later we were at the mehendi lady's salon. It was a tiny place with a small selection of gifts and jewelry up front, and a beauty parlor at the back. I grabbed a handful of glittery stick-on bindi packets, and a few stacks of glass bangles in vivid pinks, blues and greens. No telling when we'd need some bright accessories.

Usha, the woman who ran the place, came out to talk business.

'We will have about forty people, I think' I said. 'Most of them will get henna, but they'll be fine with simple patterns. Just a central motif and a few decorations on the fingers maybe. How much will that cost?'

'I'll do the bride's henna myself,' Usha said. 'And bring an assistant for everyone else. The brides henna will be five hundred dollars. And we'll charge by the hour for the assistant.'

'How long does it take to do a pair of hands?' I asked.

'Pick a pattern and I'll have her do it,' Usha said. 'You can time her. Here's the pattern book.'

It seemed like a good plan to try out the henna tattoos before we hired their service, but Vinnie refused to be the guinea pig.

'I'm not going back to the hospital with henna tattoos,' she

117

said. 'It's unprofessional. What impression will it make at the hospital?'

'You have to go back after your wedding too!' I protested.

'Yes, but then I'll have an excuse!' Vinnie said. 'And they'll know me by then!'

'Fine!' I picked a pattern from their design book. 'This one.'

The assistant henna lady worked quickly. She had a plastic cone filled with dark green henna paste from which she squeezed a thin string of henna onto my palm. It was like watching someone ice a cake. In no time she had finished an intricate paisley pattern with a peacock feather beside it. Amazing.

Vinnie looked at her clock. 'Seven minutes for that design!' she said. 'Wow!'

We put down a deposit. The mehendi was on!

***

Vinnie had to drive the Coop because my hand was covered in slowly drying green paste. The design was amazing, though. When we were little Mom bought us pre-made cones of mehendi at the Indian grocery store and we tried doing our own henna. It wasn't too hard actually, if you have patience, a steady hand, and a good eye for form. We weren't as good as Usha and the other mehendi ladies, of course—there was a reason they charged the rates they did.

And it was so weird to me that mehendi was not an essential part of TamBrahm weddings. In Punjab, where our family is from, 'get her hands colored' is a term synonymous with getting a girl married.

By the time we got home the paste was nearly dry. Good thing too because I had to get changed. What was good enough for the Iyers and the mehendi lady was not good for River Bend. Because Vir was going to be there. So far I'd only run into him by accident, but this time I *knew* I'd see him.

Get a grip, I told myself, *it was no big deal.*

I had the henna thing going on, so I thought I'd rock the bohemian look. A swingy summery Free People sundress, dangle earrings, a stack of bright bangles, strappy sandals, a dash of Victoria's Secret lip gloss, and I was set.

River Bend

We were an hour early for our meeting at River Bend.

Because I wanted Vinnie to see the Italianate Garden while it was lit up with the afternoon sun. The beautiful fountain, the formal flowerbeds, the Greek goddess sculptures, the brick patio with its carved wood railing—all looked outstanding at that time of day. The old mansion (in bad need of restoration, and crumbling on the inside, sadly) made the garden even more regal and princess-wedding-ish. I had taken lots of pictures for Vinnie before we booked the place, of course, but it wasn't like being there.

'I love it, Mini!' Vinnie said.

Whew!

We walked back to the carriage house. With its slate roof, copper cupola and weathervane, vaulted ceiling, and three massive glass-paned double doors, it was perfect for the reception. It was also where we were to meet everyone. Vinnie was just telling me how perfect it was when Vir drove up. In, of all things, an Indian-built hybrid—a Mirchandani Mirage.

He looked incredibly nice in khakis and a blue linen shirt. I'd only seen him in shorts (or pajamas!) before—and dressed up he looked even more … impressive.

'Vinnie, this is Vir,' I said with impressive calm. 'Vir, my sister, Vinnie.'

'Dr Vinnie, right?' he said, with a smile. 'I've heard a lot about you!'

'Strange, huh?' Vinnie said. "I've heard nothing about you."

I should probably have given her a heads up or something about Vir, I guess.

'So how did you find him, Mini?'

'I just, umm … ran into him,' I said.

'Literally!' Vir said. The memory seemed to amuse him.

'And where did you run into him?' Vinnie raised an eyebrow.

'Near Lake Waban,' I said, answering with geographical precision.

'The first time Yogi was chasing Roshan, my mum's cat,' Vir said. 'And then another time Mini lost her k—'

'Way!' I said, hurriedly. 'I lost my way! While walking Yogi!' I'd kept the losing of my keys episode under wraps so far. I'd never hear the end of it if it all came out. 'And Vir showed me how to get back to the Lake trail,' I finished.

'Exactly!' Vir said, covering valiantly. 'The trails are so confusing.'

'How d'you know the trails?' Vinnie said. 'You don't *sound* local.'

Wow, Vinnie was totally grilling the guy! I turned my back on Vir and gave her the Look. Vinnie ignored me.

'Right,' Vir said. 'I lived in the UK until seventh grade, and the accent may be permanent.'

'His mom is the dean of Fellsway,' I said. 'She's amazing!'

'Oh, nice!' Vinnie said. 'Have you met her?'

'No,' I said, at the same time as Vir said, 'Not yet!'

'Uh huh!' Vinnie said, thoughtfully. 'Funny what you miss when you don't live in the same state anymore.'

'Cool ride, by the way,' I said, changing the subject. 'I didn't even know you could get these things in the US.'

'It's my mum's car,' Vir explained. 'She's pretty committed to being green.'

'But how did you even import an Indian model here?' I asked. 'Mirchandani Motors is Indian, isn't it?'

Vir waved a hand, vaguely. 'It was a gift from—the Indian Embassy, I think. She didn't have to deal with bringing it over.'

'That's awesome!' I said. 'Bet Dad would love to take a look at it.'

'I'll bring it around if you like,' Vir said immediately. 'I'd like to meet him again anyway.'

'Again?' Vinnie asked, eyebrow hitched to her hairline again.

'Yeah, we met at the British Car Show,' Vir said.

'Really?' Vinnie said.

'There's Sudha Moorty!' I spotted a four-wheel drive in the distance.

'I'll go look at the power outlets in the hall,' Vir said. 'And measure the walls and stuff.'

'Hello beta!' Sudha Moorty leapt out of her jeep, exuding energy. 'I had forgotten what a beautiful venue this was! Only last year we had two weddings here.'

'Hi Sudha!' Caroline Kelly the event manager opened the door to the carriage house. 'It's great to see you again!'

I guess those two did know each other! What a small world this wedding business was.

Meanwhile Vinnie was still looking at me with a how-could-you-not-tell-me-about-that-guy stare.

'Mini,' she said, arms crossed. 'We need to talk!'

'No we don't,' I said. 'And don't jump to conclusions!'

'Yeah, right!' Vinnie said.

***

Three o'clock, and we were still waiting.

Caroline Kelly, Vinnie, Sudha Moorty, and even poor Vir, had gone over the tables, the chairs, the dance floor, the restrooms, the rain plan (we'd use the tent attached to the carriage house, in case of rain—it could seat one hundred and eighty people), the mandap, the aisle design, the fire extinguishers to be kept on hand before the ceremonial fire could be lit.

But no discussions about the food, the kitchens and the serving staff could happen because there was still no sign of Mr Sunny Sondhi of Curry Cuisine.

I called his main office and his son at least three times. They promised me he was on his way, but I was beginning to have my doubts.

'He'll be here!' I smiled manically at the assembled group. 'He will!'

'Why are you booking this guy?' Vir asked, when no one was looking. 'He seems dodgy.'

'Vinnie wants him to cater,' I whispered back. 'Curry Cuisine did Manish's sister's wedding and the Iyers really liked his food. Manish is Vinnie's fiancé,' I added, since Vir was looking lost.

My cellphone rang.

'This is Sunny Sondhi,' said an irritated-sounding voice.

'It's him,' I mimed to Vinnie. 'Mr Sondhi! How far away are you? We're all waiting for you to arrive!' A car turned around the corner as I spoke. That had to be him.

'I think I see you,' he said. 'I'll park and be there in a minute. Just wait.'

Sunny Sondhi was tall, fat, and dapperly dressed. We'd been waiting around for him for hours, but he showed up with an annoyed expression as if we were the ones who had kept *him* waiting. No apology either.

I knew he was busy—of the five or so Indian caterers to pick from in the Boston area Curry Cuisine was the biggest name—but this was ridiculous.

'Hello Mr Sondhi.' At least one of us seemed to know the Curry Cuisine guy well. He actually cracked a smile at Sudha Moorty.

'Hello, hello!' he said. 'I didn't think we had catered here before, but I remember this kitchen. So, do the catering vans have to pull up here?'

'And where are the tables?' We went over the table and dance floor setup, where we'd put the buffet table, where the dosa chef could set up his live dosa station—outdoors only, as per the fire marshal. 'That's all I need to see,' Mr Sondhi said. 'Thank you, I have another appointment.'

And we were done!

'I'll call about the music selection,' Vir said. 'It was nice meeting you, Vinnie.'

'Likewise,' said Vinnie.

The questions started before we'd pulled out of Mass Bot's rambling drive.

'Why didn't you tell me about that guy?' Vinnie asked.

'Vir?' I asked. 'No reason. Just because he's cute you don't have to jump to conclusions.'

'You're so cute and awkward around each other,' Vinnie said. 'Something has to be up!'

'Wait,' I lifted a figure, because my cellphone was ringing. 'Can you grab that?'

'Sure,' Vinnie pulled my phone out of my satchel. It was Jackie. Her car was in the shop and I was supposed to give her a ride home from River Bend. Only, what with all the waiting around, I had forgotten.

'We'll be there in a minute, Jackie,' Vinnie said. 'Sorry we forgot you!'

When we got Jackie, Vinnie started interrogating *her* about Vir instead.

Jackie, being Jackie, was only too happy to spill.

'He went to school in the UK,' Jackie said. 'Then he moved here with his mom and went to school in Cambridge, then he went to boarding school in India. He's going to MIT in the fall. And his parents are divorced. I don't think he has any siblings.'

'Thank you!' Vinnie was suddenly grinning. 'Smart too, huh? Did we pay him a deposit yet?'

'No!' We hadn't as yet officially signed up with Vir. 'He doesn't have any references! I don't know how we can trust him to do a good job. This could be a disaster!'

'Nah,' Vinnie said. 'DJ-ing isn't rocket science. He can handle it.'

'Hey, Rachel needs a DJ too!' Jackie said. 'For Jason's Bar Mitzvah. Didn't you hear about that?'

'Rachel is back?' I asked. 'I thought she was still in Israel!'

'She's been back for ten days,' Jackie said. 'And you'd know if you weren't busy with this whole wedding thing—sorry Vinnie, but it's true. Everyone's been talking about Jason's Bar Mitzvah band getting sick.'

Yikes! I really hadn't been to Amy's Attic for two whole weekends? Amy would be well within her rights to revoke my staff discount! And I hadn't even heard what Rachel had gotten up to in Israel. I guess they'd been busy grappling with Jason's Bar Mitzvah situation.

'What happened?' I asked, horrified for not having known.

'Amy had hired a band, like, last year or something,' Jackie said. 'But half of them just got the flu—in the middle of summer—and they can't perform. They've been calling about but all the good DJs already have gigs for this weekend.'

'This weekend?' I said.

'Yeah, they're kind of desperate,' Jackie said. 'Do you think Vir is free?'

'We could ask ...' I said. 'But how would he know anything about Bar Mitzvahs? He was in India the past four years.'

Mazel Tov!

So, apparently, during the two years of middle school Vir spent in the US, he went to no fewer than *nine* Bar and Bat Mitzvahs.

'Mum graduated from Brandeis,' Vir said. 'What can I say? Her friends have kids my age, and we moved here when I was thirteen. I'm kind of an expert on Bar Mitzvahs.'

'I thought she went to Fellsway,' I said. 'Isn't she an alumnus or something?'

'She went to Brandeis for grad school,' Vir said. 'She has a lot of degrees.'

'So, you'll do it?' I asked.

'Depends,' Vir said. 'Are you going?'

Now what did that have to do with it?

'Of course,' I said. 'Rachel is one of my oldest friends, and Jason's practically like my little brother!'

'Sign me up then,' Vir said. 'That way you can see if I'm good enough for Vinnie's wedding.'

'You'll have to get the kids to do party games, and teach them dance moves,' I warned. 'The limbo, the chicken dance, and the YMCA, the …'

'Electric slide?' Vir said. 'Sure, no problem. Whatever gets them moving, right?'

'Right,' I said. I had a feeling that he was laughing at me again.

***

Rachel and I caught up before the party. She looked great, natural tan, cool new cut and highlights from Tel Aviv. She was always up for a new look—the availibility of her glossy head for trials was the reason I could do *anything* with hair. And she brought back enough Dead Sea mineral creams and potions to last us all a decade. Jackie must have briefed her about Vinnie's wedding and about Vir, because she was up to speed with everything.

She was up on stage now, reading in fluent Hebrew and looking radiant in an Alice and Oliva bubble dress. I smoothed down my dress nervously—it was a periwinkle lace frock from the 2010 Tracy Reese Holiday Collection. I had worn it for Vinnie's graduation too—in Chicago, appropriately—where Tracy is from. OK, Tracy is from Detroit but that's close enough.

Throughout the service I had butterflies thinking about Vir setting up at the sports club where the party was scheduled. Amy had hired him on my recommendation. What if he wasn't good?

'Dad, I'm going to go ahead in case Amy needs help,' I said. Dad looked cute with a yamaka cap tilting precariously on his greying head.

'I'm not going to the party, Mini,' he said, pushing his glasses up. 'I have a conference call set up in an hour. I'll see you back home.'

The sports club was the perfect venue for a Bar Mitzvah party. The kids would have their choice of activities—swimming in the pool, rock climbing on the indoor rock wall, mini golf, or shooting hoops on the basketball court. The staff directed me to where the dinner tables and dance floor had been set up—the indoor tennis courts which had been transformed with decorations, balloons and lights.

Vir was already there setting up his DJ gear when I got there. It seemed to consist of a MacBook, a complicated-looking deck with tons of dials and buttons, and a pen drive. He was deep in conversation with Amy, going over the music, games, and announcements, but they stopped when they caught sight of me.

'Mini, thanks for telling us about Vir,' Amy said. 'He's been amazing. It was so nice of him to step in on such short notice.'

'Just good luck, I guess,' I said. 'Vir, is that everything you need?'

'Yes,' Vir said. 'I've set up the speakers and done a sound check. And the lights too—do you like them?'

The roof of the tennis court was lit up in blue and pink pastels—it looked awesome—I was impressed.

'I have to go make sure the appetizers are being served, honey,' Amy said, 'but stay and chat with Vir. Rachel and Jackie will be here soon!' She had the happy glow of a mom who has made it through half of a long-planned Bar Mitzvah, and has full confidence that the second half would go off without a hitch.

'You look nice,' Vir said, after she left. 'Nice hat.'

I put my hand up to my twenties-style beaded fascinator in the same periwinkle as my dress. 'You think? I made it, you know.'

There was that amused look again. 'You did not!'

'Did too! And it's a fascinator, actually,' I said, 'not a hat.'

'Fascinating,' he said. 'Though it does look a bit like a cat toy—my mum's cat would love it.'

No one had ever compared my handiwork to a kitty toy before.

'He has nice taste then,' I said.

'There are a lot of them here today, aren't there?' Vir said, looking around. Other guests had started filtering in, holding drinks and snacking on appetizers.

'Uh huh,' I said, surveying the headbands, cocktail hats, and fascinators bobbing around on the dance floor with quiet pride. 'They're all mine.'

'No way!' he said.

'It was for a fundraiser,' I explained, 'for the American Cancer Society. I have an online Etsy store that I sell stuff on. The money goes to my favorite charities—the American Cancer Society, The Jimmy Fund, the MSPCA. And the royal wedding was a great time for a fascinator sale. I sold everything I had in five days. Lots of local people bought some.'

'I think my mum might like one,' he said. 'How do I find the store?'

'Just Google "Megha & Me"—that's the name of my Etsy store,' I said. 'There isn't much left right now, but I could make her a custom one!'

'Thanks,' Vir said. 'You better go—I think they're serving dinner. I'll see you after the party.'

'Listen, Vir,' I said, suddenly panicking about his upcoming performance. I mean, Vir wasn't really the loud high energy emcee type, was he? He was more kind of … laidback. 'Please do your best? It's not like I don't trust you, but this is a *big* deal for Jason.'

'Don't worry,' he said, completely unfazed. 'I've got this.'

***

'How're you guys doing?' Vir said, mic in hand. 'I don't know about you, but I've got a feeling, that tonight's gonna be a good night!'

It's all in the attitude, I guess. He made even something as overplayed as the Black Eyed Peas—Jason's pick if I had to guess—feel fresh.

Fill up that cup—MAZEL TOV!

Look at him dancing

Just take it—OFF!

In the end I felt really stupid for worrying—because, honestly, he was outstanding. You couldn't have asked for a better emcee. Limbo, Twist, Congo line, Hora, he made that group of kids cover everything, Brit accent and all. And the candle-lighting ceremony was so incredibly touching—Jason spoke about his grandparents, aunts, uncles, cousins, friends, and his parents and

Rachel, of course—and they all came up, one by one, to help him to light the thirteen candles on his spectacular Bar Mitzvah cake. I swear I cried. And I wasn't the only one.

'You can't just stand there!' Rachel grabbed me from the edge of the dance floor. 'You've got to dance!'

'OK, OK,' I said. 'I'm doing it, aren't I?' By doing it, I meant dancing the YMCA. It's ridiculous, but I defy anyone to not feel happy while doing it. I had a silly grin on my face—just like everyone else on the dance floor.

The music had changed to a slow sweet song. Perfect for shy middle school kids—including our new Bar Mitzvah Jason Siegel—to muddle through their first slow dance.

Vir left the console and came over to where I was standing. He held out a hand. 'Would you like to dance?'

'Sure,' I said. I was glad the lights were low because I'm pretty sure I looked horribly self-conscious—is it actually possible for the whole body to blush? Then both his hands were around my waist, and both mine on his shoulders. *Breathe, Mini*, I told myself.

'Do you have grandparents?' Vir asked, as a sweet old couple—Jason's grandparents—swept by on the dance floor looking blissfully happy. Vir was a good dancer; I looked like I knew what I was doing just by following his lead.

'I have three grandparents,' I said. 'My nanaji is an old army man. He retired back in the eighties, around the time Mom and Dad got married. He's off the grid half the time, visiting old friends, travelling, doing his own thing. So I don't see him that often, but when he does surface—he's awesome. But my nani passed away when I was four.'

I was aware that I was babbling, but I couldn't stop—sheer nerves, I guess.

'Who else?' Vir asked.

'Dad's parents, Beeji and Bauji,' I said. 'They moved here when Dad was two.'

'Do they still live here?' he asked.

'They moved back to India four years ago,' I said. 'To help Bade Bauji, my great grandfather, with his business. Have you heard of KDH Spices?'

'Kake Di Hatti, right?' Vir asked. 'KDH Spices—the taste of India! Don't tell me your great grandfather is Kake!'

Kake is Punjabi for little boy—like buddy, or laddie. Kake Di Hatti would translate to Buddy's Shop, I guess.

'No, he's not Kake.' The idea of my tall, refined, white-haired great grandfather being Kake made me laugh. 'He named it after his son!'

'Your grandfather is Kake, then?' Vir asked.

'No, Kake Tauji is,' I said. It was kind of funny that the name had stuck to my dad's uncle. I guess people do have buddy uncles too, don't they? 'Will you stop laughing at my family?'

'I'm not laughing!' Vir said. 'I think very highly of KDH Spices. They made my boarding school meals almost edible! And I've been to the restaurant they have in New Delhi in … what's that market …'

'Karol Bagh,' I said. I had happy memories of the place

where Bauji grew up. Mom had grown up there too, but her family—Nanaji was minor Rajput nobility—lived in the huge old houses around the park—far from the bustle of the main market where the Punjabi refugees got their start. But things reversed over the years—the old houses crumbled, and the Punjabi entrepreneurs made fortunes. 'I haven't been there since I was seven.'

'You should go back,' Vir said. 'It's changed a lot in ten years.'

The music had stopped, but the pounding in my ears kept on—Vir still had his arms around me, you see. For a minute we just stood there as people milled around us in the dim light.

'Duty calls,' Vir said, and let me go.

Wedding Lehenga

Yogi's barking broke through my concentration as I slogged through yet another SAT prep sheet.

'What is it, boy?'

I should have known even before I looked out the window—yeah, the DHL van was parked at the curb.

I scanned the box as I signed for the package. OMG, it was from Masi—it *had* to be Vinnie's lehenga!

The box was nearly as big as I was, and heavy too. I got it in the door, tottered upstairs with it, and laid it carefully on Vinnie's old bed. Yogi sniffed it thoroughly—it must have had some really interesting smells.

'Wait,' I told the dog. 'This has to be opened *very* carefully.'

I sliced through the packing tape and opened the box—carefully scrunched up tissue paper hid the contents from view. The crisp smell of packaging paper and … sandalwood, filled the room. It smelled like India. It smelled like Masi's office.

Casting off the tissue I got my first glimpse of the lehenga.

Wow! The gold organza fabric was beyond *anything*! And the

exquisite hand-stitched embroidery made it look so rich, and yet so understated, if it's even possible for spun gold to look understated. It was stunning!

I lifted it—the weight of it was surprising. Beneath it was the dupatta—a light-as-air red silk, edged with the same old gold embroidery as the lehenga. It looked like something royalty would have worn two centuries ago, not something Vinnie would wear in four weeks!

A sense of calm washed over me. It was all right. Whatever else happened with the wedding planning now, Vinnie would be a gorgeous bride. And the dress was made to showcase Mom's jewelry. Vinnie was really, actually getting married, and things were going to turn out fine. Thanks to Mallu Masi.

Fifty points to Gryffindor.

Just to be sure, I held the lehenga up to me. Way too short, but I'd worn enough of Vinnie's hand-me-downs to know that it would fit her. The top was loose too. Not much at the waist and bust, but a lot on the shoulders. It would *totally* fit Vinnie.

I did a twirl, swinging the heavy edge of the lehenga out slightly, and threw some packing peanuts in the air in celebration.

I folded the lehenga and put it back into the box. That's when I noticed the blue silk in the box—there was another lehenga beneath.

It was firozi blue—the color of turquoise, late summer evenings, and sea glass washed up on the beaches of Cape Cod. It had once been my favorite color. Masi remembered?

The lehenga was an ankle-length circle skirt, lavishly embroidered in gold and silver dabka, and semi-precious gemstones. It reminded me of the first time I had ever seen a lehenga being embroidered. It was in Mallu Masi's workshop in Rajasthan. A circle of blue silk fabric had been stretched into a massive embroidery frame, and four of Masi's best embroiderers were working on it simultaneously with spools of golden thread.

'See the pattern, Mini?' Masi had said, showing me the intricate lines stamped lightly on the fabric. 'That's my design.'

I'd watched as the men painstakingly brought Masi's design to life—one stitch at a time. It would take months to finish that one piece. That's when I fell in love with fabric.

But something was wrong. It was much, much too big.

The drawstring waist meant I could tighten it to fit, but that would make the fabric bunch up. And that's the thing with a circle dress design—once it's been cut and stitched, you can't size it down without ruining it. There was no way I could wear it and look good.

I smiled ruefully. Scratch those points already.

Masi still thought of me as the tall, chubby, gawky thirteen-year-old I'd been when she saw me last. Partly my fault, I suppose. After she and Beeji had their last spat I stopped communicating with her completely. And things had changed a lot since then.

The year I went from being a size ten to a size zero started with my Beeji and Bauji packing up and going to India. Bade Bauji was undertaking a major expansion at KDH Spices—he wanted our Bauji's help to set up the automated plants. Also, both my grandparents were sick of the snow. Other snowbirds go to Florida, my grandparents went all the way around the world instead.

The good thing about this was a) my dad started cooking all our meals, and b) he sucked at it, so food stopped being fun and I stopped eating so much of it.

I'm not saying he didn't try to cook well. He tried very, very hard. But most of his efforts were aimed at making sure there were enough nutrients, antioxidants, and vitamins in our food, and minimal amounts of trans fats, free radicals, and other nasty stuff—with cancer in our genes he wasn't taking any chances with my health or Vinnie's. We didn't do any fast food. The meals he made were always perfectly balanced as per the food pyramid. But, even after I flung liberal amounts of KDH spices on them, they stubbornly tasted like cardboard.

How he could be related to the founder of KDH spices, I have no clue.

About then I discovered a sport that did not involve hitting a ball—cross country. All I needed to do was put one foot in front of another, over and over and over, and some ingrained tenacity made me good at it.

So between Dad's suckish food and cross-country practice I lost a ton of weight, and re-achieved my former skinniness.

Masi still hadn't got the memo, I guess.

On the positive side Vinnie literally had tears in her eyes when I showed her the lehenga via Skype.

'What about *your* lehenga?' she asked.

'It's really, really beautiful,' I said. 'But it doesn't fit. Masi still thinks I'm a size twelve or something.'

'That's tragic!' Vinnie said.

'I'll fix it, if I have time,' I said. 'But I've been thinking, Vinnie—what about getting saris for all your bridesmaids—including me!'

'We can't possibly pull that off as well,' Vinnie said. She was dressed in loose-fitting blue scrubs. She'd just come off a night shift and looked completely exhausted.

'We can,' I said. 'Saris are free size, so we don't have to worry about fittings.'

'What about the blouses?' Vinnie asked.

'I can stitch them,' I said. 'I'll just buy an extra sari and use the silk for the blouses. That way they'll match perfectly.'

'I'll ask the girls if they'll wear saris,' Vinnie said. 'But won't it be a lot of work to stitch the blouses?'

'Yeah, but it's doable,' I said. 'And imagine how great it'll look in the pictures? Do you think they'll wear red silk saris with a gold border? It'll make such a nice contrast to your gold lehenga. I can order them in bulk from this desi fashion website I found!'

'I'll email everyone, Mini, and CC you,' Vinnie said. 'Can you make sure they're OK with it?' She yawned and stretched. 'I'm sooo sleepy.'

'Go to bed!' I ordered. 'I'll email them!'

'No Mini, you're already doing so much!' Vinnie said. 'I'll

email them tomorrow. I'm sorry the lehenga Masi sent didn't fit you. Why didn't you send measurements?'

'Because I thought she was sending me a sari!' I said. 'I've been thinking though ... I could alter it.'

'Maybe you should send it back.' Vinnie said. 'What if you ruin it?'

'I won't,' I said.

'How's Vir?' Vinnie asked. 'Did he end up DJ-ing Jason's Bar Mitzvah?'

'Uh huh.' My heart did a backflip, and, I'm pretty sure a YMCA as well. 'He did great. But you do need to go over the schedule and the songs and the announcements with him, OK? So think about it!'

***

I spread out the lehenga fabric into a perfect circle on the living room floor. It looked like a pool of blue silk spangled with gold and silver.

Then I raised my best pair of scissors.

Normally I'd be petrified to chop up something so well-tailored and expensive and *new*, but I was mad. Mad enough not to care how it would turn out, if I did end up ruining it. In fact, I was sure that cutting the lehenga up was going to be positively therapeutic.

With steady hands I cut out a quarter slice of firozi blue silk like a piece of a giant pie chart.

There. Done.

Sue had said I could stitch the skirt on her sewing machine, and take in the top too. It would work, I knew it would.

***

141

In a bid to shake off the blues (no pun intended) I packed my watercolors, bottle of water and brushes into my French easel and headed to Fellsway with the dog. Painting 'en plein air' always helped me slay whatever was bothering me. Besides I had to add to the portfolio that I'd been neglecting for weeks. So much for having a good body of work before the end of summer!

I set up the easel by the small stone bridge at the far end of the lake. The water lilies were blooming in the creek below, and if I was lucky a few of the lake's resident swans would visit to inspire me. Yogi flopped down on the ground and watched the ducks sailing by, resigned to his fate. He knew what to expect after I set up the easel—hours of sitting around for him, while I messed around with paint and ignored him.

An hour later I stepped back and surveyed my work.

Not bad! I always did my best work when I had something to work out of my system. My low spirits were gone too. I wiped my hands on a rag and decided to let the paint dry before doing more with the scene.

'Hey, that's awesome!' Vir had somehow materialized next to me and was examining the painting with interest. 'Is that for your portfolio?'

'It is,' I said, playing it cool, even though my heart was doing the YMCA again, instead of pumping blood like a normal organ. 'Do you like it?'

'You had better not give this up when you go to Uni, that's all,' he said. 'Did you decide which design schools you're applying to?'

Through strategic breathing—short, shallow breaths worked

well, I found—I was able to get enough oxygen to my brain to actually function.

'No,' I said. 'I don't want to go out of state.'

'But you're selling yourself short,' he said. 'Seriously!'

'My dad won't even consider it. Do you want me to move away or something?' I meant it as a light comment, but something shifted in his eyes that sent a shiver down my spine. In a good way.

'No,' he said. 'I don't want you to move, actually.' Before he could say more Yogi started a low warning growl that made me jump.

'NO!' A bolt of black fur dashed towards Yogi. It was that danged black poodle again.

I moved to block the poodle's path and he swerved to get around me, with a laser focus on Yogi who had his fighting face on—hackles up, lips drawn back in a snarl. Then it happened so fast I could do nothing to stop it—the dog slammed into my easel and sent it flying.

'Whoa!' Vir had stepped on the dog's trailing leash, bringing him to an abrupt halt, more by accident than design and grabbed my canvas with his other hand.

How fabulous was he?

'Good save!' I said.

'Shadow!' the owner came into view at a flying run. 'Oh, I'm so sorry.'

Vir handed her the leash, adding a stern request to keep that 'blasted beast' under control in the future.

She had dragged Shadow out of sight before I saw the damage to my easel. One of the legs was completely destroyed!

'No!' I crumpled to the ground where the splintered wood from the easel's leg lay, looking totally and irreparably smashed.

'Is it expensive?' Vir asked. 'That woman should pay for it, you know.'

I spread my fingers helplessly, at a loss for words.

'Are you OK?' Vir asked.

It was all too much. I wrapped my arms around myself and burst into tears.

'Hey, hey.' Vir put a heavy arm around me. 'It's OK, it's just a … stand or whatever. You can replace it, can't you?'

'No,' I said, fiercely. 'I CAN'T.'

'Ok,' Vir said. 'Then … we'll fix it.'

'You can't fix that!' The tears came fast and furious and I couldn't talk at all. Yogi's whining brought me back. 'It's OK, Yogi, the bad dog's gone.'

'It's special somehow, isn't it?' Vir asked. 'Your stand?'

'I got it on my thirteenth birthday,' I said. 'From my mother.' The tears started up again.

To his credit, Vir thought it through before speaking.

'You said your mom passed away when you were ten,' Vir said. 'Do I have it wrong?'

'No,' I said, wiping my nose on his sleeve. 'She bought it before she died, and asked Dad to give it to me on my thirteenth birthday.'

'Really? That's kind of cool,' Vir said, putting an arm around me.

'She did that a lot,' I said. 'She even bought a handbag for Vinnie's med school graduation. Dad kept it locked up all these years and we gave it to her in May. It was a Dooney & Bourke Doctor's satchel, really classic. From their 2004 line, but it looks cool even now—in a vintage kind of way.'

I stopped on a hiccup, aware that I was babbling.

'Wow!' Vir said, as if handbags were the kind of thing that wowed him normally.

'And she designed some amazing gold jewelry for Vinnie's wedding,' I said. 'That's why I want the wedding to be perfect. She's not around to do it, but *someone* should, right?'

'Right,' Vir said. 'She loved you both a lot, clearly.'

'Uh huh,' I said. And then I didn't speak for a while, just sat there on the grass with Vir and Yogi next to me.

'I can fix it, you know,' Vir said. 'Bit of wood glue, and some screws and splints—piece of cake.'

'Really?' I said.

'Yeah,' he said. We picked up the pieces together and put them into my easel handbag. 'It won't look exactly the same, but it'll stand, I promise.'

I kind of believed it would.

You, Actually

Vinnie never sent the email to her bridesmaids about the saris.

She had a whole week of double shifts—what were they trying to do? Turn her into a physician, or kill her? But I had the names and addresses from the guest list so I called and emailed until they were all on board. Except for one holdout (who said she'd wear it anyway) they approved of the sari we liked—a wine-red silk with a thin gold border—and they insisted on paying for them. In took only a week for the saris to arrive.

Our house looked like a reunion of the WHS Class of 2004 Girl's Field Hockey Team, since they all came over to be fitted for blouses. The good thing about custom blouses was each girl could pick a design that suited her. Someone wanted spaghetti straps, others cap sleeves, or a simple sleeveless blouse. I was happy to give them the cut they wanted—but it took a big chunk of time out of my summer, even if I did one or two a week.

I was especially psyched when Jenna, the goalie, and sole holdout, said she liked how she looked in it.

'I was just afraid of all that material, you know,' she said.

'But it looks nice the way you wrap it. Just don't expect me to wear it on my own!'

'It's easy,' I said. 'If we pin the pleats at the right spot for each of you, and you practice a bit—you'll get it. But you don't have to. I'll help you the day of the wedding.'

'I'll give it a try …' Jenna said. 'I'm turning, I'm tucking, I'm flinging—OK, how does it look?'

Success! With some practice they were all getting the sari on themselves. Whew! For a minute I thought we'd have to buy them the Eazy Pleats thing they keep advertising on the bridesmaids' sari websites I'd been frequenting. Can you believe such a thing exists?

EAZY PLEATS: SARI AND PALLU PLEATER

Tired of asking your mom or an aunty to help you put on a sari? Sick of sloppy sliding pleats that make that gorgeous sari look like a hot mess? Upset that the pins in your pleats are shredding the delicate heirloom silk your grandmother left you?

Try EAZY PLEATS and you'll never need help putting on a sari again!

TIE A FLAWLESS SARI BY YOURSELF IN FIVE MINUTES WITH OUR PLEATMAKER AND EASY CLIPS! Easy Clips are classy, magnetic clips for holding your sari together. They are the simplest, safest, and quickest way to hold together your pleats, palla, chunni, lehenga, dupatta, and more.

With Eazy Pleats it's EAZY-PEAZY to look fabulous in a sari, anytime, anywhere!

Thirty dollars for a piece of plastic and a bunch of rhinestone clips? Honestly, unless you're completely clueless you should be able to make a pleat on your own—especially if you actually own a sari to practice on! They teach you to fanfold in kindergarten for heaven's sake. Still, I admit, I sent Vinnie a link. Let's face it—she never got the fanfold thing in kindergarten either.

***

The caller ID said 'Private' but it was Vir.

'Hey,' said Vir. 'You haven't been to the lake lately. What's up?'

His voice sounded so close, so deep. 'I've been busy with the bridesmaids' outfits—for the wedding. '

'You're making them yourself?' he asked.

'Just the blouses,' I said. 'I'm nearly done. Just two to go and they are out of state, so it'll have to wait.'

'Have you been painting at all?' he asked.

'No,' I said. 'No time!'

'Come over to the lake and finish that painting,' Vir said. 'I promise I'll keep a watch out for the poodle. I'll even walk Yogi while you're working so he isn't bored.'

'Really?' I asked.

'Really,' he said. 'Your easel is nearly done—the glue still needs to dry though and I don't want to rush it.'

I felt a warm rush of gratitude for him for taking the trouble to fix it.

'OK,' I said. 'I'll see you in a bit!'

***

All my good clothes were in the laundry—but I didn't want to be dressed up today. I was too tired to make the effort and it was hot hot HOT. It was time I stopped dressing up for Vir anyway.

I dragged on a paint-covered T-shirt and a pair of Vinnie's old volleyball shorts, and turned over the waistband so they wouldn't slide off—which made them even shorter. They said 'Westbury' across the butt, but it was ninety degrees out—at least I'd be cool.

I didn't have my easel back yet anyway, so I left the paints behind. I wanted to get in a sketch of the Fellsway campus from across the lake—charcoals would do. Vir said he'd meet us by the topiary garden so I found a shady spot where a low stone ledge ran along the edge of the water. If I sat on the ledge I was practically invisible to anyone walking along the path, and I could dangle my feet in the cool clean water of the lake. I planted myself there and opened my sketchpad.

After a peaceful half hour getting some stellar sketches done I heard footsteps coming my way. Vir! I peered over the wall just as he walked up to me. But why was he carrying a towel?

'Hey!' Vir said. 'Nice spot!'

My heart rate escalated to the point of being audible, or so it seemed. And the short, shallow breaths didn't seem to be working today. I took a deep breath instead.

'It's cooler here,' I said, and held up my hands to frame the scene I was trying to capture. 'And the perfect vantage point.'

'Yes, it is,' he said and pulled off his shirt to reveal an

impressively firm and muscled torso—and caused my heart rate to go from highly escalated to practically flatline.

What was he *doing*?

He climbed down to the ledge and took off his shoes. Then sat down next to me and dangled his feet in the water—while I concentrated on not being asphyxiated from the proximity to his extremely attractive and half-clad self.

'Not bad,' he said, talking about the water temperature, apparently, and waded into the lake, leaving the towel and a pile of his clothes and shoes next to me. 'I'm going for a swim.'

I took a gulp of air. 'Are you sure the water's clean?' I asked.

He just laughed and dived deep. He came up ten feet out and clawed away from the edge of the lake with long muscled arms. The water rippled away from him in circles.

Yogi waded in after him, but stopped when the water lapped his chest.

He treaded water and waved at Yogi. 'Come on, Yogi!'

I jumped up. 'Vir—no!'

'No?' he asked. 'Why not?'

All the nerves I'd felt earlier vanished. 'He doesn't swim. I mean, only if his *life* depends on it. He fell in once where it was deep and just *sank*! I thought he was going to drown, but he managed to paddle back. But it put him off the whole thing.'

Vir had swum back while I'd been talking.

'Hey, chill!' he said wading out of the lake, his wet hair plastered to his neck. 'He just needs someone to swim with him. That way he'll feel safe.'

150

'Well I can't take him to the pool,' I said. 'Most beaches on the Cape don't allow dogs in the summer. And I refuse to get into this water. It's probably full of germs … and fish poop.'

He laughed. 'I swam in the Ganga a few months ago,' he said. 'In Haridwar.' He said Ganga, not Ganges, and he pronounced it right. 'This looks like drinking water after that. Let Yogi try … maybe he'll swim with me.'

I wasn't sure a dog as old as Yogi could learn to swim.

'Come on, Yogi,' he said. He grabbed a stick floating a little way out and threw it further. 'See the stick? Go get it!'

'No,' I dumped my notepad and pulled off my shoes. 'What if he's forgotten?'

I waded out until I was next to him, fish poop be damned, but he grabbed my hand to stop me from going further. 'He's doing fine,' he said quietly, 'see?'

Yogi was paddling back with the stick clamped between his teeth, looking pleased with himself.

I couldn't believe it!

'Good dog!' I was so proud I was skipping around in the water. 'Good, good dog!' He climbed onto the ledge, dropped the stick, and shook himself—spraying us with lake water.

Vir handed me the stick. 'You throw it,' he said.

I flung the stick out and Yogi went right after it again. He really had lost his fear of swimming.

'This is great!' I said. Then I promptly lost my footing and slid sideways in sickening slow motion until I slammed into Vir. 'Oops,' I said grabbing his arm to steady myself, 'I'm so sorry.'

'Can *you* swim, by the way?' he said. 'Or do you need instruction? Because I'm kind of good at this I think.'

He had his arm around my waist and I was inches from his chest—this was making me somewhat weak in the knees. 'I can stay afloat,' I said, with dignity.

He set me on my feet at arm's length and looked me over. 'Not bad—a little skinny, but very attractive.'

'Excuse me,' I said, outraged. 'Are you, like, checking me out?'

'Of course!' he grinned at me. 'You're pretty.'

'That's …' I grasped for words, 'that's just messed up. How can you be so direct? What would your mom say?' I waved an arm towards the house in the background.

'She'd be fine with it,' he said. 'See, the thing is, you can check me out too.'

He struck a pose with both biceps flexed and looked at me challengingly. 'Well?'

The whole thing was stupid enough to make me laugh.

'You know,' I said suddenly, 'I thought Vinnie would marry someone like you,' I flexed my own arm, 'all ripped, and buff, and sarcastic.'

'Really?' he said with interest. 'Do I detect some disapproval of Manish? He isn't perfect like me, I take it?'

'You're not perfect!' I said. 'And he's great, he really is. I just thought you're the type she'd go for, but instead she fell for him. I mean, he's really, really nice, and he is so funny as well, but he's also … skinny, and musical, and not into sports, and …'

152

'You're pretty skinny yourself!' he said.

'I'm a girl!' I said.

'I noticed,' he said. 'So … what's your type?' From his tone I could tell he wasn't kidding around anymore.

'I don't know,' I lied.

Because, the right answer was—*you, actually.*

The sun had gone behind a cloud, and a drizzle had started. The waist-deep water around us was dancing with raindrops.

He still had both hands on my arms. Which were goose-bumping, and not exactly from the rain.

'How about ripped, and buff, and sarcastic?' he suggested, softly.

It felt like my heart was pounding in my ears. I was dimly aware that he was waiting for an answer, but I just stared at him. Behind him Yogi was sitting on the ledge and chewing on his stick.

'I like you, Mini,' he said. 'A lot.'

He looked so vulnerable. Something inside me melted, like a marshmallow in hot chocolate.

'I …' I could feel a shy smile coming over my face. 'I like you too, Vir.'

He took a step towards me and put an arm around my shoulders, which I'm really positive would have felt great, probably, but the momentum of it pitched us both into the lake.

'Oh no!' I tried to get up but the rocks were slippery beneath my bare feet. He fell too, and when we helped each other up we were both laughing like idiots.

We sat out on the stone bench, the towel around us both, and Yogi next to us, damp and reeking of wet dog fur. There was no need for the towel really, since the summer sun was beating down again by then, but it felt nice to cuddle. We made plans to see a movie on Thursday after my Kumon shift. And we didn't talk about Vinnie's wedding. Not even once.

First Date

'You're looking sharp today, Mini,' Sona said. 'What's going on?'

I smoothed down my dress nervously. 'Really?' I said. 'It's not too much?'

It had taken some dedicated sorting through the racks at Amy's Attic—which I had to do anyway to catch up with my hours—plus my entire staff quota for August to pay off the dress. It was a cute-as-a-button navy blue Marc Jacobs, and it looked great with the red Tory Burch ballet flats I had scored last month. It had also taken Rachel an hour—I *so* owed that girl—to work my hair into Zooey Deschanel style long, loose waves. They looked great even without her epic bangs.

'No, no, your dress is very pretty,' Preet said, before asking pointedly. 'Are you going out with friends?'

Honestly, I was having Vir pick me up at work so Dad wouldn't cross-examine me, but the Kumon moms were worse than him.

'Yeah,' I said.

'What's his name?' asked Sona.

'Vir ...' I stopped because a) she had tricked me into admitting I was going with a guy, and b) because I wasn't sure what Vir's last name was. It had to be Chabra, right? 'Vir Chabra.'

'Nice name,' Preet said. 'Punjabi too.'

'Really?' I said. 'I didn't know Chabra was Punjabi.'

'Yes,' Sona said. 'Are you going to see a movie?'

'Uh huh,' I said. '*Deathly Hallows*, part two—I can't believe he hasn't seen it.'

'Is that him?' Kaveri's mom peered out of the store front. A Mirchandani Mirage was pulling up to the curb.

'That's him,' I said. 'I better go!'

'No,' Sona said. 'Let him in. Here, do some paperwork, so you look busy.'

I stared at her as if she had two heads. 'Why?'

'So we can see him,' Sona said. 'Do it!'

'OK,' I said and sat down at the desk and stared blankly at a fractions worksheet. This was nuts!

Vir got out of the car and scanned the shop fronts looking for me. He knew I worked at Kumon. He spotted the sign and walked to the door.

'Yes?' Sona said, sounding completely normal. 'Can I help you?'

'I was looking for Mini,' Vir said. 'Mini Kapoor. She works here?'

'Mini,' Sona said, 'there's someone for you.' I looked up to see Vir standing in the waiting area, knee-high in little kids, with

156

every mom's eyes on him expressing unanimous approval. My heart swelled with pride.

He looked awesome in dark wash jeans, a polo shirt and leather lace-ups. He had dressed up too.

'Hi Vir,' I said. 'Sorry I wasn't outside. I had to finish up here …'

'Take your time,' Vir said. 'I already bought the tickets.'

'Are you and Mini Kapoor going on a date?' Rahul asked. The room erupted in muffled giggling. I was mortified!

'Um … yes,' Vir said. 'Are you Rahul?' I had only mentioned Rahul once, but he remembered.

'Yes, I am Rahul Singh,' Rahul said. 'Have a good date, Vir and Mini.'

'Thanks, Rahul,' he said. 'Bye, Sona, Preet.'

He remembered their names too!

'That kid's cute,' Vir said as we walked to the car. 'So, did I pass?'

'What do you mean?' I said, feigning ignorance.

'They were making sure I was good enough,' he said, 'for you!'

'Nonsense!' I said, smiling.

It was a good thing he didn't turn around to see the aunties giving me winks and thumbs-ups through the glass pane.

'Hey, the driver's seat is on the right!' I said. 'Shouldn't it be on the left in an Indian car?'

'It was for an American trade show,' Vir said, 'I think.' He held the door to the passenger seat open for me, and I climbed in.

'That's so cool,' I said. 'I bet my Dad would like to look at it!'

'I'd be happy to show it to him,' Vir said.

'What does your father do, Vir?' I asked as we pulled onto Route 9.

'He … umm, he's into farm equipment,' Vir said.

'Farm equipment?' I asked. What was that—tractors, and harvesters and stuff? 'In India?'

'Yeah,' Vir said. 'The agricultural sector is huge. So, is this movie hall your local hangout or something?' OK, I got it. He clearly didn't want to talk about his dad. 'You must have gone there all your life.'

'Yeah, I saw my first movie in here when I was … three,' I said. 'I had a high chair and an extra-long straw to drink my apple juice with. Vinnie was ten, and she made Mom take us. I don't really remember it, but Vinnie does. I wish I could remember it though …'

'I have something for you,' Vir said. 'It's in the boot. Don't let me forget to give it to you when I drop you home.'

By boot he meant the trunk, I assumed. 'What is it?' I asked.

'The easel,' Vir said. 'I fixed it.'

He fixed it in a week—seriously? Dad usually overshot any fix-by date he promised me by at least a month. I could get used to this.

'Thank you,' I said.

He took his eyes off the road for a second to look into mine. 'You're welcome,' he said. 'So, *Deathly Hallows*? You don't mind seeing it again?'

'Not at all,' I said. Everything was changing—Vinnie had graduated, she was getting married. Next year I'd be in college. And this was the final curtain for my favorite childhood character. I couldn't possibly see it too many times. Hey—at least I had avoided wearing anything Hogwarts-related—a big step towards adulthood for me.

Popcorn, soda, Vir, and Voldemort having his ass kicked—could it get better than that? But due to the fact that some people ended up on the wrong end of a wand—I was glad for Vir's shoulder and the wad of tissues I had brought along in my handbag.

'Thanks for that,' I said. 'Hey, maybe next time we should see a Bollywood movie. I know a theatre in Westborough that screens all the new releases. There's one out with that new actress, KK, Koyal Khanna or something. The moms at Kumon were all raving about it.'

Vir looked genuinely horrified. 'No,' he said. A very categorical "no".

'No?' I asked. 'Just "no"? You don't like Hindi movies?'

'I do,' he said, but he sounded iffy. 'But some of them are awful. You need to pick carefully. Would you care for some candy floss?'

'Cotton candy?' I said. 'Sure!'

I guess I could add Bollywood movies and his dad to the list of things Vir didn't want to talk about. Somehow his reaction to the Bollywood movie soured the sweet happy feeling of the night.

When we pulled up to the house Dad was outside walking Yogi. That was *so* an excuse to talk to Vir—he never took the dog out after ten at night. May as well get it over with then! OMG, did Dad have to wear his high-waisted Daddy jeans and those horrible shiny white sneakers? He looked like an older desi version of Seinfeld. With glasses.

'Dad, this is Vir,' I said.

'We met at the car show!' Dad said.

'Nice to see you again, sir,' Vir said.

'Nice car,' Dad said.

'Thanks,' Vir said. 'I love your vintage Esprit too.'

'Not vintage, exactly,' Dad said. 'It's too old to be new, and too young to be vintage. Want to take it for a drive?'

'Sure,' Vir said. And with that they both vanished into the garage, which Dad had *still* not cleaned despite his promises. Way to go, Dad. Welcome Vir into the messiest part of our house. I stomped into the kitchen with the abandoned dog. Ten minutes later I heard the vroom of the Lotus backing out.

I spent half an hour waiting for them, killing time by adding coupons to my latest piece of artwork, a collage masterpiece made entirely from coupons I'd clipped from weekend sales— title: Clipping for College, total value in savings: $321.75. They still weren't back—way to hijack my date, Dad—so that's the last I saw of Vir or Dad that night. Because I got into my PJs and went to bed.

Don't Google Me

Three weeks to the wedding and my checklist was looking excellent.

Vinnie and Manish had managed to get their license while they were in the state, and Vinnie had hired the bartenders, gone over the wine list (Dad did not want me in charge of the alcohol, since I was four years away from being able to drink legally), paid for an alcohol license from the town of Dover, and organized a bus to transport the out-of-state guests from the hotel to River Bend.

She got it all done online or by phone while getting through her first month of residency—my sister is a champion! And the RSVPs were piling up. There were a few people who hadn't responded but the majority had checked in.

Work was fine, SAT prep was fine, I'd even added a few pieces to my portfolio—and I'd made progress on my personal essay for college apps (it's never too early to start as per Dad, and Vir).

Speaking of Vir ... Things were going really, really well! Dad and Vir had hit it off apparently. Why was I surprised? At some level he was just the nova-watching, technology-loving, MIT geek type Dad would approve of. And he knew an astounding amount of stuff about cars. When I stressed about Dad working late and paying no attention to the wedding preparations Vir defended him and went on about Dad's start-up, and how close they were to getting Intel Capital in the bag as far as funding was concerned. It was a little weird how they had clicked.

'In fact, I might intern with them next summer,' he said. 'If they haven't crashed and burned by then.'

'That's reassuring,' I said.

'I think they'll be fine,' Vir said. 'If the economy doesn't tank, and no competing technologies emerge, and they don't run out of funding—they'll do alright.'

'He's so tight-fisted about the wedding,' I complained. 'He loves that start-up more than Vinnie.'

'He doesn't want to jeopardize your college fund—it took him a decade in a corporate career to build it up. And he's really an entrepreneur at heart.'

'So, you're defending him?' I asked.

'I'm explaining his point of view,' Vir said.

'Hey, what's your dad like?' I asked.

'He's … fine,' Vir said.

'Uh huh,' I said.

'Actually, he's a genius in his field.'

'Really?' I said, trying and failing to imagine a genius in the field of farm equipment. 'How?'

'It's too boring to talk about,' Vir said. 'Wanna get lunch?'

I saw him nearly every day while walking Yogi—that dog was such a strong swimmer now he was fetching sticks with the Labradors!

We hung out with Jackie, and Rachel, and everyone at Panera Bread (half my AP class was working there that summer). I took him to Westbury High School even though school was out. WHS was brand new—well, nearly four years old. We were the lucky class that got to start freshman year in the new building.

'It's awesome,' Vir said. 'I can't get over how this is a government school, and it's so amazing.'

Government school? That was funny. 'It's called a public school,' I said.

'Public school in England means an exclusive private school,' Vir said.

'Yeah, like that makes a lot of sense!' I said. 'What's wrong with you people? How can it be a public school when only the rich elite can afford to send their kids there?'

'Hey, I don't make the language,' Vir said.

I looked around the familiar school campus. It looked so deserted and peaceful in summer. There was something I wanted to share with him …

'Vir, follow me,' I said, and grabbed his hand.

The front doors to the school were open because of the summer camp—I steered Vir through the lobby into the quad, the heart of the school. It was surrounded on three sides by the school building and the back was open to the lake.

'OK, we're here,' I said, and took a deep breath and pointed. 'Look down there.'

The brick pathway was made up of carved bricks with names, dates, and messages. 'What is this?' Vir asked.

'Commemorative bricks,' I said. 'When they were building the school you could buy a brick for a hundred bucks and put a message on it. Dad bought five bricks, one for each decade of her life, even though the last decade wasn't finished.'

MEGHA KAPOOR
1962-2004
BELOVED MOTHER OF YASHASVINI
WHS CLASS OF 2004

MEGHA KAPOOR
1962-2004
LOVING MOM OF MINI AND YOGI

MEGHA KAPOOR
1962-2004
CHERISHED WIFE OF VINOD

MEGHA KAPOOR
1962-2004
DARLING DAUGHTER OF COL. P. S.
RAGHAV
AND THE LATE MRS LATA RAGHAV

MEGHA KAPOOR
1962-2004
BEST FRIEND AND BELOVED SISTER
OF MALIKA

'For your mom?' Vir asked.

'Yes,' I said. Usually, I avoided coming here with anyone, walked the other way during school, and only came here alone—when I stayed late at school for something, or on the weekend—never when crowds of people were stomping all over the path. 'Look—it's these five bricks,' I said. 'So this entire section of the pathway is in memory of my mom.'

'This one is yours.' Vir knelt down and touched it with his fingers. 'How come it says "Mini" and not Padmini?'

'Because I was ten, and no one called me Padmini.' I sat down cross-legged on the grass by the pathway. 'It didn't feel right to Dad, it didn't feel right to me—so we stuck with Mini. And I insisted we put Yogi on my brick too.'

'That's cool,' Vir said. 'And it's such a beautiful spot too,'

He was looking at the town lake which was right behind the school.

'Yeah,' I said. 'We don't have a gravestone to lay flowers on, like other families, so I put them here sometimes. Just a single flower, but it makes me feel close to her.'

'Let me guess—she spent a lot of time helping out at the school?'

'She did—even volunteered while she was ill,' I said. 'They organized a town-wide referendum for the tax override. Lots of people didn't want to raise taxes to build a new school, but the old one was totally falling down, and it would have cost nearly as much to fix it. Mom was really into spreading the word, convincing people, getting the vote out—you know.'

'Did she see the school finished?' Vir asked.

'No,' I said. 'But she saw the plans. She knew what it would be like, and that even though Vinnie would have graduated, it would be finished in time for my class.'

Vir slung an arm around my shoulders and pulled me in for a long hug.

'What was your school like?' I asked him. 'The one in India?'

'Mayo College?' he asked. 'It was really regimented—uniforms, strict rules, houses—very old school. But I loved the campus. It's full of historic buildings—the first students were maharajahs, you know, and they built their own house. But what I liked best were the horses.'

'You had horses on campus?' I asked.

'Yeah, fifty horses,' Vir said. 'We had a great polo team—I was captain actually. I still miss my horse, Sultan. He was the best.'

'You know, I think my grandfather went to school there,' I said, an old memory surfacing. 'My nanaji, Mom's dad—he's the reason Vinnie and I have such valiant Rajput names.'

'Cool,' he said. 'Hey, my mom wants to meet you—tomorrow, if that's OK?'

'What?' I said, totally panicking. 'I mean, yes, of course, I'd like to meet her. But, what if she doesn't like me, or something?'

Vir kissed the corner of my mouth. 'She'll love you.'

Behind him I could see a bunch of kids canoeing in the lake—and pointing at us—I went red.

'I'm not comfortable with public displays of affection, Vir Chabra,' I said, pulling away.

He frowned slightly. 'What did you call me?'

'Vir Chabra,' I said. 'That's your name, isn't it?'

'It sounds nice,' he said grinning. 'But I use my dad's last name.'

'Oh, that explains why nothing showed up on Google,' I said. 'Only some pediatrician in Texas, and a guy in Jabalpur who collects pool tables.'

'You Googled me?' Vir raised an eyebrow. The warmth died slowly out of his eyes—weird. In fact, he looked kind of worried.

'Standard procedure according to my friend Jackie,' I said. Why was he so surprised that I'd Googled him? 'So, what's your actual name?'

Vir ran his hand through his hair. 'You know what? I'm going to Google myself to see what's out there before I tell you,' he said. 'Who knows what crap's up on Facebook? I hate all these social networking sites.'

OMG, maybe he thought I was coming on too strong? Being all sneaky and stalkerish or something? This was awkward!

'Look, whatever-your-name-is,' I said, trying to sound casual. 'I'm on Facebook as Padmini Lata Kapoor. Feel free to friend me whenever you want. I won't Google you or anything until you do.'

'Promise?' he smiled.

'Totally!' I'd do it even if I died of curiosity.

Mirchandani Motors

When Vir called and asked me to meet his mom I was covered in mud, sweat, and hot wax.

Because—this:

Vinnie and Sudha Aunty had put their heads together and come up with some complicated floral centerpiece. It was a tall glass column vase filled with water, with colored pebbles at the bottom, submerged orchids in the middle, and floating candles on top. Given a choice, Vinnie always preferred the simplest of floral arrangements so I was dumbstruck that she wanted this thing, but she'd seen it at a friend's wedding and fallen in love with the look.

I had to try it out of course. There wasn't anything as exotic as orchids on hand, but I got some hydrangeas from the garden and dug up some regular pebbles (literally, hence the mud) and some Yankee Candles tea lights.

Surprise! It only took ten minutes to fill up our biggest vase with water, throw in the rinsed pebbles and the cut flowers and float some lighted tea lights on top. I did get some hot wax on me trying to position the tea lights but OMG, it looked fabulous! No wonder Vinnie was going on about it. I took a bunch of (rather impressive) pictures and emailed them off to her. I might still need her girlfriends' help, but it wouldn't take long to put it together—whew.

And that's the reason I was a hot mess when the phone rang.

I naturally assumed it was Vinnie.

'Did you see the pictures?' I said, grabbing the receiver.

'No,' said Vir. 'It's Vir—sorry!'

'Hey,' I said. 'What's up?'

'You free now?' he said. 'Mom wants to meet you. I can come get you in an hour if it's OK.'

'In an hour?' I cast a panicked look at myself in the mirror across the hall. 'How about an hour and a half? I've been in the garden, and ... busy. Let me get showered and changed!'

'OK,' he said. 'I'll be there.'

***

'She won't eat you!' Vir said bracingly. 'Stop hyperventilating.'

We drove up the long drive to the Georgian style heritage building at the top of the hill—the dean's residence.

'She sounds so intimidating,' I said. 'What if she hates me?'

'My mom? Intimidating?' Vir looked genuinely puzzled. 'No way. Wait till you meet the rest of my family!'

I didn't point out that he still hadn't said anything about his dad or the rest of his family. But taking the high road was killing me.

Vir's mom was waiting outside, with an incredibly fat and fluffy cat by her side. I recognized him as the creature Yogi had chased up the hill the day I first met Vir.

'Mom, this is Mini,' Vir said. 'And this lazy thing is Roshan.' She didn't look intimidating, actually. She had a curly mop of salt and pepper hair, and a sweet smile, and a rather stylish dress, in a librarian sort of way. And a pair of Toms on her feet—some poor kid had decent shoes because of her purchase. I approved—I bought Beeji a pair myself every time she visited. She held out both her hands to mine. 'It's great to meet you, Mini!' she said.

'It's great to meet you too,' I said.

'Let's go on the terrace and we'll have some tea,' she said and opened the door for me, her pearl earrings swinging prettily. The cat followed us, rubbing up against Vir's sandal-clad ankles.

'You're so pretty,' Mrs Chabra said. Or was that Ms Chabra? I was in dark indigo skinny jeans, white cotton top with pretty eyelet lace—conservative, covered up, cute. 'I told Vir you were, the first time I saw you.'

'When was that?' I asked. I didn't recall meeting her before.

'When your dog had the run-in with Roshan here,' she said.

So she'd seen my microscopic spandex yoga shorts that day—so much for covered up and conservative—I felt ill!

'I'm *so* sorry about that,' I said. 'Yogi hasn't been around too many cats and ...'

'Don't be sorry,' she said. 'You did us a favor!'

171

'How d'you mean?' I asked, mystified.

'Vir had just got here from India, and he was so jetlagged he was sleeping till noon every day,' she explained. 'But after he saw you, he started getting up, shaving, and jogging around the lake at the crack of dawn.'

'He did?' I gasped. 'He did *not*!'

'Muuum,' Vir said, red in the face. So it was true? I'd never in a million years have guessed! And he had played it so cool, just nodding briefly if I did run into him.

'Yes he did,' she said. 'And then he'd say: I saw the girl with the dog today—and smile till evening.'

'I'm not sure I believe it,' I said, stunned.

'And I love your dog,' she said. 'He has such an ancient silhouette, like he stepped out of an Egyptian frieze!'

'Doesn't he?!' I said. 'Like Anubis! The Romans had dogs like him too. I went to the Pompeii exhibit last year at the MOS and saw a picture of the Cave Canum mosaic. It's a sign with a picture of a dog just like Yogi and it means …'

'Beware of Dog,' she finished. 'I know it. He's very classical.'

I was starting to like Vir's mom more and more. And yet, I was still nervous.

'Roshan is adorable,' I said. 'Can I pick him up?'

'Please! He loves attention,' she said.

It's absolutely impossible to be nervous with a giant purring cat in your lap, so I managed to relax after that—I *so* owed that cat.

We talked about school, and university, and politics in India and the US. Thanks to having to share a TV remote with my dad, I was pretty well-informed.

'I heard your older sister is getting married. Congratulations!' she said. 'How's the wedding planning going?'

'It's going,' I said. 'We have a tight budget, but I think we've managed to plan things the way Vinnie would want. She wants a small and pretty outdoor wedding, so that's what we've organized. Except for the janvasam which is going to be at the temple, we're sticking to a Punjabi-style wedding.'

'Your mother would've liked that, right?' she said.

'Yes,' I said. 'I think she would've.'

'It's not important to have a flashy wedding,' she said. 'It's important to make sure the people getting married are well matched.' She smiled ruefully. 'I should know!'

'Well, we're trusting Vinnie on that one,' I said. 'But they seem happy.'

'That's great!' she said. 'Vir says you have real artistic talent and that you like design, but you're not applying to any design programs—why's that?' That was completely out of left field.

'Err … first off, I'm not really that good,' I said,

'I've seen your Etsy shop—you're good,' she said. 'What else?'

'Okay,' I said. 'My dad wants me to get a,' I made air quotes, 'proper college education.'

'What's improper about art?' she asked. 'If that's your career of choice?'

173

'He wants me to have a comprehensive education,' I said. 'Something that will ensure I'm gainfully employed. And to be honest I'd rather stay close to home. Vinnie is staying in Chicago for another four years. I don't want to leave Dad and Yogi and go off to New York!'

'I'm sure they'll be fine,' she said. 'But have you thought about RISD?'

'That's the best option,' I said. 'But even if I get in—which is wicked hard—Dad will say design isn't enough. That I should expand my horizons, learn from the accumulated wisdom of mankind, get some marketable skills so I can actually support myself. Like RISD doesn't have a stellar placement record for their design grads!'

'They also have a dual degree program with Brown,' she said thoughtfully. 'Did you know?'

'No!' I said. 'Really? How do you apply to that?'

'I think you have to apply individually to Brown, and RISD,' she said. 'And if you get in to both you can apply for the dual degree program.'

'That sounds great!' I said. 'I mean it's really, really tough to get into either of those schools, but I could try.'

'And there's always Fellsway,' she said, smiling.

'Fellsway is definitely on my list,' I said. 'I love it here.'

'We don't have a design curriculum,' she said. 'But we've had a fashion design club since 1999, and they manage to pack in a great deal within the liberal arts framework. Vir will be happy if you go here though. And I might see more of him if you go here too!'

'Thanks, I'll think about it,' I said. 'You must be so proud that Vir got accepted into MIT.'

'Yes, I am,' she said. 'And so is his father.'

I tried to keep a straight face, but she must have seen something that made her add. 'Vir, I think you should tell her,' she waved a hand around vaguely, 'about Dad.'

'Fine,' Vir said shortly.

'Before the August 15th thing,' she insisted.

'What August 15th thing?' I asked.

'There's an event for India Day in Boston,' Vir said. 'It's sponsored by my dad's company. I want you to come, but Mum wants me to give you a heads up about the family before then.' He had a sheepish grin on his face. 'They're a bit ...' He waved a hand vaguely.

Bit *what?*

'Your dad's in farm equipment, you said, right?' I said. 'Why are they sponsoring stuff here?'

'He said his father is in farm equipment?' Vir's mom sounded strange.

'Yes,' I said. 'And that he was a genius in his field, but it's too boring to talk about.'

'That's not entirely accurate, is it, Vir?' she said. 'Well, I have to finish up some work in the office so I'll say bye now. It was wonderful meeting you, Mini. I'll see you again, I'm sure! Vir, you can't spring them on Mini without telling her. You need to talk to her—now!'

Well, that was direct. What was wrong with Vir's dad's family?

She rested a hand on my shoulder. 'I'm so happy Vir found you!'

'Me too,' I said, and she vanished into the house leaving Roshan to keep us company.

The sun was setting over the lake but it was still warm on the stone terrace.

'So, what's the big mystery about your dad?' I asked Vir.

'It's just that—I can't stand my stepmother,' Vir said. 'I really don't like her. And I was stuck in Mumbai living with them for ten months. I loved working with my dad, and I learned a lot—but I was sick of her. She's one of those socialites, you know, and she dragged me around to parties like I was some kind of lapdog, and dangled me before her friends' daughters. And then we fought about something silly. So I kind of left without telling them, and for a few hours they even thought I was kidnapped. They all got mad. It was ridiculous. Anyway, we've made up now, and Dad and her are coming to Boston in two weeks, and it'll be nice if you could meet them—so, will you?'

'Fine,' I said. 'But who is your dad?'

'Ramesh Mirchandani,' he said. He looked like he had just launched a nuclear missile or something.

'Like the ...' Why did the name sound familiar? 'Like the ... car?'

'Yeah,' Vir said. 'Mirchandani Motors is the family company. My dad and his brother run it.'

I was too astounded to speak. My boyfriend's dad was one

176

of the Mirchandani brothers who owned Mirchandani Motors. What?!

'FARM EQUIPMENT?!' I said, at last. 'Vir!'

'Hey, we're big in tractors,' Vir said. 'In fact, tractors are still sixty percent of the business.'

'So that's why your mom has a Mirage?' I asked.

'It was an exhibition car,' Vir said. 'Mom liked it, so Dad arranged for her to have it. They still, you know, communicate.'

'So, are you rich, or something?' I asked.

'Rich is relative, but yeah,' Vir said. 'My dad's side of the family is well off, by any standards.'

'Okay,' I said. 'Does that mean you don't really want to set up a DJ business?'

'That was just so I could see more of you,' Vir said. 'But I'll do Vinnie's wedding, of course. I promised!'

'You had better!' I said. I sat still, trying to take it in. 'Vir, it might take me a while to process this.'

'Can I hold you while you do?' he asked.

'Please!' I said, and laid my spinning head on his shoulder. 'You know, I may owe my Uncle Ernie an apology. I think he tried to, like, set us up, and I *totally* doubted his judgment.'

***

The surprise was that Dad knew.

'Yes, he told me that day he brought you home from the movies,' Dad said.

'When you were driving around in the Lotus?' I asked.

'That's how it came up,' Dad said. 'We were talking cars. He

177

knows a lot about automobiles, and engineering, and he's going to MIT. I like him. He doesn't act rich or anything.'

'And when exactly were you going to share this with me?' I asked.

'I thought you knew,' Dad said. 'Anyway, what's the big deal? It doesn't change who he is otherwise.'

People Like Us

I was 'officially' meeting everyone at the India Day concert.

His dad, uncle, aunt, and two cousins—all the rich, successful Mirchandanis—and also the dreaded stepmom slash socialite. No pressure, right?

Seriously, what do you even wear to something like that—a party dress, an evening gown? Nothing I owned was remotely suitable, and it was too late to order online. The only thing left to do was to a) check out Amy's Attic just in case someone unloaded a size zero designer dress in mint condition and/or b) go shopping with my emergency fashion fund clutched in my hot little hand.

I headed for the mall to scan through Nordstrom, Anthropologie, Neiman Marcus, and Macy's. No luck. The only possibility that I actually considered was a Jason Wu dress that looked like something Audrey Hepburn would have worn back in the day. But would it work for the event? I tried it on for laughs before changing back. It was fantastic—god, how I loved Jason Wu! But, alas, it was also $1200! The sticker shock was still with me when I left the mall.

But I knew how to fix that.

Mom always said when you can't buy something because it is very, very expensive, go treat yourself to something happy, and fun, and beautiful that is very, very cheap—a pretty pair of earrings, a bright scarf, or a small cup of Hagen Daaz ice cream.

So, on the way home I stopped at the little garden shop outside Building Nineteen, and bought a gorgeous bright red geranium plant in a plastic pot. For $1.20!

'Enjoy!' the guy at the checkout said to me, as I paid up.

'Thanks, I will,' I said. He was holding a sign that said 'HARDY MUMS'. 'When are the mums coming in?' I asked.

'Another couple of weeks,' he said, leaning on a rake. 'They're just about ready in the greenhouse.'

'I'll come get some when you get them in,' I said.

'You always do, honey,' he said.

It was true.

They always came in right around when school started in September. Mom used to buy a minivan load of chrysanthemums then. A present for the 'Hardy Mums' she called it, meaning mums as in mothers of course. And she dedicated the first day of school to transplanting the flowers into window boxes outside our house. I remember coming home from school to see her looking happy and rested and the front windows in our house full of bright blooms.

I was still smiling when I watered my bright red geraniums at the kitchen sink and set them in a sunny spot on the windowsill. I could buy one thousand of these plants for the price of that dress. Imagine! That was the same price tag as that lehenga that Masi sent.

Masi's lehenga! I'd forgotten about the fabric I had cut out of it! I had one quarter circle of a beautiful firozi blue silk. Maybe I could do something with it. I ran into my room and threw open my wardrobe again.

There it was. I spread it out and considered carefully. If I used the bottom half there would be enough fabric for a skirt— but what about the top? I pulled out my fabric basket filled with remnants from various craft projects. I'd collected many shades of silk while I was working on the fascinator fundraiser— including a spearmint green silk. There was quite a bit of it left over if I remembered right. Now, if only it would work with the lehenga fabric.

I spread out the two fabrics side by side. The blue of the ornate lehenga fabric was the exact same weight and saturation as the plain green silk. The contrast in color really made the pattern of the fabric pop.

Somewhere I had a pattern for a fitted V-neck bodice. It took me ten minutes of rummaging in my pattern drawer to find it. I pulled my dress form to the center of the room, found a box of pins, and my heavy scissors. This *could* work.

***

'It's genius!' said Rachel. 'You've outdone yourself, Mini.'

I did a happy twirl for Jackie and peered over my shoulder

at the full-length mirror behind the door to my room. There were strings dangling from the neck, the blue tulle I had layered beneath the skirt needed to be hemmed, the bottom of the concealed zipper had to be tucked and hand-stitched, but I was happy.

The firozi fabric had transformed into the bias cut skirt of my new dress, and the top was a fitted spearmint green bodice with a deep V-neck, front and back. It was a neat little color-block dress that was totally made of awesome.

My room, on the other hand, looked like a disaster zone. It was covered in beads and sequins (from the lehenga fabric) and snippets of green silk too—but, on balance, it was worth it.

'I agree,' Jackie said. 'Totally!'

'It's Masi's fabric that makes it work,' I said. The blue fabric really was something special—all jeweled and magical and Arabian Nights-ish—god knows how many hours of hand embroidery went into making a yard of it. 'The rest of the dress is just a showcase for it.'

'It is,' Rachel said. 'But it's not just the skirt fabric. It has great structure, classic lines, and it fits really well. It's outstanding, Mini. You look fantastic in it!'

'I don't have any shoes to go with it,' I sighed.

'I think Mom just got some Miu Miu pumps from a sample sale. They're that exact shade of blue and green—in your size,' Rachel said. 'I bet she'll let you borrow them.'

'You're making my prom dress, Mini!' Jackie said. 'I'm booking it now!'

182

'I will,' I said, covering a big yawn with one hand. 'I owe you guys!'

'Get in bed!' Rachel said. 'Zip the thing off and hang it up. You need your beauty sleep.'

And so I did.

Three days later I got dressed in the new outfit feeling like Cinderella going to the ball. I didn't have glass slippers but the Miu Miu pumps in the same spearmint green and firozi blue as my dress (Rachel had brought them over from Amy's) were even better.

My Kate Spade bag in spearmint green looked great with the dress too. Pink lips, smoky eyes, smooth hair with a lowswept retro beehive, and the pretty gold earrings from Mom's safety deposit locker stash completed the look.

I was ready, or so I thought—I had no clue how crazy the evening was going to get.

***

'Who are you wearing?' the reporter yelled at me from behind the barricade.

This was un-be-lieve-able. I had imagined a quiet cultured evening with slightly intimidating and/or snooty people. Not so, apparently!

Instead, I, Mini Kapoor was at a red carpet event, clutching Vir's arm with cold, panicked fingers, barely able to balance on my borrowed-from-Amy's-Attic Miu Miu shoes, because of nerves. It was supposed to be a concert of Indian classical music at the MIT campus. People rock up to those things in jeans. I mean, I went to summer camp here with a bunch of geeks. Who knew that Ustad Rashmikant was playing with Lady Gaga?! And that Katy Perry was one of the guests.

'Argh!' Vir muttered. 'I should have known.'

'Should have known what?' I asked.

'That it would be a media circus!' he said. 'Anything organized by my stepmother turns into that. Somehow, I thought, since it was in Cambridge, Massachusetts, instead of Mumbai, Maharashtra, that it would be different!'

'But why're they taking pictures of you?' I asked.

'Not me,' Vir said. 'They're taking pictures of you.'

And indeed they were.

'Is that a Malika Motwani?' A woman's voice said.

I was shocked enough to turn and stare at the questioner.

'It is definitely her signature lehenga fabric,' the woman pushed up her no-nonsense eyeglasses and glanced over me critically; she had a camera and a friendly grin—and a notepad. 'That scalloped hem is pretty distinctive. It's from her blue collection, isn't it? The one she unveiled at this year's DCW— Firozi Fantasy it's called I think. Could you spin please?'

I lost the deer-in-the-headlight stance and spun obediently, even managing a shaky smile—but I was secretly horrified. A fashion blogger who could id Masi's fabric! What were the odds?

'But the cut is completely different from her line,' the woman said. 'She didn't make the dress—so who did?'

'An ... undiscovered local designer?' I said. It sounded lame even to me. 'Thanks, we have to go in!'

'Sir, is it definitely over between you and KK?' someone yelled as we walked away.

My head snapped back. 'What did he say?' I asked.

'Didn't catch it,' Vir said, steering me away from the reporters. 'It does look like a Malika Motwani. Not her typical style, though. I like it!'

I stared at him in wonder. Did he say 'her typical style'? Had the world gone completely mad? How the hell did Vir know about Masi's typical style?

'What the heck is DCW?' I asked Vir.

'Delhi Couture Week,' Vir grinned at me. 'I liked the Malika Motwani show best. She wouldn't sell a lehenga that looked like your skirt to my stepmother. You know—for any price!'

'Really?' I asked. Vir's stepmother bought Masi's clothes?

'It was really funny,' he said. 'I've never seen my stepmom so upset. Wait till she sees you in this!'

'Have you met her?' I asked.

'Malika Motwani?' he asked. 'Yeah! She's such a battle axe. How did you get that dress off of her anyway? I know she doesn't do anything but Indian-style clothes—lehengas, salwars, saris—that kind of thing.'

Battle axe! A snort of laughter escaped me. He definitely had Masi pegged.

'She sent me the lehenga,' I said. 'For the wedding. And she had no idea what size I am, of course. So it was huge! I had to alter it to get it to fit—and there was all this leftover fabric. I didn't have anything dressy enough for today so I used the fabric to make this.'

'OK—what?' Vir looked shocked. 'How did you get her to "send" you a dress that's worth lakhs of rupees?' He stared at me critically. 'You look amazing in it, but this definitely cost more than your Kate Spade bag from Amy's—and you've been going on about how expensive that was! Wasn't it a waste of money to buy it if you had to alter it that much?'

'I didn't have to pay for it,' I admitted.

'And why's that?' he asked.

I slung my Kate Spade handbag over my shoulder defiantly, and raised my chin. In the background I could see cameras flash. 'Because Malika Motwani is my masi.'

***

'This is just too perfect,' Vir said. 'They're all set on disliking you, just because I found you on my own, and because Mum likes you …'

'Your mum likes me?' I asked.

'Hell yeah!' Vir said. 'But my mum and my stepmother—they don't ever see eye to eye, so I was a bit worried that things could get ugly. But this is good. It could definitely make everything easier.'

'But you said Masi was rude to her,' I said. 'How is that good?'

'Oh, it's good!' Vir said. 'She thinks Masi is an artistic genius. She doesn't get offended when she's rude to her. OK, here we go …'

A tall, slim woman in a deceptively simple georgette sari stood by a man who was definitely Vir's dad.

'Mummy,' I could tell Vir was uncomfortable saying that word. 'Meet my friend, Mini. And guess what we just found out? She's related to your favorite designer.'

'Really?!' Vir's stepmother clutched at my arm, but she was staring at my dress, not at me. 'Yes! I remember that embroidery! She wouldn't sell me the lehenga, darling. Said it didn't come in my size. I didn't know it came in a dress! How are you related to Malika, Mini?'

She finally looked at me and her gaze was friendly and approving.

Vir hadn't even mentioned Masi's name, I realized, but she knew from looking at my dress who he'd meant. Maybe Masi really was her favorite designer.

'She's my masi,' I said.

'Wonderful! But I didn't know Malika had a sister,' she said. 'Is your mother older than her, or younger?'

'My mom was older,' I said. 'But she passed away—years ago.'

Her eyes opened wide. Her sympathy was genuine. 'I'm so sorry!' she said. 'I didn't know.'

'It's OK,' I said. How could she? It's not something people talk about.

She inclined her neck graciously. 'Well, any niece of Malika is a friend of mine,' she said, as if that settled everything. 'We're even related, I think. Her husband is a Motwani and they're cousins to the Mirchandanis—the Sindhi connection, you know.'

All I knew about my Motu Mausa, Masi's husband, was that he had a contracting business that managed huge projects—government buildings, and roadworks, and what not.

'I'm very glad you and Vir became friends. We were sooo woorried about him being soooo far from home. Didn't know what type of friends he'd make here. His father and I just hoped he'd steer clear of the wrong type.'

It occurred to me that Vir's mom lived here, and yet they had no confidence in her ability to keep him away from the 'wrong' type. And what was the 'wrong type' anyway? I could see why Gulshan Chabra and Vir's stepmother didn't see eye to eye.

'I'm sure he will,' I said. I guess I had reason to thank Masi for something. The minute Vir's stepmother knew Malika Motwani was my aunt they treated me like … one of *them*!

'Mini,' Vir said. 'This is my dad.'

Mr Mirchandani was a handsome man. He looked like an older version of Vir. But Vir was browner, taller, and more athletic-looking. His dad was fairer, a little flabby around the middle, and his hair was greying at the temples. But he had a sharp, intelligent glint in his eyes which reminded me of Vir.

'Nice to meet you, Mini,' he said. 'Your masi is a big friend of my wife's, it seems. Small world, isn't it?'

FASHION
confidential

Fashion report! Cambridge Massachusetts

A college town like Cambridge is stuffed with scruffy students swotting for tests and fully dry of people with a clue about fashion, especially Desi fashion--but last night was an exception!

The celebrities who showed up for the fundraiser sponsored by Mirchandani Motors wore Desi designers in honor of India's Independence Day.

Check out the pictures below! Lady Gaga in Prabal Gurang, Katy Perry in Tarun Tahiliani and, our favorite, Vir Mirchandani's hot new girlfriend, Mini, in a dress by an 'undiscovered local designer'. Wonder what KK would say to that!

But there's a mystery surrounding that dress—the fabric is from Couture Queen Malika Motwani's newest collection—Firozi Fantasy! This begs the question—is Malika Motwani getting into the ready-to-wear business?

She last flirted with ready-to-wear six years ago, when she was in talks with Barney's New York to create an exclusive line. The collaboration crashed when Malika Motwani pulled out for undisclosed reasons, and since then she has concentrated on her core bridal and custom couture line, which is out of reach for mortals like us.

But if the delicious number we see in this picture is any clue, Malika may be experimenting with a new line—and taking on a new designer. We'll keep our ears to the ground on this one—so stay posted!

Duped

'You were wearing a dress made out of the lehenga I sent.' Masi was nothing if not direct. 'Please explain.'

'I'm sorry, Masi,' I said. 'It's just that I had nothing to wear ...'

'Who made the dress for you?' she said.

'I did! And I didn't ruin the lehenga!' I said. 'I had to take it in, so it was all leftover fabric. I just used it to make a dress.'

There was silence at the other end.

'You made that dress?' Masi asked.

'Yeah,' I said.

'And "took in" the lehenga?'

'Yes, and I got compliments from everyone. Jackie, and Vinnie, and Vir, and even Dad—not that he knows anything about it. But it wasn't a bad use of the fabric. I'd have sent it back to you if I knew you wanted it.'

'How did the lehenga turn out?' Masi asked.

I paused, confused. Wasn't that, like, off topic?

'Great!' I said. 'There's a lot less bunching at the waist now, because I changed it from a full circle skirt to a three quarter. I could send you a picture, if you like.'

'That would be nice,' Masi said. 'When did you learn to sew?'

'In seventh grade,' I said. 'And I also did a nine-week summer course at the School of Fashion Design—the one on Newbury Street? That was two years ago. And I should probably tell you I've been using your fabric for my Etsy shop too. Just in case that's an issue.'

'What's an Etsy shop?' Masi asked.

'It's a website where you sell handmade items,' I said. 'I give a portion of my sales to charities I like—MSPCA, ACS … you know.'

'Can I see it?' Masi asked.

'Sure,' I said. 'I'll send you a link.'

'Just tell me the address,' Masi said. 'I want to see it now.'

I felt a twinge of irritation breaking through my guilt. Did she have to be so demanding?

'If you Google "Etsy" and "Megha & Me" it should come up,' I said.

There was silence at the other end.

'That's the name of your shop?' she asked. 'Megha and Me?' She'd lost the bossy tone.

'Right,' I said. 'Did you find it?'

'Wait …' she said. 'Yes, I see it.'

'I didn't really use a lot of your fabrics,' I said. 'Just recycled bits and pieces from the clothes I'd outgrown. It seemed such a pity to throw them away. I hope that's OK …'

'It's fine, Mini,' Masi said. Her side of the phone fell silent; all I could hear was static crackling.

'Do you still want a picture of the lehenga?' I asked.

'Don't worry about it now,' Masi said. 'I'll see it at the wedding.'

I nearly dropped the phone. 'You're coming?' I said.

'I'm invited, aren't I?' Masi said. 'I got a card and everything. Nice card, by the way—did you design that too?'

'Yeah,' I admitted. 'When are you, umm, arriving?'

'On Tuesday,' Masi said. 'And how come you were with Vir?'

She knew him, I guess.

'He asked me out,' I said.

'Where did you meet him?' Masi asked.

'He's DJ-ing Vinnie's wedding,' I said, not wanting to get into the whole long story.

'You're paying Vir Mirchandani to DJ Vinnie's wedding?' Masi sounded incredulous.

'Yes,' I said.

'Mini, do you have any idea how much that kid is worth?'

'Masi, I know his family is wealthy,' I said. 'But kids take jobs even when their family is well off. It teaches work ethic. What's wrong with that?'

Masi sighed in exasperation. 'Nothing at all, Mini. I'll see you on Tuesday.'

***

'She can't come now, Vinnie,' I wailed. 'She'll spoil everything!'

Vinnie was no help. 'It's time you stopped trying to keep her out of everything. And anyway, it's my wedding and I want her here.'

'What help can she possibly be? And I haven't kept her out!' I said. 'She's the one who's always kept herself out. She didn't even come when Mom …'

'Mini,' Vinnie said sharply. 'That wasn't her fault!'

'How can you say that?' I asked. 'She was always flying around the world, she could totally have come. You're the one who ended up doing everything.'

'I didn't …' Vinnie said.

'You did! You even dressed Mom. God, Vinnie, I don't know how you even …' I fell silent, overcome by memories.

'It wasn't hard,' Vinnie said, at last. She was always a rock of strength in an emergency. 'I wanted to be a doctor, remember?' She'd make a great one too. Funny, we had not talked about any of this—ever. Why it came up then, I have no clue. But, now I couldn't stop.

'You put Mom in that long dress she wore when Dad and her first met—I remember. How did you find it? How did it even fit her after all those years …'

'It fit because Masi made sure it did,' Vinnie said quietly. 'She sent it.'

'Masi sent it?' I asked. 'No! It was always here.'

'Masi went to the old house in Karol Bagh,' Vinnie said, 'and dug through all the steel trunks in the store room. The ones that hadn't been opened since Nani died.'

I have a vivid memory of those trunks. Large, black, painted iron trunks that had been over the length and breadth of India on Nana's army postings. They said Lt. Col. P. S. Raghav in crisp white letters. Mom's whole childhood was stored in them. Masi had to dig through them?

Vinnie was still talking. 'And she found the outfit and she had it altered so it would fit and she couriered it here a month before it happened.'

'She did?'

'Yes,' Vinnie said. 'Mom told her that's what she wanted to wear at the end. How do you think it feels to mail your sister's clothes for her funeral?'

'But she didn't come,' I said. 'Beeji said …'

'Beeji never liked her,' said Vinnie. 'And after Masi told her to stop feeding you fried food, she didn't have one nice thing to say about Masi. And you believed her.'

'But still … she didn't come!' I insisted.

'Mom didn't want her to,' Vinnie said. 'She didn't want a big deathbed scene. She just wanted one more normal day at home with us. As normal as she could make it. So Masi didn't come. But she talked to her every night after we went to bed.'

I was probably fast asleep by then, and no one ever told me.

'And when Mom was so drugged at the end because of the pain, the doctor said someone should tell her it's OK to let go—even if it didn't feel like she could hear. Masi did it. She talked to her all night that last night before she died. Mom could hear her, I know.'

I had tears streaming down my face. 'I didn't know,' I said.

***

Shut. Up.

That's why he didn't want me Googling him!

How could he? Really—how *could* he?

I didn't even mean to pry—the trusting lovestruck sap that I was. I was just curious about how I looked in the picture Masi saw on that fashion blogger's website. Can you blame me? I've never been on any kind of fashion blog before, so I had to see if they got my good side, and how my dress looked in the picture, and if anyone had commented on it, or liked it, or hated on it, or whatever.

So I searched for the event and there it was—a super-flattering picture of me in my color-block dress, alongside Vir—who also looked gorgeous, though it kills me to admit it. But next to it were pictures of Vir, my Vir, with Koyal Khanna—the Bollywood actress Koyal Khanna! That was why he didn't want to watch that movie I asked him about. SHE was in it. And she was his girlfriend—at least according to the news reports.

And those pictures! Vir and Koyal on a white sand beach in Goa—with her in a tiny bikini that I would never in a million years have the chutzpah to wear. Vir and Koyal at a movie premiere—the movie premiere of that movie I tried to get him to watch, in fact! Vir and Koyal wearing preppy, sporty outfits at some IPL match (whatever that means).

I dropped my head onto my desk—which I had decoupaged with photocopies of Mom's jewelry notes—with my luck they'd turn out to be forgeries too. How does one deal with something like this?

I should have called him and demanded an explanation, but I just felt like climbing into a small dark hole and never coming out.

I ignored Vir's texts that day. And I didn't meet him at the lake as we'd planned. I cried into Yogi's fur before falling asleep.

My heart was broken.

Totally.

***

I carried on.

Now that Masi was coming I had to make sure that the mehendi—the one event we were having at home—was perfect. I threw myself into planning it, which also helped keep my mind off Vir. We'd booked the mehendi lady already—so the next most important thing was food.

That meant a trip to Sher-e-Punjab.

'I'm so sorry I can't give you the contract for the wedding,' I said. 'Ladkewale Tamil hein ...' He smiled at my accent as I tried to explain that we had to have some TamBrahm dishes at the wedding—rasam, sambhar, payasam, etc.

'No problem, *ji*,' he said. 'We'll cater your mehendi. Anything else we can do to help? Have a lassi and samosa before you go. No payment needed.'

I sat down in the pink diner with the plastic flowers and ate the best samosa I had had in a long long time. In fact, I finished everything they put before me. They didn't have a lot of stuff on their menu, but what they made they made well.

Manic mad-at-Vir energy (as well as lassi and samosas) fueled my mehendi-planning efforts. Next stop, Taylor Rental. They rent everything—tents, tables, chairs, linens, china, stemware, silverware, heaters, air conditioners, carpets, lights—anything you can think of.

I was sure we couldn't fit everyone in the house so we needed tables and chairs. I had a look at the linens as well—just to see—even though it was smarter to get disposable paper and plastic from the Party Store instead.

But you know what I found? Curry Cuisine was overcharging for the linens! We'd picked the simplest linens and china and silverware—white floor-length table covers, burgundy napkins, simple gold-rimmed china—and he was charging double what Taylor Rental advertised. What was up with that?

There wasn't much I could do—we had accepted his quote, and put down a deposit. We were stuck with him, I guess. I felt deflated. Not only was that Sunny Sondhi a pompous ass who gave us the run around but he inflated his prices as well.

I'd call Ragini Aunty and ask about the rates he gave them last year, I decided. And check with Sudha Moorty too. Good thing I had her number on speed dial.

'The rates are fine, beta,' Sudha Moorty said. I could hear loud music in the background—no surprise, she was at a wedding. 'But don't be late paying him, OK? Did I tell you what he pulled at Mishra Ji's son's wedding last year?'

'No—what?' I asked.

'The balance was due the day of the wedding. The parents were sitting in some ceremony with their older son, and the younger son didn't have his checkbook—so he threatened to take all the food away!'

'What?' I asked. 'Did he?'

'No, the younger son went to the ATM and took out cash. I thought he was going to knock him down, he was so angry.'

'That's not good,' I said.

'And I *told* him! I said: Mr Sondhi, it's their son's wedding. Don't do this. I said I would give him a check myself, and that he knew my credit was good. But did he listen? No!'

'I'll pay him on time, Aunty,' I said. 'Thanks for telling me!'

'And beta, I never knew that Megha's sister was Malika Motwani!' she said. 'So many of my brides want her lehengas for their trousseau. Is she making Vinnie's lehenga?'

Could she sound any more worshipful?

'She is, Aunty,' I said. 'She definitely is.'

Ragini Aunty had nothing but praises for Curry Cuisine, though.

'He was on time, and the wait staff was excellent, and the food was delicious,' she said. 'It was buffet style, not *ilai sappadu*. Most practical, you know, over here. But we didn't have to worry about annnything.'

She spoke really fast. My brain could barely keep up with

198

decoding her accent in time to hear her next sentence.

'Everything else going well, yes?' Ragini Aunty said. 'I was just telling Uncle, Vinnie is sooo lucky to have a sister like you. You're doing so much for her wedding, managing everrrything. Is your grandmother coming from India soon? And your Aunty?'

'Beeji and Bauji are coming on Thursday, and Masi is coming tomorrow,' I said. 'Actually, I better go. Aunty, I have to clean and stock up before they get here. Beeji and Bauji's house has not been opened in ten months—it must be covered in dust!'

'You'll go clean it, and stock it?' Ragni Aunty said. 'Such a good granddaughter! I tell you, they're very lucky to have you!'

'Thanks, Aunty,' I said.

'Wait, wait, Padmini, there's one thing I want to ask you,' she said. 'It's about the priest!'

'What about the priest?' I asked warily.

'Do you have the list of what he needs for the wedding?' she asked. 'It's better to get it beforehand instead of leaving it to the end.'

'You're right, Aunty,' I said. 'Do you have his number?'

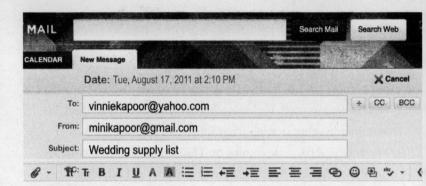

MAIL   Search Mail   Search Web

CALENDAR   New Message

Date: Tue, August 17, 2011 at 2:10 PM   ✗ Cancel

To: vinniekapoor@yahoo.com   +   CC   BCC

From: minikapoor@gmail.com

Subject: Wedding supply list

Hey Vinnie,

Here's the list of stuff for the wedding ceremony as per the priest:

Haldi (Turmeric)

Kumkum (Red powder)

Chandan (Sandalwood)

Agarbatti (Incense Sticks)

Kapur (Fire starter)

Coconuts x 5

Bananas x 12

Rice 2 lbs

Ghee (Clarified butter) 1 lb

Flowers

Garlands x 4 (2 will do too, he said)

Betel leaves

Pan supari nuts

$25 change in quarters

Sugar (a little)

Mithai (sweets)

Mangalsutra necklace

Bichua (toe rings)

Stone (the size of a brick)

Kopra x 2 (dry coconut, halved)

Plates x 5

Small bowls x 8

Spoons x 8

Aluminium Foil

Paper Towels

Matches

Deep oil lamp (brass)

Puffed Rice

Vegetable Oil

Cotton wicks

He said there should be mango leaves in the mandap. No point getting this stuff until a couple of days before the wedding or it might spoil. I'm emailing this so we have backup if the scrap of paper I wrote things on gets lost. We can get everything at Patel Brothers in Shrewsbury.

Xoxoxox

Mini

P.S. Did you really play basketball with him at Neela Aunty's house years ago or did I dream that up?

Masi in the House

Vir called—again.

And this time he called the landline instead of my cellphone. And when Dad handed me the phone without explaining who it was, I got tricked into speaking to him.

'Mini!' Vir said. Hearing him say my name was bittersweet. I'd been deleting his messages without listening to them because I couldn't deal with hearing that voice. I should have hung up—but I didn't.

'Where have you been?' he said. 'I've been calling every day. Can you just tell me what's going *on*?'

'I don't want to talk,' I said. Dad took one look at me, and vanished into his office.

'OK,' Vir said. 'OK, fine. But can you tell me why you don't want to talk?'

'No,' I said. A tear slipped down my cheek. Odd—I hadn't even realized I was crying.

'When I saw you last time everything was fine,' he said. 'What happened since then, Mini?'

Why did he sound so dang cute? It just wasn't fair. But I couldn't even think with those images swimming before my eyes. The ones of him and the perfectly beautiful Koyal Khanna. I swallowed the hurt resolutely.

'What happened, Vir Mirchandani, is that I *Googled* you,' I said, and hung up.

***

Manish was supposed to talk to Vir about the music, this week. I told him instead that we didn't have a DJ anymore. To avoid actual contact I'd dropped Vir a note in the mail—yes, in the actual USPS mailbox, stamp and envelope and everything. Manish took it well—in fact, he sounded pretty excited about arranging all the music himself. And now, thanks to his musical talent and that of his friends—he played in two bands, apparently—it was all going to be live.

Yay, I guess.

'Thanks for picking such a kickass venue, Mini,' he said. 'It rocks. And the acoustics in that carriage house are great.'

He was even having a piano trucked in so he could serenade Vinnie with a song he had written specially for her. No wonder Vinnie loved the guy. I bet he never even looked at a Bollywood star with Vinnie around.

'Did I tell you I booked the horse?' Manish said.

'You did?' I asked. I had sent the link with the wedding horse to Manish. He had to OK it, obviously, since he had to ride the thing.

'Yeah,' he said. 'It's a surprise for Vinnie. I told her that

Tamils don't do a baraat, so she isn't expecting it.'

'That is *so* sweet,' I said.

'I was nervous at first, but Vir was great!' he said.

'Vir?' I asked.

'He went with me to the farm,' Manish said. 'And walked me through the whole thing. Even brought Benadryl, because of course I was allergic to the horse, or maybe it was the hay.'

Talk about dedication—this guy really loved my sister, didn't he?

'Vinnie will love it!' I said. 'Is there anything you need as far as equipment?'

'I've talked to Caroline at River Bend,' Manish said. 'What they have is pretty basic, but with that vaulted ceiling and everything it'll be fine.'

'We just won't have the lighting that we'd planned on,' I said. 'But if you want we can rent the stuff from Taylor Rental. I have Vir's notes on where to put the lighting so it looks best.'

'He sounded like a nice guy,' Manish said. 'I mean, I've only spoken to him once, but he did sound cool. Why isn't he doing the lighting again?'

'Because I fired him,' I said.

'Oooh—that's harsh,' Manish said. 'Bad break-up?'

'Yeah,' I said.

***

OK, I wasn't even seeing him anymore, and now my *grandparents* knew about Vir! Could it possibly get any worse?

Mallu Masi was not the only one who had seen the pictures

of Vir and me. Beeji, my grandmother had turned into a page three addict ever since she had moved to India. But she hardly expected her granddaughter safely back in the US supposedly studying hard for her SATs and teaching little kids their mathematics, to feature in it.

Needless to say she'd told Bauji. And Bauji gave me a long, stern lecture, via telephone, and now they were both coming ten days early for the wedding—with Bade Bauji, her father, in tow!

'Mini, you have to be careful who you're friendly with,' Beeji said on the phone. 'That boy is not like you. He's spoilt and rich and he's had so many girlfriends.'

'Look,' I said. 'I'm not seeing him anymore. So, can we forget about this?'

'OK, OK,' she said. 'Just be careful, bachche, that's all.'

'Beeji, why is Bade Bauji coming?' I asked. 'Isn't it too much for him? He's ninety two, and he's never even left India before.'

'I told him there's no need,' Beeji said. 'But he wants to come.'

'How did he even get a visa?' I asked. 'Isn't it really hard to get a tourist visa for the US, if you haven't been there before?'

'Of course he got a visa,' Beeji said. 'They know he has a big business in India.'

So that was three more confirmed guests to add to the guest list—one hundred and eighty guests invited, one hundred and fifty confirmed.

Oy vey.

***

Mallu Masi was the first overseas visitor to arrive.

Dad and I took the minivan to the airport—nothing else could transport the luggage Masi was sure to bring. We waited at the customs gate for Masi to come into view. After a long stream of British tourists (the flight was from London) she appeared—and she had not changed a bit! Same artfully highlighted shoulder-length hair, same bouncy striding step, and smooth olive skin. How could she step off a plane after a day-long journey looking that fresh and unwrinkled?

'Mini!' she said and grabbed me into a long hug. 'Look at you! You're tall like your dad, but you look just like Megha!'

'Err … thanks,' I said, extricating myself. 'It's good to see you, Masi.'

Stupidly, it actually felt true.

'Malika,' Dad said, grinning boyishly. Wow, I couldn't remember seeing Dad smile like that in years. He and Masi had always gotten along well.

'Vinod,' she said. 'So good to see you, ya!'

'Wish you'd brought the boys with you,' Dad said. By which he meant Motu Mausa (Mohan Motwani, Masi's husband) and her twelve-year-old twin boys, Avinash and Arvind.

'Ari and Avi are at school,' she said. 'Their school reopened on July 1st, Mini, otherwise I would have definitely brought them. But they'll come next week, and Nana is coming too!'

'Nanaji is coming too?' I squealed. 'That's awesome!'

Nanaji, my other grandfather—Mom and Masi's dad—didn't travel overseas as much as he used to. And he was hard to contact because he was usually off visiting his army buddies who had retired in every remote corner to be found in India—none of them had internet access. I didn't even know he had got the wedding invitation I'd mailed to his Delhi address.

'Of course he is,' Masi said. 'Your Bade Bauji can make it, when he's what—ninety two? So why can't Nanaji?'

**

The atmosphere at home was suddenly festive. Masi breezed into the house, threw her stuff all over the master bedroom (Dad had lived in his study for the last seven years), put on loud Bollywood music, and forbid poor Yogi to 'shed all over my pashminas'.

We ordered take-out and Dad went off to pick it up.

'Show me how you altered the lehenga, Mini,' she demanded. 'I just have to see what you did with it!'

'It's in my closet,' I said. 'I'll get it.'

Before I could get over to my room she was already there, and, having flung my closet door open, was oohing and aahing over various items in it.

'Where did you get that?' she asked.

'Careful,' I said. 'It's vintage.'

'I can see that!' she said.

'And here's the lehenga!' she said. She pulled it out and examined it with interest. 'Nice work, Mini. Clean sewing too. You have a machine which can handle fabric this thick?'

'I don't,' I said. 'But my friend Jackie's mom is a quilter and she let me use her sewing machine. I just have this ...'

207

'… Megha's old machine?' she said, taking in my sewing corner in the far end of the room. 'I remember it now.'

'I love the lehenga, Masi,' I said. 'Thanks for sending it to me. I didn't realize it was your signature piece, otherwise I would never have taken it apart.'

'Is this the dress you wore where when you went out with Vir?' she asked.

A shard of hurt stabbed at me when she said his name.

'Yes,' I said. 'Yes it is.'

'It's excellent,' Masi said. 'I'm proud of you.'

It shouldn't have meant so much, but it did.

'Thanks,' I said.

'Do you know I've had a ton of orders for this design already?' she asked. 'They all want the dress that Boston girl was wearing.'

'Get out of here!' I said, shocked. 'Really?'

'Really,' she said. 'Mini, what's this?' She held up a tiny firozi blue double-breasted pea coat. 'This can't be yours.'

Oh no! I snatched it back. 'It used to be,' I said. 'But I never wore it. Here's Dad now, Masi. Let's go eat.'

***

So here's the lowdown on why I was still upset with my Masi. The September Vinnie left for college was probably the hardest time in my life. Worse even than when Mom died because right after it happened I was so numb it didn't even feel real. And Vinnie was there that spring and summer to cushion me from it. But when she left for college—it really hit hard—and the only thing that kept me going was the promise Masi had made me.

She said she would come to visit in December and I would go to India with her. I believed her. Because she had *promised*—more than once! She was going to New York for work—it was an exciting collaboration with Barney's, and possibly Saks Fifth Avenue. She was finally going to launch a ready-to-wear collection in India and overseas. And after her meetings she would come to Boston and take me back to Delhi for three weeks. I'd miss a week of school, sure, but that was hardly a big deal in sixth grade.

I was so excited about that trip. It was my Golden Ticket. When Vinnie came home for Thanksgiving, she took me shopping for it. I hadn't had a birthday party that November—Dad and Vinnie took me to see *Harry Potter and the Prisoner of Azkaban* instead. But Vinnie bought me a double-breasted pea coat—in my favorite firozi blue with bright gold brass buttons—just for my trip to Delhi. Mom had told us how cold it could be there in winter, and how the houses were not built for the cold weather, and how no one had central heating. I didn't remember being there in winter, but Vinnie did.

Vinnie went back to college after Thanksgiving, but I looked at my new clothes, and my suitcase, and packed and unpacked them. Then held the jacket to my face and dreamt of India. It felt soft and smelt of pure wool, excitement, and adventure. I just knew that my trip would be incredible. I'd drink Thums Up in Masi's office, and visit her sewing units, and babysit my cute twin cousins—it would be epic.

But a week before Mallu Masi was supposed to come to New York she canceled her trip—just like that. No explanation. Nothing.

It was just like that morning I found Mom, or the day I saw Vir's pictures with Koyal. Everything went dark, and I had to cope.

I finally wore the new clothes to school in January. But I never wore the beautiful blue pea coat. That's why it still hung in my closet as a warning—never trust Mallu Masi.

Old Secrets, White Lies

I went over to air out Beeji and Bauji's house and stock up their fridge—it's no fun food-shopping while jetlagged. Masi offered to help—I had no clue how much help she would actually be. I mean, when was the last time she used a vacuum cleaner—if ever? But she was determined to come along, so I was stuck with her.

'I like your car,' she said. 'It's cute.'

'Thanks,' I said. A good word about my car or my dog always got through—even from Masi.

'I still remember when your nanaji taught Megha how to drive! He made her use that tank of a car he had—the Ambassador. Did you ever see it?'

'I've seen photos,' I said. The Ambassador was the first car to be manufactured in India, I knew.

'Yeah,' she said. 'He set up *gharas*, you know, the terracotta water pots? Arranged an obstacle course in a field at our farmhouse and made her drive around them. By the end of her first try the she had flattened them all!'

'Wow, did she blow a tire?' I asked. It was good to hear something about Mom I didn't already know.

'No, but she scared a herd of buffalos!' Masi said. 'Nanaji's farmhand swore they wouldn't give any milk that day because of the incident.' Tears of laughter were streaming down her cheeks. When she was like that it was hard not to like her.

Beeji and Bauji's place looked dusty and smelled stale—it had been sitting in the baking summer sun for months. They should've really rented it out, just so it would be looked after. It took three hours of vigorous vacuuming, throwing open windows and doors just to freshen the musty air inside.

'What's down there?' Masi asked as I flipped on the light to the basement and walked downstairs.

'Just storage,' I said.

I stared at a stack of suitcases—vintage hardcase American Touristers—struck by an idea. Beeji stored her old saris in them. Maybe Mom's wedding lehenga was here instead of at home? Dad and I had been through every box in our attic and found nothing.

'I'm just going to look in these, Masi,' I said. 'If they're open.'

I took down the first one, snapped the clasps open and lifted the lid. Beeji's old saris, dupattas, and salwar kameezes, neatly packed. But no bulky silk lehenga. I shut it and opened another one. This one had old linens hand-embroidered by Beeji half a century ago. I passed a hand over them—they felt crisp and new, even now—why had she never used them to set a table? Or displayed them in her china cabinet? What a waste!

'Look!' Masi had been opening suitcases too. 'That's Megha's lehenga.'

Brilliant pink silk spilled from Masi's hands—Mom's lehenga. I knew it right away even though I'd only seen it in pictures. The pink was an unusual crushed raspberry spangled with silver tilla work—hand embroidery done with metallic thread, a specialty of Punjab.

'We've been looking for this everywhere!' I said. 'In the garage, in the attic, in all the storage boxes at home. I didn't realize she left it here!'

'They lived with Vinod's parents the year they got married, right?' Masi said. 'Before they bought a house. I guess she must have given it to Beeji for safekeeping.' She paused. 'And your Beeji never even told you.'

'Do you think it'll fit Vinnie?' I asked.

'Yeah,' Masi said. 'If it needs any fixing I can do it. I designed it after all. I was so proud of it! You're looking at the very first Malika Motwani, Mini. And I wasn't even a Motwani then!'

'You made Mom's wedding lehenga?' I asked.

'With input from her of course,' Masi said. 'Megha was great at it, but Nanaji didn't let her study design. There was no future in it, he said. But when I finished class twelve NIFT had just opened in Delhi.'

'National Institute of Fashion Technology?' I asked.

'Yeah,' Masi said. 'It opened in 1986, and Megha talked them into letting me apply. If it wasn't for her I'd have been doing

B.Com at SRCC! Hey, will Vinnie wear this for the reception if we fix it?'

'Yes!' I said. 'That's why I was looking for it! I'll have it drycleaned and then we can fix it. She'll be thrilled!'

'Let's finish up here!' Masi said, clearly done with housework.

It was still light as we drove home.

'So, I'm thinking of the ready-to-wear line again, Mini,' she said, over the music station I'd turned on to discourage conversation. 'I haven't thought about it for a while, but, after six years, the time seems to be right again.'

'What happened last time?' I asked. 'Why did you pull out?'

'You remember that?' she asked. 'You were so little!'

'Remember?' I asked—she thought I'd *forgotten*? 'Of course I remember. I was really excited about going to India, you know.' That had to be the understatement of the decade. 'Vinnie helped me shop when she came home for Thanksgiving. I bought gifts for Ari and Avi with my allowance. And then you canceled …'

I could feel her eyes on me, but I kept mine firmly on the road. 'Vinod said you took it well,' she said, finally.

'What does Dad know,' I said. 'The pea coat you saw in my closet—Vinnie bought it for me as a birthday present, for that trip.'

'It looks brand new,' she said.

I shrugged. 'I was so disappointed about the trip that I never wore it.'

'OK,' she said. '*That's* just tragic. You would have looked so cute in it, Mini.'

'It's too late now,' I shrugged.

'I don't think I ever talked to you properly after that,' Masi said. 'The summer I came to see you when you were …'

'Fat?' I asked, teeth clenched.

'Chubby,' she said. 'Your Beeji was so hostile when I tried to explain that she should feed you healthy food, and encourage you to exercise.'

'She was just taking care of me the best way she could,' I said.

'Vinod understood,' she said. 'He started running with you after that, right? And he supported their move to India.'

Wait—that was because of her?

'I just thought, you know, teenagers,' she said. 'Can't force them to talk. If you wanted to accept my friend request—you would. If you wanted to talk to me you'd call.'

'I didn't …' There were tears glinting at the end of my lashes but I didn't brush them away. 'I didn't *want* to talk to you. Before, I thought that you were the only person who got me. Dad and Vinnie were always on about engineering and medicine and stuff. Beeji didn't understand either. You were the one creative person in my life, and you clearly wanted nothing to do with me.'

'I wasn't happy about missing that trip, Mini,' Masi said. 'It was hard to disappoint you …'

'Then why did you?' I flung at her.

She said nothing.

I waited in bitter silence. What possible reason could she have?

'You want to know?' she said. 'OK, I'll tell you!'

Oh, this ought to be good.

'That November—they found a cyst in my mammogram,' she said. 'A large one, and it was irregular so they were afraid it could be something more.'

No! The word screamed in my head. My knuckles were white, I was gripping the steering wheel so hard.

Of course! The hushed phone conversations with Dad that I tried so hard to overhear—that's what they had been about. How bad had it been?

Meanwhile Masi went on explaining—how it changed her priorities, how she put her business on the backburner, let her nanny go, started packing lunch for Ari and Avi with her own hands, how she made sure she picked them up after school (meaning in her chauffer-driven car, of course), how she made sure she had check-ups every few months for years.

'The first time they put me through a bunch of tests, including a biopsy. It looked like it might be cancer ...'

My heart was pounding. Please—not that!

'They removed it, but it turned out not to be malignant. But that's why I canceled the trip, the deals, and your holiday. It wasn't even a year from the time Megha passed. I didn't want you to know—it would have scared you. Vinod agreed.'

Fear gripped me. Was there any danger of a reccurrence? The car behind me changed into the next lane because I was going way too slow. I'd better pull over before I drove into a tree. An exit was coming up and I took it and parked at the first gas station off of the road.

'What's wrong? Do you need petrol?' Masi asked.

I climbed out of the driver's seat and walked over to her side. She had got out, looking puzzled and concerned. I probably confused her even more by wrapping my arms around her in a tight hug.

She hugged me back, and then I was sobbing all over her pashmina wrap. She felt so tiny and fragile. But she was there.

'You're OK now, right?' I asked her. 'It never came back?'

'I'm fine, beta,' she said. 'I'm fine—really!'

I let her go and stood there awkwardly trying to explain.

'Masi, I never tho—' I said. All these years I had blamed her and refused to communicate with her, and she had just been trying to protect me, while dealing with way more crap than anyone deserved. And she'd been right about Beeji too—though it was hard to admit. I may be taller than her but right then I felt about two inches high.

'Silly kid,' she said, her eyes wet with tears too. 'I'm clear now. It was just a scare. There's no need for you to worry, I promise.'

***

Apparently I'm not so great at figuring things out. I jump to stupid conclusions and clam up and stop communicating.

So, this time I called him.

'Mini?' Vir said. 'Is that you?'

'Yeah,' I said. I looked down at the notes I'd made to get me through the call.

'I know I've been acting strange, but I saw the pictures of you with Koyal, and other, umm … girls—and I freaked.'

'Understood,' he said. 'I should have warned you.'

'It was a total shock,' I said, my voice kind of broken at that point. *Hold it together, Mini*, I told myself.

'I agree,' he said. 'But Mini,' and here his voice took on an injured tone, 'you should have heard me out, instead of just *assuming …*'

Really?

After all the things he kept from me this was *my* fault? I hung up the phone, my hands shaking.

This was much, much harder than I thought it would be.

The phone rang.

'What?' I snapped.

'Look, I know this is not the best time!' Vir said.

Damn right it wasn't.

'It isn't,' I said. 'I'm really busy right now, Vir. I want to get through the wedding; we're having all kinds of problems with the …'

'… weather, I know,' Vir said. 'I've seen the news reports. And I'd like to help—please. If there's anything I can do, just let me know.'

'Fine,' I said.

'And when this is over let's sit down and talk about this rationally,' he said. 'It's not how it looks—I promise.'

It better not be, Vir Mirchandani, it better not.

THE NEWS

www.thenews.com   August 22, 2011

HURRICANE IRENE HITS PUERTO RICO

Hurricane Irene has hit the US Caribbean territory of Puerto Rico, knocking out electricity lines and ripping up trees. More than 800,000 homes were left without power including in the capital, San Juan.

Irene, which is the first hurricane of the 2011 season, then swept just north of the Dominican Republic.

Tropical storm watches and warnings were also in effect for the US Virgin Islands, British Virgin Islands, the southeastern Bahamas and the Turks and Caicos Islands.

Residents of the southeastern United States were urged to monitor Irene's progress as the storm headed their way. Computer forecast models showed Irene moving northwest over the Dominican Republic and then heading towards the Florida peninsula, possibly arriving there on Thursday.

Current forecasts suggest that Irene poses no threat to US oil and gas installations in the Gulf of Mexico.

Evil Eye

'Hurricane Bob!' Dad said. 'That's the one I'm thinking of!'

We were driving to the airport to pick up Beeji, Bauji and Bade Bauji. The weatherman on the radio seemed torn between analyzing the earthquake we felt earlier that day—it wasn't much more than a jolt, if you ask me—and recapping the hurricanes that brushed New England in the past. There had been a grand total of two in the last half century—Hurricane Donna in 1960, and Hurricane Bob in '91.

So there *had* been a hurricane in New England in my lifetime—who knew! According to the radio guy there was some possibility that the hurricane in Puerto Rico could hit New York, and even make it all the way to Massachusetts.

As if!

This was the first hurricane of the season and they were all just panicking for nothing. Weren't they?

'Was it bad?' I asked Dad. 'The one in 1991?'

'Hurricane Bob?' Dad asked. 'It did a lot of damage, but on the Cape mostly, not *inland*. We just got rain and wind. I don't even think I took the day off work.'

Which isn't saying much—Dad never took a day off work for anything. And yet, I had to admit, the spinning storm system they showed on the evening news looked like the evil eye Beeji always warned about, coming to life.

'So, is Bade Bauji going to be wearing jeans and a jacket instead of his khadi kurta?' I asked. It had been ages since I'd seen him.

'He said he didn't want to risk being frisked by security because of his clothes, so he bought a special outfit for the plane trip,' Dad said.

I couldn't imagine anyone frisking Bade Bauji. He commanded respect even at ninety-two. Granted, the last time I saw him I was only seven, but I'd been very impressed. And I knew his life story of course—the story of how he founded KDH spices.

He left West Punjab with nothing after the partition of India. All their family property was lost after West Punjab became part of Pakistan. He started from scratch in the refugee camps in Delhi, setting up a business that sold pre-ground spices to housewives. And then his Punjabi spices became famous. He pioneered the selling of boxed spices, basically. For all kinds of Indian dishes—chana masala, rajma, muttar paneer, sambar, tandoori and so on. And through it all Bade Bauji always wore the simple homespun Gandhian fabric—khadi—that he had put on as a symbol of the Independence movement in the forties. Except now he was wearing Levi's to avoid getting cavity-searched in an American airport. I bet he looked adorable, though.

'There he is,' Dad said, smiling. Bauji was wheeling the cart with Beeji and Bade Bauji, who looked amazingly on-trend in khakis and an L.L. Bean jacket. Wow. Where does one even get L.L. Bean jackets in India?

Beeji was in a starched salwar kameez, ambling along like a ship in sail. No concessions made there—and I wouldn't want to be in the shoes of any security person who decided to frisk her!

'*Peri pona*, Bauji.' Dad swiped a hand in the direction of Bade Bauji's feet. I made a half-hearted attempt to follow suit, feeling kind of ridiculous. I meant well, but it just didn't look or feel right if I did it.

'No, no, beta,' Beeji said. 'No need. How are you, Mini? You are looking fine!'

Beeji was an odd mixture of very traditional and very American. She'd lived here for forty years until Bauji decided he wanted to help modernize the KDH Spices grinding operations, and also help launch the new ayurvedic spices line.

Bade Bauji examined me carefully. 'You look like your mother,' Bade Bauji pronounced at last in his slow, deep voice and careful English. 'You have your father's height, but you are Megha through and through.'

'Thanks!' I said. I knew I always liked him, even when I was five.

'Minnni!' Bauji said. Bauji had not changed. Same lantern jaw, same big grin—he looked like the builder he was—even though he had now decided to dedicate his life to researching and bringing ayurvedic spices to the world. A strange thing for an engineer and builder to be into, but hey, whatever works, right? 'How's the house looking?'

'It could do with some work!' I said. This was our old joke. Dad couldn't be bothered to fix anything around the house so Bauji always sent his sub-contractors over to help out whenever anything was seriously in need of repair. When the boiler died, when the water pipes froze, when the toilet made a weird whistling sound when it flushed, when the door stuck, when the roof tiles blew off—it was Bauji's trade friends that showed up and fixed the plumbing, retiled the roof, and hammered open the door.

Bauji and I also convinced Dad to replace the windows, finish the three-season porch, expand the deck and do various other home improvement projects. It was his way of being there for us. I missed having him around.

'I'm here now,' he said. 'If there's anything you want done before the wedding, we still have time!'

***

Vinnie was here!

Manish picked her up at the airport and brought her home after a visit at his parents' in Newton. He even came inside the house and gingerly petted Yogi. Even though Vinnie said that it was stupid to risk breaking out in hives five days before the wedding, he scored major points with me and Dad. He was trying—I had to give him that—he was definitely trying.

223

As soon as he left we went upstairs with Masi and looked at the lehenga. Vinnie hadn't even seen the real thing yet, except in pictures and on Skype!

'Masi, what if it doesn't fit?' Vinnie said.

'*Arre!*' Masi said. 'We're here, no? We'll make it fit!'

'OK, but what if I hate it?' Vinnie said.

'*That* we can't change now,' Masi said.

'But you won't,' I added. 'I promise, Vinnie!'

'OK,' she said. 'Here goes!' She opened the box and lifted the tissue.

Silence.

'Well?' Masi said.

'Say something!' I said, dying of suspense.

'Masi!' Vinnie looked stunned. She opened her arms, being at a loss for words, and squeezed Masi. 'It's so much more beautiful in real life. Thank you, Masi! Thank you!'

'Put it on first,' Masi said, all smiles, 'before you start thanking me!'

'But it's so, so beautiful,' Vinnie said, cradling the dress.

'Yes, it's beautiful,' I said. 'But put it on, Vinnie. Now. We want to see—does it even fit or what? OK, go!'

'OK, OK!' Vinnie grabbed the box and vanished into her room. Masi grabbed my hand and squeezed. 'I've dressed so many brides, beta, that it's all old to me now. All this fitting-shitting.' How I kept a straight face while she rhymed fitting with shitting, I don't know, but she was obviously sincere, so I did. 'But this is Vinnie, and I'm nervous. I'm actually *nervous*, about this. What if she hates it, huh? Haven't been this nervous since I made Megha's lehenga in ... 1986?'

I patted her hand, but I was a wreck myself. Masi may have designed it but I picked it out and convinced her it was the one. What if she did hate it? The door opened.

A vision in gold and red stood in the doorway. My sister Vinnie!

The choli fitted her perfectly, setting off her curves; the old gold glowed against her tanned, toned arms. There was a small amount of bare midriff before the lehenga hugged her at the waist and flared out in a froth of gold. The heavy embroidery at the hem made the skirt swing at the slightest movement.

Oh shoot! She had thrown the pretty red scarf in a horrible bunch over one shoulder, but we could fix that.

'Vinnie!' I literally had tears in my eyes. 'Have you *seen* yourself?'

'No,' Vinnie said. 'It feels good,' she said, and gingerly walked a step or two in the not-too-high heels I had put out for her. 'But how does it look?'

'OK, wait, first let me fix this,' Masi said. 'Turn around!' She ordered and laced up the back of the choli properly and started to drape the red scarf over Vinnie's head.

'Wait! Put this on first!' I put a blue velvet jewelry box down on the bed.

'Oh, right,' Masi put down the scarf and snapped open the jewelry case. 'I had forgotten about this. Oh, look at this! It's Megha's design!' She lifted the gold necklace reverently. The

225

gold glittered in the light. 'Just look at this!' She clasped it gently around Vinnie's neck, as I held up my sister's glossy black hair (shoulder-length now, thankfully). Masi held out the earrings and Vinnie put them in. I pinned the maangtika into place so it dangled high on her forehead, and Masi arranged the cranberry red scarf over her hair.

'Remember, with the hair and make-up you'll look even better,' Masi warned.

'Just look, Vinnie,' I said and turned her around so she was facing the full-length mirror at the back of my door.

'Wow, that's me?' Vinnie gasped.

'Sure is!' I said.

She turned this way and that. 'Manish is not going to believe this,' she said. 'I look amazing!'

'OK, let's show Dad!' I said, steering her out of the door and downstairs. 'Dad, get a load of this!'

'What?' Dad said. He was wandering around with an open plastic cup of low-fat yogurt in one hand and a spoon in another, oblivious to the excitement upstairs.

'This could get on her lehenga!' I said, taking the yogurt from his hand and setting it on a table. 'OK, Vinnie, come through!' I opened the door to the kitchen. 'Ta-da!'

Vinnie floated in, smiling happily.

'Vinnie!' Dad was suddenly all smiles. 'You look like a million bucks!'

'Doesn't she?' Masi said and pulled out a fifty dollar bill, waved it around Vinnie's head before putting it in the slot of my

226

MSPCA collection box. 'Nazar na lage!'

'What are you doing?' I asked. 'All that waving thing?'

'Warding off the evil eye,' Masi said. 'Vinnie, come! We have one more outfit for you to try.'

'I don't need another outfit!' Vinnie said.

'It's for the reception,' Masi said. 'Mini, go get it.'

I knew what it was of course—but we had not told Vinnie about finding Mom's lehenga. I followed them upstairs and grabbed it out of my closet where it was hanging, shrouded in a plastic drycleaning bag.

Vinnie pulled the plastic off. 'No way!' This time she had tears in her eyes.

'Way!' I said. 'Masi fixed that too. Go try it on!'

We waited for her to get in it and soon she was back incased in the raspberry pink and silver outfit.

'How does it look?' Vinnie asked.

'Brilliant!' I said, reverting to Potter speak. 'Bloody brilliant!'

It was very vintage, like something Madhuri Dixit would have worn, but Vinnie's fresh young face updated it immediately. There was a lump in my throat. It's not that she looked like Mom exactly, but there were flashes of Mom in the way she moved, and smiled, and sounded even. And with that lehenga on, there was no mistaking it.

'Do that thing with the evil eye, Masi,' I said. 'Do it immediately!'

If we were very lucky it might turn the storm that was

coming into a bit of light rain.

***

'It's very grand!' Ragini Aunty said. 'It will be beautiful, Padmini. Beauuutiful.'

'I didn't even know this was here,' Manish said. 'Vinnie played field hockey and soccer here, Amma.'

No, it wasn't the wedding rehearsal—that was on Friday— but most of the immediate family was here now, so we brought them to River Bend anyway. Vinnie and Manish, Masi, Beeji, Bauji, Bade Bauji, Dad, Ragini Aunty, Manoj Uncle—and me.

Luckily Masi and Beeji had called an unspoken truce and decided to present a united front to the Iyers.

'The mandap will go here,' Vinnie said. 'Sudha Aunty will be draping it in rust and dark red sheer fabric, and there will be flowers above the *mandap* on all four sides.'

'It sounds very pretty,' Ragini Aunty said.

'Group photo!' Manish said. And everyone arranged themselves into two lines in front of the graceful marble fountain—they finally had it working, thankfully—and smiled dutifully for the camera. Ragini Aunty in her bright red kanjivaram sari, Beeji in a very Punjabi lace salwar kameez, Bade Bauji in his homespun cotton kurta, and the rest of us in jeans.

'Let me,' Caroline Kelly said. Manish explained the way the camera worked and then took his place in the family line-up, his arm around Vinnie in spite of the presence of all the parents and grandparents, and a great-grandparent. To their credit they took it in their stride.

228

Did I mention that there wasn't a cloud in the sky?

'Say cheese!' said Caroline.

***

We were invited to Beeji's for dinner. I was on the phone the whole way trying to get a hold of the remaining two bridesmaids who did not have sari blouses as yet. With four days left! I left messages on the phone, via email, and on their FB pages and with their mothers. 'Please call today!' I said into the phone. 'Otherwise you're knotting a strip of cloth over your boobs for the wedding!'

'We're here!' Dad announced, and we spilled out of the minivan onto Beeji's driveway. Dad, Masi, Vinnie, me, and Yogi of course. 'Something smells good!'

My grandparents' house is a 1960s split level in a subdivision of 1960s split levels. It's the neighborhood my Dad grew up in. Bauji built huge 5000 sq. ft. mansions in wealthy suburbs—the kind with four-car garages and floating walkways and two-storey atriums with crystal chandeliers. Once in a while when he had one sitting on the market he contemplated selling off the split level and moving into it. But it's so not him. This house, where Dad planted the now towering pine trees on either side, and helped Bauji put in the garage, and filmed sci-fi pictures with a super 8 camera in the backyard—this is them. That's why they were holding on to it even though they lived in India most of the year.

Bauji did gut the interior and remove a few walls and put in granite and hardwood and marble to upgrade the place whenever his building crew had downtime. The bathrooms were remodeled during the recession of 2005, and the new kitchen was put in the year Bauji couldn't sell a fully finished house. And you'd think Beeji would have been thankful for the gorgeous new kitchen he had built for her—but no—she was perfectly happy with her harvest gold kitchen from the '60s, thank you very much. Complete with avocado green oven and fridge and dishwasher. She had kept them in mint working condition for four decades. The new granite and rosewood kitchen with the recessed lights and slide-out pantry weren't really her cup of tea. But she could make magic in any kitchen anywhere.

Knowing Beeji I was expecting an extravagant spread with the newest KDH Spices showcased in every dish.

She didn't disappoint.

Chana masala, with fresh bhatooras, okra, kadhi, vegetarian rice pulao—yum! 'And I'm making laddoos,' she said, and uncovered a couple of platters with the flourish of a sorcerer. 'For the wedding!'

'LADDOOS,' I said, gazing incredulously at the hundreds of fist-sized golden yellow balls that had magically appeared on trays all over Beeji's kitchen. It was clearly a work-in-progress. There was a giant pot full of fresh golden brown boondis soaked in syrup on the countertop that were yet to be rolled into proper fist-sized laddoo balls. 'You are making laddoos for the wedding? What are we paying that Sunny Sondhi for then?'

I mean the woman had just got here—how did she even make this much food in such little time?

'But there should be some homemade sweets from the home, no?' Beeji said. 'This is Vinnie's favorite.'

'It is good hospitality,' Masi chipped in unexpectedly. 'Anyone can buy sweets, but homemade is from the heart.'

Was that a tagline from one of the KDH masala advertisements?

If there was sarcasm behind that quote, I couldn't detect it. Masi had resolved to be nice.

Which was a good thing, because Beeji didn't look like she would be up for a verbal scrap. It was completely unnecessary for her to have cooked dessert for an entire wedding party before she was even over her jetlag.

'Beeji, no one makes sweets at home anymore,' I said. 'Even in India they get a halwai to make it if they really want it fresh. And anyway we've ordered a massive wedding cake.'

'Those South Indians ...' Beeji started.

'Tamilians,' I corrected.

'Yes, Tamilians,' she said. 'Some of them don't eat eggs, you know. And Manish is allergic to nuts, and with that kind of thing it's better to have homemade—always. These caterers put nuts in everything. In sweets more than anything.'

For all her complaining about their dietary restrictions she had the 'South Indians" needs in mind—typical Beeji.

'And that's why Curry Cuisine is bringing nut-free payasam for them,' I said. 'They catered for Manish's sister's wedding, remember, and Manish ate their dessert and survived. Let's just put this away for now, OK?'

231

Beeji looked mighty offended, so I added, 'I'll help you squeeze the rest of them after they've left. Just please go get dressed, and Vinnie and I will set the table and everything.'

***

When we were full of Beeji's, in Ragini Aunty's words— 'excccelent cooking'—we turned on the weather channel and watched the forecast. Yeah, the storm was definitely headed our way. If we were lucky it would swing west and inland and give Westbury a miss, or it would swing east and out to sea, but right now it looked like it was beating a path to Vinnie's wedding mandap. Go figure!

'We have a rain plan,' Vinnie said. 'Right, Mini?'

'Yes they have a tent that we can set up for the ceremony. It's semi-attached to the carriage house where the reception is going to be held. We'd just have to put the dance floor in the tent and put the mandap on top of it and the white chairs for the guests grouped around it. And when it's done we'll have to skip cocktail hour and go straight to the reception.'

'The rehearsal is on Friday at River Bend,' Vinnie said. 'We'll talk about it then.'

Dad's cellphone rang and he walked out of the room, only to return two minutes later grinning from ear to ear.

'… great news,' Dad said. 'Intel Capital finally called, and … they're giving us all the funding we asked for!'

'That's awesome, Dad,' I hugged him. 'That's epic!'

'You can spend anything you want for the wedding now,' he said. 'And I won't say a thing!'

Maybe the tide was turning for our family after all.

I ran upstairs and fetched a platter from Beeji's kitchen.

'Laddoos for everyone!' I said.

***

THE NEWS

www.thenews.com　　　　　　　August 25, 2011

HURRICANE IRENE HITS PUERTO RICO

Hurricane Irene: Massachusetts, Rhode Island. Prepare for Impact August 25, 2011 1:08 PM EDT

After experiencing an out-of-the-blue earthquake earlier this week, New England residents must prepare for another natural disaster: Hurricane Irene.

The storm will likely be the first to make landfall in the area since Hurricane Bob assaulted coastal communities in 1991. While New Englanders prove year after year that they can handle their share of poor weather, authorities are taking no chances with Irene, and preparing for the worst ahead of time.

Hurricane Irene, currently a Category 3 storm, ripped through the Bahamas on Wednesday night with 120-miles-per-hour winds. Irene is expected to reach Category 4 strength as it nears the Carolinas, before downgrading to a Category 1 or a weak Category 2 by the time it makes landfall in New England on Sunday.

Terry Francona, manager of the Red Sox, told the newspaper the team is attempting to reorganize three weekend games with the Oakland Athletics in order to fit them all in before the hurricane approaches. The Massachusetts Emergency Management Agency (MEMA) has been consulting with other New England states, the Federal Emergency Management Agency (FEMA) and the National Weather Service to ensure the region is fully prepared, CBS News reports.

MEMA's website offers a series of hurricane preparation tips. The agency recommends that every home and business stock an emergency supply kit—which should include a flashlight, batteries, non-perishable foods, bottled water, a first aid kit and a portable radio—and prepare a disaster 'Go Bag' with essential items in case of a sudden evacuation.

Rain Option

I. CAN'T. EVEN.

I can't even *begin* to explain what it was like. When we found out that the dang hurricane was headed straight at us at the exact place and time of Vinnie's wedding. Just like that. BAM.

EPIC FAIL doesn't even cover it.

The only hope left was that it could weaken into a tropical depression and just be a big rainstorm instead of hitting us in hurricane avatar.

If I was the praying type I would have been praying, but what was the use? Miracles had stopped working for the likes of us a long time ago.

All we could do was wait. We'd know by Friday, definitely. Until then there was nothing to be done except wring hands, write place cards, and go on as if nothing the size of Texas was barreling down at us at 120 miles an hour.

So when we headed to the wedding rehearsal at River Bend on Friday there was a lot weighing on our minds.

Instead of just the event manager there was a group of

people waiting for us at the venue.

'This is my boss, Karen Cummings, the general manager of the Massachusetts Botanical Society,' Caroline said. 'I thought we should have her in on the discussion in case we need to get her approval on anything. We've been monitoring the weather too.'

'It looks like the storm will hit on Sunday, for sure,' Karen said. 'We will do everything we can to make sure your event still runs smoothly, but as of now the outdoor part of the event has to be canceled.'

Vinnie and Manish held hands tightly—they were adorable. 'Of course,' Manish said. 'We want everyone to be safe.'

'Can we move to the rain plan?' Vinnie asked. 'Move the wedding ceremony under the tent and skip cocktail hour to go right to the reception?'

'That would be the best solution,' Caroline said. 'The only problem is …'

'If the storm is predicted to have winds over fifty miles an hour,' Karen continued, 'then we have to pack up the tent.'

'Pack up the tent?' I asked. 'But it has a concrete floor, it has metal scaffolding. It's not like a pop-up tent or anything. I've seen it up in snow!'

'Yes, it's pretty sturdy,' Caroline admitted. 'But fifty-miles-an-hour winds are too much for it to take. We can't take the risk of it collapsing on a party of people.'

'Of course not,' Dad said. 'But this is hypothetical, right? If the storm takes a different track, we're good.'

'That's correct,' Karen said.

'If we do have to take the tent down,' I asked, 'where can we have the ceremony?'

'Well,' Caroline said, sounding apologetic. 'An open fire is not allowed inside a heritage building. And all the buildings at River Bend are heritage sites. They can have candles, yes, but not an actual fire or anything.'

'So we can't get married at River Bend at all?' Vinnie asked.

'If you promise that the fire will be very, very small then we could make an exception,' Karen said. 'It's a very unusual situation, and we want to be as accommodating as we can.'

'Am I late?' A tall young man in a business suit walked through the double doors of the carriage house. He had a pleasant face but the resemblance to Sunny Sondhi was unmistakable. 'I'm Vicky Sondhi, from Curry Cuisine.'

'Was Mr Sondhi too busy to come?' Dad asked.

'My dad's busy, so he sent me,' Vicky said. 'I guess we have a weather situation on Sunday. Just want to make sure we're on the same page as everyone.'

I'd been thinking about the time of the wedding—maybe that was the solution. We had scheduled it for 3:00 pm with the reception at 7:00 pm. It was traditional in the North to have weddings in the evening.

'How about we reschedule the wedding to 9:00 am?' I asked. 'We can have the reception at noon and serve lunch instead of dinner. We have the grounds and buildings booked for the day, right?'

'That may not be a bad idea,' Caroline said. 'The storm is supposed to hit hardest late afternoon and evening. By then your guests could be on their way home if you're lucky.'

'Can you serve lunch instead of dinner?' I asked Vicky Sondi. It was great that he was here after all. 'It's just a six-hour difference, but it would solve everything.'

'We'd have to call the bus transportation company, and all the guests, and the bartender, and the priest, and Sudha Moorty,' I added. 'She said there was a big wedding in Boston on Saturday. Remember, the horse was booked for it too?'

'The Bernstein-Patel wedding,' Vicky Sondhi nodded knowledgeably. 'Everyone's talking about it. They've booked four white horses to pull the wedding carriage.'

So the horse Manish had booked was a carriage horse too.

'Good for them,' I said. 'We have to call Sudha Aunty, but if she's good with coming out early and getting the decorations done, we'll handle everything else. How does that sound?'

'Excellent,' said Vinnie.

'I don't know,' Manish said. 'I have some friends coming in from California on Sunday afternoon. They won't be able to make it.'

'How many friends?' I asked.

'Six or seven,' Manish said.

'They'll have to miss it then,' I said. 'Odds are that their flight will be canceled anyway, so there's no point waiting for them.'

'Not so fast,' Manish said. 'Let me think about it.'

'OK,' I said. 'I do think they're closing Logan Airport for the storm though, Manish. Can they take an earlier flight?'

'Maybe … I don't know,' Manish said.

Leave him alone, Vinnie mouthed at me. *Fine*, I mouthed back at her.

'How about you guys continue discussing this?' I said. 'I still have a lot of work to do at home for the mehendi.'

The mehendi was still tomorrow, and I didn't have Sudha Moorty to help decorate the house. Masi was at home madly stitching the blouses for the remaining two bridesmaids. Beeji was madly making laddoos for absolutely no reason, except it made her feel like she was doing something. They were so worried they weren't even fighting.

I ordered five gorgeous umbrellas via Dad's Amazon Prime account. They have free next-day delivery so at least we'd have some umbrellas that wouldn't clash with our Malika Motwani couture.

Then I snapped shut my laptop. Enough! First I was going to walk my dog. Then, I was going to get my hair done. They had my cellphone number. If something went crazy wrong they could always find me.

***

I had booked Katrina, my regular hairdresser to come to the house to get Vinnie ready—but she wasn't coming until 4:30 pm. I wanted to be done before then so I could help get her dressed without worrying about myself. So, I went to the mall and walked into the Dellaria and got an appointment with a random hairdresser. Not the smartest of moves, usually, but for some reason it paid off. My hairdresser was an excellent listener.

I hadn't even known how stressed I was until I started to talk to her about Vinnie's wedding and the storm, and Mom's jewelry, and my family, and Vir and so on.

'Don't you worry, it'll all come right,' she said. 'At least everyone is here for her.'

'So many of the guests are stranded in airports all over the country,' I said. 'My grandfather and my two little cousins are in London—their flight has been delayed too. I don't want them to miss the wedding.' I leaned my head back so she could shampoo my hair.

'Whoever is meant to be there will get there,' she said, rinsing out my scalp in warm water. 'Don't you fret. It's better that they're safe on the ground somewhere, isn't it?'

'OK,' I said. 'But,' I spread my hands hopelessly. 'So many guests had flights canceled—in Miami, Dallas, San Francisco, and Chicago. No one will get here.'

'Your ninety-two-year-old great-grandfather got here from India,' she said.

'Right, because he came early,' I said.

'He was meant to make it,' she said, wrapping my head in a towel and pointing me to a chair. 'They weren't. So, what's next?'

'The janvasam at the temple—that's tonight,' I said.

'That's the engagement sort of thing,' she said. 'And then?'

'Then the mehendi tomorrow,' I said.

'At your house?' she asked.

'Yeah, but we're prepared for that. They're delivering the tables and chairs tonight and we're setting everything up in the morning.'

'And the wedding is on Sunday,' she said.

'Sunday *morning* now,' I said.

'Three events in three days,' she said, as she clipped the last rollers into place. 'Just take it one step at a time.'

'OK,' I said.

'You have half an hour under the dryer,' she said, turning on the dome-like dryer over my head. 'Read a magazine, and I'll get you some tea.'

I had five minutes of peace—the calm before the storm—before the phone rang.

It was Vinnie. Vinnie sounding perfectly calm and clinical as she broke the horrible news. Massachusetts had declared a state of emergency and all state parks were to be closed on Sunday— including River Bend.

The wedding was off.

***

'What's wrong?' the hairdresser asked.

I was still sitting in stunned silence when she checked on me forty minutes later. I told her.

'It's my fault,' I said. 'I planned it, and now it's all gone wrong.'

'Nonsense,' she said. 'My grandparents got married in a Nor'easter, you know. There was no one there but ten people and a preacher—it can be done.'

'Even if we find another venue,' I said, 'how are we ever going to let people know and change everything around?'

'You can't do it without help,' she said. 'So, anyone who's ever said they want to help, call them. Tell them what you need. They will feel better if they can do something—anything.'

'OK,' I said. 'I will.'

'That's the spirit,' she said. 'Now let's make your hair look gorgeous.'

An hour later I emerged rested, and determined, and ready to stick it to that storm.

THE NEWS

www.thenews.com   August 26, 2011

Gov. Deval Patrick Declares State Of Emergency Ahead of Irene

WBUR News & Wire Services August 26, 2011 BOSTON

Gov. Deval Patrick has declared a state of emergency in Massachusetts and is mobilizing 2500 members of the National Guard as Hurricane Irene approaches.

Patrick told a briefing at the state's emergency management headquarters in Framingham on Friday that Irene is expected to have a significant impact on Massachusetts, arriving Saturday night with the brunt of the storm expected on Sunday afternoon.

'As we all know, Mother Nature is unpredictable, and the forecast may change for the better or the worse,' Patrick added later.

As of late Friday afternoon, Irene was a Category 2 storm with winds of approximately 100 miles per hour. It could downgrade as it continues north.

Also Friday, the White House said President Obama will cut his Martha's Vineyard vacation short because of Irene. He'll return to Washington on Friday night instead of Saturday afternoon.

In a statement on Friday, Obama said that all indications suggest Irene will be a 'historic' storm.

Change of Plan

'They don't have a choice,' Vinnie said. 'The State of Massachusetts has ordered them shut.'

'So ... we'll find an alternative venue,' I said. I didn't even believe it. We both knew how far in advance places got booked.

'We tried,' Vinnie said. 'Dad's been on the phone ever since we left River Bend. Everything outdoor is canceled and everything indoor is booked.'

We had to think outside the box. Outside the room. Outside the house.

'How about here?' A wild idea was taking hold of me. 'At our house! Tomorrow—before the storm hits hard!'

'Are you crazy?' Vinnie said. 'We can't fit over a hundred people in here. Even with the people cancelling we'll have at least that many people.'

'Maybe not inside,' I said, and grabbed my car keys. 'But we have the yard—at least until it starts raining. I'll be back, Vinnie!'

'But where are you going?' Vinnie wailed.

'Just get ready for the janvasam,' I said, and gave her a kiss. 'I have a plan.'

I hopped in the car and pushed a button on my cellphone— it's a good thing I had Taylor Rental on speed dial. The ringtone buzzed at the other end. Pick up, pick up, pick up—dang it! Someone rapped on my car window as I reversed slowly out into the street.

Vir!

I had nearly run him over—if you can run anyone over at 2 miles an hour.

Let them help. The hairdresser's stern voice sounded in my head.

I stopped the car and jumped out.

'Vir, drive the car!' I said. 'I have to make a phone call.'

'You'd trust me with your car?' he said, looking warily at me.

'Are you kidding me?' I said. 'My dad let you drive his Lotus!'

'Fine, fine, I'll drive,' he said. 'If I can fit behind the wheel.'

There was a charged silence in the car as he eased the Mini up the hill. My call went to voice mail—I hit redial.

'Err ... where exactly are we going?' Vir asked.

'The Westbury Town Hall,' I said. 'If they're still open!'

He was an excellent driver—even I sometimes stalled at the top of the hill, but not Vir. Meanwhile someone at Taylor Rental answered the phone. 'Hi,' I said. 'I'd like to book a tent for tomorrow, please.'

'What kind of tent?' the girl asked.

'Twenty foot by forty foot tent,' I said after consulting my notepad. Yeah, that was the largest size I could fit on the front lawn. The backyard had trees, and the sidelawn was sharply slanted—so they were both out.

'OK,' she said. 'Do you want sidewalls for the tent?'

'Yes,' I said. 'The ones with the arched windows.'

'What date is this for?' she asked.

'Tomorrow,' I said. 'Saturday the 27th of August.'

'What town?' she asked.

'Westbury,' I said. We had made it to the town center and Vir was parking by the library. I jumped out of the car, and sprinted for the Town Hall. They usually closed at four-thirty. I still had five or ten minutes—if they hadn't changed their schedule for the summer. Many of the town services did. And if they had shorter summer hours my plan was toast.

'And do you have a dig-safe permit?' she asked. That was the question I'd been dreading.

'No,' I said. 'But I am trying to get to the Town Hall. With any luck they'll still be open and ...'

There were no lights on in the Town Hall. The door was bolted. Shoot! Of all the days for the Town Hall to close early!

'I'm here, but they're closed,' I said. 'Can we still get a tent?'

'We can't put up a tent without a dig-safe permit, ma'am,' she said. 'I'm sorry.'

'It's my sister's wedding,' I explained dejectedly. 'It was

supposed to be at River Bend on Sunday but they've canceled because of the hurricane. So we're trying to move it to our house. But we can't do it without a t...tent,' my voice broke. I *so* didn't want to cry—not with Vir watching. But what on earth were we going to do *now*?

'Your sister's wedding got canceled? That's terrible!' the girl said. 'Look, hold on a minute, let me talk to someone.'

'OK,' I said. 'I'll hold.' Vir had caught up with me. He took one look at my face and pulled me firmly into a hug. I was too surprised to resist—and I had to admit, it felt good.

'You there?' the girl said. 'OK, I checked with my boss and he did say that we can't put up a tent without a permit ...'

I rested my head on his shoulder for a minute before regaining my sanity and pushing away. Vir let go.

'Thanks for trying,' I said. 'It's really nice of you.'

'... no, wait,' she said. 'We can't put up a tent, but *you* can.'

'What?' I asked. Maybe my brain had stopped functioning due to all the impossible things it had had to process lately. Did she just say we could put up a tent?

'We can give you a tent. We just can't put it up,' she said. 'Do you still want it?'

My heart was racing. 'YES!' I said. 'Yes, and there are other things ... I need ten tables, a hundred chairs, floor-length tablecloths, napkins, china, silverware, stemware ...'

'One at a time,' she said. 'I have to take this down. How many table covers and what kind?'

'Ten round, white, floor-length for the eight-foot

roundtables,' I said. 'I'll need a buffet table too …'

Vir was looking at me as if I'd lost my mind. But he waited to question me until after I got off the phone with her.

'What was that about?' Vir said.

'Getting a big tent,' I said. 'So we can have the reception at home.'

'But who's going to put up a forty-foot tent?' he asked.

'That's not a problem, trust me,' I said. 'But food, I need food.'

'What about Curry Cuisine?' he asked.

'That Vicky Sondhi cashed the nine-thousand-dollar check my Dad gave him,' I said. 'And he's not returning calls.'

'WHAT? He gave him a check?' Vir asked. 'For the full amount?'

'It's my fault,' I said. 'I insisted that he pay the guy in advance because Sudha Aunty told us that he threatened to take away food at this other wedding because he *wasn't* paid in advance. We never imagined this!'

'I don't blame you,' Vir said. '*No* one expected this!'

It hit me then. Like a hot samosa.

'I should call Sher-e-Punjab,' I said. 'Right now!'

I scrolled through the contacts on my phone, and found the number. 'Sher-e-Punjab? Rajendar Singh Ji?' I said. 'Thank God! Badi problem aa gai hai—aapki help chahiye. Can you double our order?' I counted on my hands to get a grasp of the numbers. 'Triple our order? Forty nahin, one hundred twenty logon ka khana chahiye. Haan ji, hurricane ki vajah se cancel karna pada.

Kal shadi hamare ghar se hogi. Haan ji. Thank you ji.'

'What did he say?' Vir asked.

'He's going to start cooking,' I said. 'Right now!'

'That's great!' Vir said. But I was already dialing another number.

'Bauji!' I said, when Bauji picked up at the other end. 'You heard, no?'

'Yes,' Bauji said. 'What can be done now, I don't know …'

'I do,' I said. 'But Bauji …We. Need. Help. Do you have the utilities map of our house which shows where the gas lines are and everything? You do? Great! And can you get hold of your old construction crew?

***

Vir and I drove back in silence. I knew what to do as far as the wedding—but I was lost when it came to him. The way he hugged me, the way he sounded so concerned … But there was all that other stuff. I couldn't even *think* about it now.

'Can I do anything else?' he asked quietly when we got home.

'I'll let you know,' I said. 'And thanks, Vir.'

'I mean it,' he said.

'I know,' I said, and then paused. 'Actually, I just thought of something …'

'Anything,' he said.

'Can you pick up some chrysanthemums in the morning?' I asked. 'From the garden center next to Building Nineteen? They call them "Hardy Mums".'

'OK,' Vir said. 'What time do they open?'

'8:00 am,' I said. 'I need at least a dozen large pots. Two dozen if they have them. Any and all colors you can find.'

'They'll be there!' he said.

***

At home, Masi and Katrina had worked their magic to make Vinnie look outstanding.

'Mini!' Masi said. 'Go get changed, beta. We're late! We'll have to go ahead and your dad and you can catch up later.'

'OK,' I said. 'I'm going! But I have to tell you …'

'Not now!' Masi said. 'We'll talk at the temple.'

So even though everything about the wedding and the mehendi—the date and time and venue—was up in the air, we still had to get to the one event that was going off without a hitch—the janvasam. They all piled into cars and headed for the temple.

Dad and I would have to catch up.

I wore the gorgeous kanjivaram sari that Ragini Aunty had given me. It was a luscious double weave—pink from one angle, purple from the other—and shot all over with sprays of gold. I had a basic pink blouse that went well with it, as did Nani's anklet necklace.

***

The Sri Laxmi temple in Ashland is the hub of the Indian Hindu community in New England. I hadn't been to it since Mom's death. None of us had. Because that's when Dad decided that the idea of a concerned and compassionate deity was laughable in the light of recent family history. And in case we ever doubted it there was (*drumroll*) the uninvited hurricane at Vinnie's wedding.

Still we went. And as we turned off Route 128 and the whitewashed spires of the temple came into view, I felt stirrings of old memories. This is where I had my first dance performance at the age of five. It must have hit Dad even harder—I could feel him freeze as we stopped at the temple.

I cast around for an ice-breaker.

'Look, Dad!' I said. 'The car-blessing spot!'

That's where the priest would come out and perform a prayer for an automobile—sprinkle holy water on its hood, and break a coconut in front of it for good luck. I remember coming after we bought the minivan. Mom had insisted.

Needless to say my Mini Cooper had not had the treatment and neither had Dad's Lotus Esprit.

There was a sign in the car-blessing spot which said 'THE TEMPLE IS CLOSED TOMORROW AUGUST 27 DUE TO THE HURRICANE'.

'Want to update the minivan's blessing?' I teased.

'It's cheaper than insurance!' Dad said—a Mom quote—and he even cracked a smile. It had been a good day when we had gotten the minivan blessed. We had lunch at Udupi afterwards and felt safe driving home in our newly blessed car.

'Come on,' Masi said. 'Vinnie's hair is getting messed up in the wind.' Vinnie's hair had been put up in a bun and Masi had carefully draped her in a beautiful Benarasi sari, the staple of North Indian brides for centuries. She looked like an ad for Eazy Pleats Sari pleater or something—perfect.

Manish's family was waiting for us at the front of the temple. I smiled because Manish had decided to go shirtless after all.

'Hey, Manish has some decent abs under the scrubs and lab coat!' I ribbed Vinnie. 'Who knew?'

'Will you stop it?' Vinnie said, red in the face.

I have to admit that on the right guy a *veshti* looks nice. Vir for example, with his swimmer's physique.

'Vanakkam, vanakkam,' Manoj Uncle said. Which is a Tamil greeting, apparently.

They walked us to the long room that ran along the length of the temple. It had been set up with rows of chairs.

'Mini,' Bauji said. 'I called Alan Brown and Ritchie. They'll be at your house at 6:30 in the morning. What time did you say Taylor Rental opens?'

'They don't start delivering until eight,' I said. 'But we can pick up at six-thirty if we haul it ourselves. Do they have something big enough to carry everything?'

'Yes,' Bauji said. 'They have a pick-up truck, and I'll bring mine.'

'When can they have the tent up?' I asked. 'I've asked Sher-e-Punjab to bring lunch at noon.'

'They'll be done by noon,' Bauji said.

I relaxed enough to finally look around. Bade Bauji was sitting in the front row, the red turban on his head adding a few inches to his tall frame. Beeji, Dad and Masi were sitting next to him.

Ragini Aunty was holding Vinnie's arm and chatting with a priest. It was Krishna Ji, the head temple priest, the one she said was an Iyengar. He had really gone gray in the last seven years, but otherwise his face was the same—kind, wrinkled, smiling, with a white V on his forehead like the Hare Krishnas. I guess they stole it from the Iyengars.

'I didn't know that Manish was marrying Vinnie,' he said. 'Ragini Amma, I've known this family for a long long time. Both the girls I know.'

I was smiling without meaning to. He was always so sweet to us. 'How is Rama Ji?' I asked. 'Very good,' he said. 'OK, the mahoorat is now, kanna, let's start the nischayatartham.'

They had set up for the ceremony with a red carpet, gold chairs, a gold and white brocade backdrop, and stacked pots with mango leaves and coconuts atop—definitely Sudha Moorty's handiwork! It was traditional but it had a bright and happy wedding vibe.

Manish and his family sat to one side of the priest and Vinnie and Dad to the other. In the center was the small firepit for the *homum*. 'Amma, please,' Krishna Ji said to Masi. 'You come and sit and complete the rituals for the girl's mother.'

'Sure,' Masi said. 'Vinnie is my daughter too.'

'Pssssst,' someone said in my ear.

'Yes?' I turned around to see an imposing woman in a gorgeous lilac sari and a cascade of jasmine flowers in her glossy black hair. 'Come with me.'

Her tone was pretty authoritative so I followed her out.

She pulled me into the main temple hall. 'I'm Kanika, Manish's mom's friend. You are Mini?'

'Yes,' I said. 'It's nice to meet you.'

'We were thinking ...' An older man in a stately silk kurta joined our huddle. 'Natarajan and I think the wedding can be performed at the temple.'

'Isn't the temple closed tomorrow?' I asked.

'Yes, yes,' Kanika shook her head impatiently. 'But it is open in the *morning*.'

I looked at the sign behind her, and this one said: Due to the storm, the temple closes tomorrow August 27, at NOON.

'If they start early they can be done by noon,' Kanika Aunty said. Yes, Kanika *Aunty*—I was totally adopting her after her brilliant plan. 'We could have the reception another day.'

'We have the reception at our house!' I said. That could work. 'But will they let us have the wedding here, on such short notice?'

'Not normally,' Kanika Aunty said. 'But my husband Natarajan is on the board of the temple. He can talk to them.'

The TamBrahms made up half the board apparently. And now we were in the inner circle. Lucky us!

Natarajan was smiling encouragingly over her shoulder. 'You come with me and fill out the forms.'

'But shouldn't I ask Vinnie, or Dad?' I asked. 'Or Manish!'

'No time,' Natarajan said. 'Ragini and Manoj are fine with it. If Manish and Vinnie don't like it we can cancel, but we should book it just so we have something.'

254

There was a small office window behind which a plump lady sat. Even with my kanjivaram sari I didn't seem to meet with her approval.

'Yes?' she asked.

'Now ask for the wedding booking form,' Natarajan instructed, from behind me. 'In English, *not* in Hindi, OK?'

'OK,' I said. 'Err … could I please have the form to book weddings?'

Suddenly the woman was all smiles. 'You are Ragini's son Manish's fiancée's sister!' she said. It took me a minute to figure out that this was correct. 'Yes!' I confirmed. Natarajan Uncle was doing nothing but smiling and nodding in the background, but clearly his presence was helping.

'Tomorrow morning,' she said. 'Yes, we are open!'

Something about the way she said it made me think that the open-till-noon thing had to do with various strings being pulled on the temple board as well.

I concentrated on the simple paper form in my hand. Bride's name, Groom's name, Temple member making the booking's name—that would be Dad, right? I didn't know if he technically was still a member of this congregation.

I looked back at the form. Temple donation: $500. Was that *all*? Dang, it was cheap to book a temple hall! But I didn't think I had that much money on me. 'Err … I'm not sure I have …' I started.

'Make the payment tomorrow,' the lady said obligingly.

'Sure, if that's OK with you,' I said, handing back the

completed form. 'So are we booked for tomorrow?'

'Yes,' she said. 'Krishna Ji will perform the ceremony.'

I smiled. Those simple words made the whole crazy day feel better—*Krishna Ji will perform the ceremony*. Maybe this was also meant to be.

***

'Do we have a time?' Kanika Aunty asked.

'Yes, 9:00 am tomorrow, here,' I said, clutching the booking form paper to me. 'Followed by the reception at 21 Andrea Road, Westbury, at noon.'

'Write it down,' she instructed. 'Quickly!' I jotted down the details and handed it to her. She walked to the front and handed it to Dad. Dad looked at it, looked up at me and mouthed: ARE YOU SURE?

I nodded.

He stood up and cleared his throat, and proceeded to read.

'We, the families of Vinod Kapoor, and Manoj and Ragini Iyer declare the intention of our daughter Yashasvini Kapoor and our son Manish Iyer to marry at 9:00 am tomorrow, the 27th of August, 2011, at Sri Laxmi Temple, Ashland. The ceremony will be performed by Krishna Iyengar Ji, the head priest. A reception will follow at noon at the Kapoor residence at 21 Andrea Road, Westbury.'

I suppose the announcement is usually a formality at these things because everyone already knows the details. But this was no formality—everyone was hanging on Dad's words—including the bride and groom.

He looked up. 'You may be aware that there has been a slight change of plan due to the hurricane. We need to let everyone know the new date and venue so they can get here. Please spread the word.'

With that Dad handed a platter of gifts to the Iyers, who in turn presented gifts to him. Manish took the Punjabi sherwani we had bought him and went off to change.

'Mini!' I looked up to see Vinnie pass by amidst a flock of smiling Tamilian ladies. I guess they were going to help her get dressed. I got up, but Masi put a hand on mine— 'Let them,' she said. I hoped they realized that Vinnie was incapable of putting on a sari without help, or an Eazy Pleater!

There was a hush in the chatter behind us so I turned to look.

Vinnie! OMG—she looked amazing! They had dressed her in a green and red sari, put strings of jasmine flowers in her hair, and some gold temple jewelry too.

A choking sound next to me alerted me that Dad was on the verge of tears—and ready to bolt. Luckily I needed him to do something.

'Dad, you know the Indian grocery store in Framingham?' I said, handing him a scrap of paper. 'Go there and get this!'

'Now?' he asked.

'Yeah, now,' I said. 'We're just going to be eating now; you won't miss anything.'

***

'Where's Dad?' Vinnie asked.

'You look stunning, Vinnie!' I said. She did. 'Manish, you too!' Manish looked even more transformed in the buttoned-up sherwani and pants than Vinnie did in her sari.

'So ... the wedding will be here and the reception at home?' Vinnie asked, trying to keep up. 'Will that *work*?'

'Yeah,' I said flippantly, trying not to let her guess the general state of panic under my smiling veneer. 'Absolutely!'

'We need to let everyone know!' Vinnie said. 'As soon as we get home I have to call everyone!'

'Vinnie, what about the mehendi?' I asked.

'Well, we have to cancel that of course.' Vinnie looked puzzled.

'But you have to have mehendi on your hands before you get married,' I said. 'Look at them!'

Her palms were clean and tan and decidedly un-bride-like. 'Ohhh!' Vinnie said. 'Do you think I could go to the mehendi lady?'

'I've called and canceled, and she said not to worry and that she'll stay up late and put it for you whenever you can get to her,' I said.

'But she's all the way over in Lexington, right?' Vinnie said. 'That's an hour and a half just to get there and back, and how long to put it on?'

'One hour,' I said. 'If she does a rushed job.'

Vinnie looked resigned. 'Guess I'm getting married without the mehendi then. No way I can spend two to three hours on just that tonight. We won't even be out of here before ten-thirty—it's more important to get the word out.'

'Or,' I said. 'We can put it on you—Masi and me. It won't be great but at least it will be mehendi.'

'You're forgetting that we don't *have* any mehendi,' Vinnie said.

'We will,' I said. 'Dad's on it. This is delicious, by the way!' The vadas and rasam and curd rice they served up after the ceremony were to die for.

'There is so much food left,' Ragini Aunty said. 'Maybe you can take it home? It might come in handy tomorrow.'

'Sure,' I said. Good thing I had cleaned out the entire fridge last weekend. We had plenty of room to store stuff.

'Where's your father?' Manoj Uncle asked. 'I want to introduce him to my brother-in-law.'

'He had to run out on an errand, Uncle,' I said. 'He'll be back soon!'

'Oh yes, there he is now,' Manoj Uncle said. So soon! Either Dad had floored it all the way to Framingham or the store was closed. I must have looked worried because Dad held up a grocery bag in one hand and gave me a lopsided grin.

Yeah, he had floored it.

***

Late at night, Friday, and Masi and I were with Vinnie in her hotel room. She had a room at the Westbury Marriott where the make-up lady was supposed to come in the morning to fix her up and drape her sari. We had forced Dad to go home to bed, since there wasn't much he could do. Vinnie was typing, texting and calling with one hand while I held a tube of henna over the other.

'Hold still, dammit!' I said.

'OK, OK,' she said. I was attempting to execute one of the designs she had picked off the Internet. Thankfully for all of us her tastes ran to simple symmetrical florals and paisleys. Masi had recused herself from the task of actually putting on the mehendi on the grounds of having bad eyesight and shaky hands.

As if! She confined herself to critiquing my efforts, not that I wasn't already nervous enough or anything, and also helping Vinnie type and take her calls—which was actually very handy.

'So is Sudha still decorating?' Masi asked.

'Yes,' I said. 'Even though tomorrow is also the Patel-Bernstein wedding.' They were probably dealing with the same crazy weather scenario as we were.

'Oh, the poor things,' Vinnie said.

'I'm just glad Sudha Moorty is willing to do our decorations before rushing off to do theirs,' I said. When Vinnie called her and explained the situation, she had asked for an hour before she could confirm about the decorations at the temple in time for a nine o'clock wedding. Then she had called back and said she would—in spite of the other wedding. She would have to be there at 5 o'clock with her team of carpenters and handymen. Pure steel, our Sudha Aunty.

'Turn over your hand,' I said, and continued the design over the back of Vinnie's hand. 'Ooops! Masi—toothpick!' Masi handed me one and I carefully wiped off the blooper.

'OK, done. There, now hold your palm outstretched, don't smudge it while it's wet, and don't wash it off in two hours,' I said. Vinnie held up her hands and scanned my work. 'That looks totally legit, Mini,' she said. 'You're a pro.'

'Yeah, yeah,' I said. 'You're only saying that because you're stuck with it. Do you want some on your feet too?'

'Just a little …' Vinnie said. I worked a trail of vines and flowers from her big toe across the top of her foot to her heel and wrapped around her ankle. 'How's that?'

Vinnie nodded so I finished the other side, before putting down the cone and yawning and stretching. 'I gotta get home and crash.'

Luckily Vinnie was already in her PJs before starting the whole henna thing so she just had to roll into bed. I had to drive back.

'You go home,' Masi said. 'I'll stay here and help Vinnie get ready in the morning. And all the bridesmaids.' They were all either staying in the hotel or coming in the morning to get help putting on their saris. I was supposed to have helped them but now …

'What about your clothes?' I asked.

'Send them with Vinod in the morning,' Masi said. 'I know you have a lot to do, with the house. I won't be much help there, but I know how to get a bunch of girls runway-ready.'

I gave her a hug. I was actually getting used to randomly giving her hugs. I think she even enjoyed them. Yes, she totally did.

And then I went home. I wasn't going to bed anytime soon!

***

River Bend—Canceled. Full refund.

Curry Cuisine—Canceled. Need to get a hold of them to discuss refund.

Bus service—Canceled. Full refund.

Bartender—Canceled. Full refund.

Florist—Canceled. Full refund.

Wedding Cake—Canceled. Full refund.

Wedding Horse—Canceled. Full refund.

Red Maple Photography (Manish's friend Kristan)—ON

Sringaar Wedding Stylists—ON

Namaskar Wedding Decorators—ON

Sher-e-Punjab Caterers—ON

Taylor Rental—ON

Kapoor Construction (Bauji's crew)—ON

Game On

It was going to be legendary—or a disaster.

Either way, no one would ever forget it.

Game. On.

I sent off an email to all the gals invited to the mehendi, explaining things. I sent off a more detailed email to Jackie and Rachel. I sent off emails to all the neighbors on the street giving them a heads up about the traffic mayhem soon to descend on Andrea Road the next day—and inviting them all to the reception. There is a saying in Hindi—*pittey par doh joot aur*—what's two more blows if you're already having your ass kicked. So, what were a few neighbors when I'd already invited a whole wedding party?

The doorbell rang. I went downstairs to find Dad opening the door to Bauji. Bauji was holding a big cardboard box that said Amazon.com. 'These were outside, Vinod,' he said.

'Umm … Mini, what are these?' Dad asked.

'Umbrellas,' I said.

'Don't we *have* umbrellas?' Dad asked.

'Not ones that complement Vinnie's dress,' I said. 'And the bridesmaids'!'

'Ookaay,' Dad shook his head, and turned to Bauji.

'Are your guys here?' he asked. Bauji nodded towards the driveway where two pick-up trucks were parked. 'Here's the list of things I've ordered,' I said, handing it to him. 'It *should* fit in those trucks.' I must have sounded worried because he said, 'Don't worry, we'll make it fit,'

'I'll go with them,' Dad said.

'No, you have to get ready!' I said. 'And they'll have more room if you don't go.'

And then they were gone. 'Go have a shower,' I ordered Dad, 'and I'll put on the coffee.'

I was just going up the stairs when a Mirchandani Mirage screeched to a halt on the curb.

Vir stepped out holding a pot of absolutely brilliant pink chrysanthemums.

What with my late night I probably resembled something his mom's cat would drag in, but he looked rested, and showered and ready to go.

'I brought your flowers,' he said.

'Awesome,' I said, tucking a few strands of hair behind my ear in a vain attempt at tidying up. 'They were open this early?'

'7 am,' he said, and started bringing in pots and pots of the most glorious vibrant colors of chrysanthemums—pink, yellow, white, red, orange.

I forgot to be self-conscious and starting hopping around in my flannel pajamas.

'Oh, they're perfect, Vir!' I said. 'Thank you!'

'Is there anything else you need?' Vir said.

'Will you come to the wedding?' I asked.

'If you want me to,' Vir said.

'I do,' I said, and smiled warmly at him. Whatever those gossip magazines said, my gut said different. And today, I was going to go with my gut.

'Was someone just here?' Dad asked. That had to be the quickest shower ever.

'Just Vir, bringing some flowers,' I said. 'Coffee?'

***

'Vinnie is dressed and ready!' Masi said, giving me the update at the hotel. 'We'll go directly to the temple, Mini. Are you dressed?'

'No,' I said. I was outside watching Bauji and the guys unpack the gear from Taylor Rental. 'But Dad just left. Bauji and I will get there as soon as we're done.'

Bauji and the dudes had a ton of stuff to unload off of the pick-up trucks. Alan put down a rack of china and the plates clattered alarmingly in the rack.

'Careful with that!' I yelled. 'Careful!'

'Don't worry,' he grinned. 'We've got this!'

'The tent goes here, Bauji,' I said. 'It should fit, I measured it. Did you bring the diagram of the gas lines and electrical lines?'

'Yeah,' Bauji said. 'I have it right here. There's nothing at all at the front. They all come down the side of the house, down

265

the hill. We can put stakes as deep as we like in the front yard. Alan, Ritchie, come here.'

The guys had got everything off the trucks.

'OK, you know we're short on time,' Bauji said. 'We need the lawn mowed.'

'Do we have time for that?' I asked. The grass wasn't that high, but Bauji was a perfectionist—I had forgotten.

'Yes, we do,' Bauji said. 'Mow the lawn first and then get the tent up. I want it weather-tight just in case we have rain. Mini, how d'you want the tables and chairs set up?'

'Like this,' I said, handing them a layout I'd sketched. 'I don't know when we'll have time for the place settings …'

'We can do it,' Alan said. 'Do you want us to set up the tables and the plates and things? We can do it real nice.'

Could they? They had hands the size of Christmas hams. But they were quick and smart and careful.

'OK,' I said. 'I need ten chairs per table, and ten place settings. Tablecloth first, then plates, silverware, wine glasses, napkins …'

'We can do that,' Ritchie said. 'Do the flowers go in the middle?'

'Yes!' I said. Wow, these guys were bright. 'Exactly! And if you have time after that, could you get string lights from the party store and hang them on the trees?'

'Like for Christmas?' Alan asked.

'Just like that!' I said. 'But only if you have time.'

'Go change, beta,' Bauji said. 'I need to get that list of things

266

the priest wanted to the temple. Your Dad forgot it in the garage. You change and come fast, OK?'

'OK,' I said.

***

I tied on my red bridesmaid sari and secured it with a bunch of safety pins. Apart from Mom's plain gold chain I didn't put on any jewelry. I didn't want to look more dressed up than the rest of the bridesmaids—I had planned to change into the firozi lehenga for the reception, but now I didn't know if I'd even have time for that.

By the time I finished doing my hair and make-up it was eight. The guys had already mowed the front lawn and started to raise the tent—which was HUGE!

I rushed to the Mini and started the engine. Tried to start the engine, that is. I had been so tired last night I'd left the headlights on—the battery was toast! And Vinnie's wedding started in an hour!

I called Dad.

'Dad, my car's dead; I need a jumpstart!' I said.

'What?' Dad said. 'OK, don't panic. Call AAA, they'll get you going!'

'They'll take ages!' I wailed. 'I'm not going to miss Vinnie's wedding!'

'Then take a taxi,' Dad said.

'That'll take ages too,' I said.

'There are jump cables somewhere in the garage,' Dad said. 'Maybe the guys can jumpstart your car. Or take Alan's pick-up truck!'

'They can't stop working—they've too much to do,' I said. 'Maybe Vir …'

'Vir is here,' Dad said. 'It'll take too long for him to get back.'

Sounded like everyone was there but me.

'I'll see if Jackie's up. Maybe she can give me a ride.'

'Fine,' Dad said.

'Pick up, pick up. Pick. Up. The. Damn. Phone!' My pleading was for nothing because Jackie was not doing any picking up of the phone on a Sunday. She had to be up at six for the summer camp every weekday—she was sleeping in.

So what were my options to getting immediately mobile?

Only one.

I pushed the button for the other side of the garage and it rolled open to reveal Dad's car.

Cue the James Bond theme song—I was taking the Lotus Esprit.

***

The headlights lifted noiselessly from the sleek hood of the car as I started the engine and backed into the street.

The stick shift style was different, the clutch a bit tight, and the visibility weirdly low, but other than that—there was nothing to it. And what a sound that machine made!

I won't lie—it was fun driving the Lotus!

Dad had only ever allowed me to take it down the street and back. The speed and power of the thing was incredible. It was almost too soon for me when I got there. I shifted gears and turned into the long wooded driveway that led up to the temple.

Vir was standing there with two other guys—OMG, was that really Chintu and Mintu Patel? All of them had their eyes bulging out at the sight of me in the racecar.

'Sweet ride!' Vir was the first one to speak when I rolled down the car window. 'So, are you with the bride's party or the groom's?'

'Vir!' I said. 'What are you doing?'

'Directing traffic, of course,' Vir informed me. 'I'm helping out, along with these guys—family friends, I gather? We're putting the groom's side in *that* car park and the bride's side in *this* car park. Of course some people are just here to pray and they're completely confused.'

'So I have to go to the car park at the top of the hill?' I asked.

'Correct,' Vir said. 'You look beautiful, Mini.' I was about to feel flattered when he added. 'Especially in that car!' Way to destroy a perfectly heartfelt compliment.

I got to the top of the hill only to be flagged down by a frantic Sudha Moorty. A bunch of capable-looking guys, wearing tool belts, and carrying silks, drapes, and flowers, surrounded her.

'Mini, go down to that car park!' she said. 'Go now!'

'But I thought the bride's side was supposed to go here?' I asked.

'Yes, but that car, Mini,' she breathed. 'That car is perfect!'

'For what?' I asked. Had she totally lost the plot?

'For the wedding,' she said. 'We're not getting the horse because it's booked for the Patel-Bernstein wedding, so how to make an entrance?' she paused for impact. 'I thought we can decorate the white Ferrari ...'

'Lotus,' I corrected.

'Whatever. It's a good-looking car, that's all,' she said. 'Manish really, REALLY wanted to surprise Vinnie with a Punjabi baraat, but it doesn't work unless the guy has a nice ride. We don't have a horse, but, once we've decorated it, this will be perfect!'

I could see Dad approach us from the corner of my eye.

'Dad won't like it ...' I said. If I told him we were going to sticky-tape rosebuds on his beloved car's impeccable fiberglass exterior he would lose his mind.

'Then don't ask him!' Sudha said. 'Just go! I'll be there in five minutes.'

'OK,' I said, hurriedly changing gears into reverse and backed out of there before he could get to us.

The temple driveway is a circular one-way, so I had to pass by Vir at the entrance again.

'Everything OK?' Vir said. Did I mention that he was wearing a dark Nehru collar dinner jacket—more 60's Beatles than Pandit Nehru—and he looked strikingly handsome in it? No? Well, he did.

'Get in,' I said.

'Ooookay,' Vir said. 'Carry on without me, guys!' This last to Chintu and Mintu Patel.

'Can you drop me off at the top of the hill and then drive this to the groom's side?' I said. 'Sudha Aunty is going to decorate it—watch her and make sure she doesn't ruin the finish? If I have to let it out of my sight I'm putting it in hands I trust—yours.'

'I'm happy that you trust me,' Vir said. 'But I don't know a single person on the groom's side.'

'They're nice,' I said. 'And please give them these red turbans.' I handed him a stack of starched and ironed turban cloths, no tacky pre-tied turbans if Beeji could have her way. 'Oh crap!'

'What?' Vir asked.

'They're not *tied*,' I said. 'Bade Bauji was supposed to tie the turbans for us so they could just put it on their heads. Do you think those Iyers know how to tie a turban?'

'They may not,' Vir said. 'But I do!'

'How?' I asked. 'Isn't it really hard?'

'It was part of our dress uniform at Mayo College,' Vir said. 'We had to wear it to temple and all formal events. So how do you want it tied—Jodhpuri style, or Jaipuri?'

'Vir,' I said. 'Thank you!'

'You're welcome,' he said.

***

Back in the bride's side car park I finally got a good look at Vinnie. I needn't have worried because of course Masi had done a spectacular job—Vinnie looked ravishing. She didn't look overdone like some brides. Despite all the gold and red her look was simple and classic—contemporary chic with a hint of traditional. Timeless.

Best of all her gold lehenga with the cranberry red veil set off Mom's jewelry to perfection. Masi, Beeji, her bridesmaids, and half the aunties were fussing around her and for a moment I felt left out. Then she caught sight of me and her face lit up.

'Mini, where have you *been*?' she demanded.

'Taking care of stuff,' I said. 'You look ready to get married, Dr Vinnie!'

'You better believe I am!' Vinnie said. 'Did you get a look at Manish?'

'I did,' I said mysteriously. 'But I can't tell you anything.'

A flash went off next to my face and I looked over to see an intense young woman behind a huge camera with an extra-large lens attached.

'Kristan?' I asked. This had to be Manish's friend Kristan who was to do the photography and videography. What a relief! By the look of her equipment she was more than qualified.

'You're the sister.' Kristan had no trouble identifying me. 'So can we *finally* take group photographs?' I didn't realize they'd been waiting for me. Kristan was already giving directions.

'Vinnie in the center, dad to the left, Mini to the right, Aunty left, grandparents right,' she directed. 'OK, perfect. Say "to hell with Irene"!'

All of Vinnie's bridesmaids were picture perfect in their red saris—and they had the most awesome twenties-style headbands and fascinators in their hair.

Where on earth did they get those?

'I had some made,' Masi said. 'With the leftover material

from Vinnie's lehenga. Your designs inspired me I guess, and the girls thought they were fun so they decided to use them.'

'Wow,' I said. 'Just wow! But where's mine?'

'Right here,' Masi said. She produced a hair comb with an antique gold flower mounted on it and pushed it into my hair. Her hands were gentle as she fastened it firmly with bobby pins.

We had time for a few more photographs and then dhol beats announced that the groom's party was advancing up the hill.

'The baraat is coming,' Dad said. 'Places everyone!'

What a beautiful sight!

The Lotus was climbing the hill slowly and smoothly without stalling out once. Vir was at the wheel, evidently. Red roses and festive gold tassels hung from the sleek hood of the race car— Sudha Moorty's work. I could hear Dad make a strangled sound in his throat at the sight—but he didn't say anything. And driving was not the only thing Vir had done well—Manish's head was crowned by a flamboyant red turban.

'No way!' Vinnie said. 'Red turban, white *car*! This is even better than a horse, Mini.'

'It adds four moons to his glory,' I said, translating one of Beeji's favorite Punjabi phrases.

Vinnie laughed. 'It's a proper baraat! Dad, I can't believe you let Manish use the Lotus!'

'The horse wasn't available this morning,' I said. 'So, obviously, there was no other option.'

'Manish was going to ride an actual horse?' Vinnie asked.

'After consuming a massive dose of Benadryl,' I said. 'But this is better, no? At least he won't fall asleep at the mandap!'

Ahead of the baraat came two real Punjabi dholis with large wooden drums and a bunch of Iyer relatives dancing in a happy, if not very Punjabi, way.

Beeji greeted Manish with a lighted lamp, and a ceremonial red tilak on his forehead. Masi handed Manish a wedding garland (FancyFlowers.com had done their job well!) and he stood there waiting for Vinnie.

'Come on girls!' I said. 'Now!'

Vinnie's bridesmaids and I held aloft the ceremonial red and gold canopy high above Vinnie's head. Vinnie walked beneath it holding her wedding garland, Dad beside her, and we walked slowly out towards the groom's party.

I could hear gasps of admiration. Vinnie looked every inch the glowing bride, and I think the bright red the rest of us wore added to her splendor.

In the background Kristan was clicking away earnestly. Then Vinnie garlanded Manish and the ceremony was under way.

Sudha Moorty had done an outstanding job—the mandap was just like Vinnie had wanted. Beautifully draped in tasseled silk, with a flower-bedecked welcome arch, and a red carpet down the center aisle. I looked back from the mandap and saw row upon row of smiling faces. Beeji, Bauji, Bade Bauji, Dad, Vinnie's friends from high school and med school, old teachers, Beeji's Arya Samaj friends, the Tamilians from the Iyers' side.

And—it took me a moment to place her—the bank teller from the Westbury Bank of America branch. She had been at the temple to pray and found herself caught in the wedding. She had been happy to stay.

In the confusion no one asked Krishna Ji to perform the ceremony the Punjabi way so he went ahead and followed the Tamil ceremonials instead.

There was a bit when Manish opened an umbrella and pretended to go off to Kashi and stay a bachelor, until he was persuaded to come back. And another when they reenacted the garlanding ceremony but both Vinnie and Manish were lifted up by family members to make the garlanding more difficult for the other person—like a sort of competition. Vinnie didn't get very high with only Dad and Bauji holding her until Vir, Chintu and Mintu chipped in.

And there was the part when they had Vinnie sit on Dad's lap—not something they do in Punjab, but sweet anyway. They also performed some of the more familiar rituals—the seven steps around the fire and so forth.

And before we knew it they were done!

'You're all invited to our house for the reception,' Dad said. 'The address is posted on the temple bulletin board.'

So it was.

***

I had been getting calls throughout the ceremony. Jackie and Rachel had gone over to our house soon after they got my email, just to keep an eye on things. Then they promptly called in their moms, so Sue and Amy were there as well. Everything was going well, they reported. The tent was up, the tables set, the flowers arranged. Jackie had walked Yogi—the poor dog had no idea why he had been abandoned since early in the morning and why strangers were swarming over his yard and putting up large scary things.

But I was still worried about the food! It was to come at noon and it was already 11:50 and I was nowhere close to getting home. I called Sher-e-Punjab. No one answered. I called Rajinder Singh's cellphone—no response. In desperation, I called Preet.

'Why didn't you call me?' Preet demanded. 'All day long I've been worrying about your sister's wedding. Give me your address. I'll go now and talk to Rajinder.'

'Thanks so much, Preet!' I said. 'We've not even been paid a single cent so far. And if he gets to our house and there's no one there to give him a check—I'm worried he might ...'

'Don't worry about anything,' Preet said. 'But I don't have anywhere to leave Rahul—is it OK if I bring him? And Sona wants to help too.'

'Of course!' I said. 'And I'll be there as soon as I can!'

After the final group photos they didn't need me anymore so I hurried home. It had been bright when we took the group pictures and the baraat came up the hill to the temple, but now the sky was getting dark and the wind was picking up. The radio was full of stories about what was happening in New York— none of it good. Over a hundred people were about to descend on our house—I had good reason to worry.

Big Tent, Small Miracles

The tent was up!

Jackie had told me it was, but it was something else to see it myself. Festive and bright with yellow and white stripes and clear arched windows—it was beautiful to behold. And it was perfectly level, lashed down tight, and looked ready to take on the weather—rain or shine.

The inside was shipshape too—neat, sparkling table settings with their burgundy fanfolded napkins (how *did* Bauji's guys manage that?) and bushels of colorful chrysanthemums in place of centerpieces.

'It's a miracle!' I said faintly as Alan and Ritchie beamed at me. They were still up on step ladders looping reels of string lights through the three maple trees that framed our yard—they'd look bright and festive once it got darker outside and we turned them on. If we still had power.

Construction workers, my *jooti*. The guys were clearly in the wrong damn profession.

Also, the buffet table was covered in a floor-length table

cloth, and arranged on it were sparkling silver chafing dishes filled with mouthwatering curries, rice, and naans—I could smell them even though the lids were shut. So Sher-e-Punjab had come through too!

Wahe Guru Ji ki fatheh!

Bauji had ridden back with me in the minivan, and he looked proud of his crew.

'So, basically we're in good shape, right?' I said to no one in particular, hoping they couldn't sense my panic.

But Preet, Jackie, Sona, Rachel, and Ernie Uncle (where did he come from?), and even little Rahul—looking adorable in a cotton kurta—were looking at me with goofy grins—the way people look at adorable babies.

'Awww, check you out!' Jackie said. 'The girl in the red sari!'

'There are nine more of those at this wedding,' I said, but I was flattered.

'So the tent's up, the food's here.' Jackie laid a friendly arm over Preet's shoulders. 'Preet here talked to the caterers—awesome-looking guys in beards and turbans, Mini—and she organized everything. They let her have the chafing dishes and extra serving spoons and stuff to make it easier to serve the food. And I've walked Yogi. We've pushed back the furniture inside too so there's plenty of room for everyone to move around. Both our moms have vacuumed everything, and cleaned the bathrooms, and put out fresh towels and stuff.'

So that's where Amy and Sue had vanished!

'So, what else do you need?'

'Alcohol!' said Bauji. 'We don't have any alcohol!' Other people may say beer, wine or champagne, but Bauji went straight to the point in his businesslike way. And he was right—we didn't have a drop of alcohol.

'There's a liquor store at the intersection of Route 9 and 27,' I said to Alan. 'Do you know it?'

'Sure do,' Alan said, with a grin.

'We need their best champagne for the toast—lots of it. And beer—any idea what type, Bauji?' I asked. Here was a topic I knew nothing about.

'We'll get a selection of beer and wine,' Alan said. 'They'll take back what we don't open if we're buying bulk. What else?'

'Sparkling cider for the people who don't drink,' I said. In any Indian group there's bound to be a few of those. 'That's all!'

That's when I noticed that my car was parked on the curb instead of blocking the driveway. That had to be Uncle Ernie's work. 'Did you jumpstart the Mini?' I asked.

'Yeah,' he said. 'I heard the Lotus got bedazzled—what did Vinod say to that?'

'It's standing in for the wedding horse,' I said, grinning. 'It had to have some bling.'

He just rolled his eyes—like Dad. 'Mini, you have plenty of room on the street for parking but not if you have over fifty cars,' Ernie Uncle said. 'Do you need people to valet the cars?'

'That would be awesome!' I said. I hadn't even thought of that.

'I'll call a couple of my guys,' he said, pulling out his cellphone. 'It might cost you, though.'

'It's cool,' I grinned. 'We're liquid, Ernie Uncle—Dad's start-up just got funded!'

A couple in a Honda Accord pulled into our driveway. The woman in the passenger seat was wearing a sari and carrying a baby—we had our first guests.

'I can greet them for you, but what do I say?' Jackie hissed into my ear.

'Just say welcome and come inside,' I said, as nervous as her.

'Inside?' Jackie said. 'I thought they were eating in the tent?'

'We can put the appetizers in the house and move them out for the lunch after Vinnie and Manish arrive,' I said.

Soon the house was full, the samosas were nearly gone, and I was starting to panic. 'There's more downstairs!' Preet said. 'Go fetch them!'

In the laundry room I found buckets, no really, BUCKETS of extra curry, and platters of samosas and chutneys. And they were heavy and hot—there was no way I could carry them up. I stuck my head out of the laundry but couldn't see Dad, or Vir, or Bauji, or even Chintu or Mintu. 'Excuse me!' I said. 'Could someone please help carry out some food?'

A tall boy who was clearly related to Manish, given his familiar smile, and one of Vinnie's bespectacled med school friends took charge, and carried steaming hot samosas out to the hungry hordes.

In the kitchen Preet manned the sink, washing used snack

dishes; Amy and Sue dried them. Around them people were eating, chatting, laughing and mingling. In spite of the tight squeeze everyone had a smile on their face.

'This is going better than I thought,' Amy said with cautious optimism. 'They're all so sweet!'

'Sweets!' I said. 'We don't have them! We canceled the cake!'

Rachel was the one who remembered. 'Didn't your Beeji make something—those yellow ball things?' she asked. 'They're sweet, aren't they?'

'Laddoos!' I said. 'I have hundreds of them and they are nut and gluten free—we're saved! Come with me.'

Manish's cousin and Vinnie's friend helped Jackie and Amy carry the laddoos from the garage where they were stacked in the largest, ugliest plastic Tupperware boxes you can imagine—Beeji specialized in them.

Inspiration struck again and I found Mom's crystal three-tier dessert stand and took it out to the tent, ducking through the drizzle that had started up. I washed and dried it and set it up on a side table next to the buffet. 'Help me stack,' I said, and cracked open a Tupperware box. Jackie helped me cover each tier of the dessert stand with golden laddoos.

A little girl in a summer dress, a golden bindi and blue glass bangles, came over to look.

She had dark hair, olive skin, and bright blue eyes. Eyes that looked red from crying.

'Do you want to help?' I asked, and she cheered up immediately.

'Yes,' she said, and started to arrange the laddoos even more carefully than us.

We turned the topmost tier into a neat little pyramid, and let the girl in blue place the last laddoo at the very top.

It looked impressive.

'What's wrong, honey?' I asked the kid. 'You look upset.'

'She laughed at my Punjabi,' she said, pointing at an older woman—one of Beeji's satsang friends.

'My Hindi sounds funny too sometimes,' I said. 'It's because we grew up here, right?'

'And I spilled curry on my jacket,' she said. 'It's a white wool jacket. Mom said it's too hot to wear it today but I wanted to. And now it's ruined.'

'Oh,' I said. 'What size do you wear?'

'Size twelve,' she said. 'I'm only ten, but I'm tall.'

'And do you like blue?' I asked. Her dress and bangles were blue—firozi blue.

She nodded.

'Then I have the perfect jacket for you,' I said. 'It's exactly that blue, and it has gold buttons, and I bought it for a trip to India seven years ago, but I never wore it. It still has the price tags on!'

'I'm going to India this winter,' she said. 'I've never been before.'

'Then you have to wear it for me,' I said. 'Deal?'

'Deal!'

***

'Mini!' It was Masi, newly alighted from Beeji's car, along with Dad, Beeji and Bade Bauji. 'Is everything under control?'

'Yes,' I said. 'The tables and the food are all set. People are having appetizers and drinks. Ernie Uncle's guys are taking care of the cars and parking. We're just waiting for Vinnie and Manish.'

'So, why don't you get changed?' Masi said.

I had to admit—six hours of running around, serving samosas and arranging laddoos—had taken their toll. I was a hot mess—my sari was crumpled, my hair damp, and make-up smudged.

'It's OK, Masi,' I said.

'No,' she said. 'It isn't. Look, Vinnie got changed at the hotel room. You go upstairs and wear your blue lehenga, and freshen up. I know the house is packed but I'll make sure no one walks in on you.'

She looked pretty determined, so I gave in.

'Fine,' I said. 'I won't be long.'

It only took me fifteen minutes to get changed and comb out my hair, which, thanks to the vast amount of product the nice hairdresser had put in it yesterday, still looked smooth and stylish once I managed to get it dry.

I opened the blue velvet jewelry box with the gold kundan set in it—necklace, bangles, maangtika and earrings. They'd look great with what I was wearing. I held it up to my neck for a minute and looked in the mirror.

This is for your wedding, Mini.

Which event would definitely be a while.

But I could still wear *some* of it. I fastened the earrings on and put the rest away—they could wait for the day Mom had meant them for.

Then I found a little paper gift bag, folded the firozi pea coat into it, and covered it with tissue paper.

Perfect!

'That's better,' Masi said when I reappeared downstairs. 'I've been waiting to see you in that dress, Mini. And I'm not disappointed. Now, have you eaten anything?'

'No,' I said. 'I'll have lunch with everyone.'

'Have a vada,' Masi said. 'Then you can go help again.'

'In a minute,' I said, looking around for the little girl.

I felt a tug at my skirt and looked down to see her right next to me.

'There you are!' I said. 'Here's the jacket I promised you.'

She rummaged through the tissue and her face lit up when she saw the jacket.

'It's bee-you-tiful!' she breathed.

'You like that shade of blue?' I asked. 'It's called firozi!'

'Thanks,' said a woman standing next to her—the girl's mother I guess 'You're welcome,' I said.

'It's time *someone* wore that thing,' Masi said, with an impish grin. 'You ready for your vada now, Mini?'

'Yes, I am!'

The samosas had finally finished and a bunch of Beeji's friends were heating up the vadas from the janvasam and serving them up. Masi fixed me a plate with a crisp golden vada on it and a dollop of chutney next to it. I must have been starving because it tasted amazing.

'Mini,' said a familiar voice. It was Krishna Ji, the priest. 'Congratulations!'

'Thanks,' I said. "Would you like a vada?"

He shook his head, but pulled up a chair next to mine.

'I was very glad to do Vinnie's wedding,' he said. 'It's been a long time.'

I nodded. 'It has.'

'Last time I was in this house your Amma was sick,' he said. 'I remember I sat right here and had tea, and you asked me—you remember what you asked me?'

I knew exactly what I'd asked him.

'I asked for a miracle,' I said. 'I wanted her to live.'

'And I told you that certainly there will be a miracle,' he shook his head sadly. 'My faith, you know? I did not think anyone could refuse the wish of such a small child, not even God. So many years gone, and I still don't understand it.'

I smiled ruefully—for what was there to say?

'But do you know what your mom asked for that same day?' he asked.

'No,' I said.

'She had accepted it then—her fate. She was only worried about you all,' he said. 'Especially you, kanna. Your mom said: Krishna Ji, Vinnie is strong and tough, and she's nearly grown up—she'll be sad, but she'll be OK. But Mini, I just want my

285

Mini to be fine. She's so little, and she doesn't *talk*—I don't want her to be damaged by any of this. If only I could know that she will be fine.'

'What did you tell her?' I asked.

'I promised her sincerely that you would be,' he said. 'My faith, you know?'

I stared at him, at a loss for words.

'I can see now that your mom's wish came true,' he said. 'You are very fine. You are taking care of so many things for your dad, your sister. God may not have heard you, but he heard your mom. She would be so, so proud of you.'

I had tears in my eyes but I smiled at him through them.

'Thanks for telling me,' I said. 'It means a lot.' Just then there was a commotion outside.

'They're here!' Rachel said, peeking out through a window.

I gulped down the last vada and hurried to the front door. I wanted to turn on the string lights before Vinnie got a good look at the house!

The Lotus (driven by Manish this time) was parked in the driveway—they had arrived!

***

Vinnie had changed into Mom's old wedding lehenga. She looked so soft and radiant in the vintage pink and silver. Just as she was stepping out of the car there was a dramatic crack of thunder and it started to rain—again.

'Umbrellas!' I said and hurried over to the designated umbrella area—the cardboard box from Amazon.com was stacked with dripping floral umbrellas that been fully used but had never even made it past the foyer. Had they only arrived this morning? I pulled a soft pastel one with Monet's water lilies on it for Vinnie and hurried over to cover her before she got a drop of water on Mom's dress.

'Oh. My. God. Mini,' she said, her eyes shining. 'Everything looks amazing!'

Kristan was in the car with them, still clicking away. I handed Manish another umbrella to hold over Kristan. Those pictures had to turn out good!

'Everyone in the tent please—Vinnie and Manish have arrived!' That was the Iyers' friend Natarajan from the temple board. For a minute I was afraid there would be a stampede out of our single exit from the house, the front door. Then I saw that people were coming out of the garage door, down the deck, through the backdoor.

Would the rain stay out of the tent? If not, I wasn't sure how we could have everyone sit down together for lunch. I needn't have worried—the tent held. A volunteer group of umbrella ushers had sprung up at the garage door, where most of the traffic was making its way to the tent.

'These are the prettiest umbrellas I've ever seen,' said a sweet-faced lady in a hot pink kanjivaram.

'You're just like Megha—same to same,' said Chintu and Mintu Patel's mom, pinching my cheeks rather painfully. 'Carbon copy!'

'Mini!' Uncle Ernie strode over in a bright yellow rain

287

poncho—no flowery umbrella for him. 'You want to see this!'

'What …' I started to ask and then screamed insanely at the sight of the rental car with Canadian plates—and my Nanaji and Masi's twin boys Ari and Avi were descending from it.

'Nanaji, you made it!'

Masi came tearing out of the tent and wrapped the twin boys into her arms. She hadn't said a word when we lost contact with Nanaji at Heathrow Airport, but she must have been crazy worried.

'We took a flight to Montreal from London,' Nanaji explained. 'And drove down from there. What did we miss?'

'The ceremony is over, but everyone is here for the reception!' Masi said.

You should have seen Vinnie's face when Nanaji walked into the tent. You should have seen Nanaji's face when he saw Vinnie all dressed up in Mom's old wedding lehenga. Some things just cannot be expressed in words.

There was a line at the buffet table and people were serving themselves and sitting down at tables and chatting and having a good time.

But there was someone missing still.

'Did anyone see Vir?' I asked Dad. 'No,' he said. 'He was there at the temple though, wasn't he? He was driving my car!' I backed away quickly before Dad could say any more on that subject.

There were people to chat with, and food to eat, and pictures to pose in, but it didn't feel complete without Vir. Where was he?

'Vir?' Chintu said. 'I think he said he had to pick up a friend from Logan Airport.'

'Is he coming back?' I asked.

'I don't know,' he said.

I guess I'd have to wait and see.

Meanwhile, there were still more people coming into the tent—my neighbor Ina from number 12, and Siggy from up the hill, and Barbara from across the road, and Maurice from next door.

'So you pre-poned it?' Maurice asked. 'I was saying to Ina, I was saying—they're in trouble now with this weather. Was I right?'

'The main thing is they pulled it off—they're married,' Ina said. 'They did get married?'

'Yes, they did,' I said. 'I'm so sorry about all the traffic and noise, but we didn't have much of a choice …'

'No, no, don't even worry about it,' Siggy said. 'If there's anything we can do, just say the word …'

'Just stay, and eat something, and have fun,' I said. 'And go talk to Vinnie—she'll be thrilled to see all of you!'

'Hey, Vir, my man!' I could hear Manish from way over in the garage. The garage had turned into the bar because Alan and Ritchie were pouring drinks for whoever asked. They had a cooler filled with ice for the drinks, because the electricity had gone with the rainstorm—and they were clearly imbibing as much of the stuff as they were dispensing.

Vir was here!

Fairy Lights

I headed over to the garage, working my way through the crowd.

'I brought some gear,' I heard Vir say. 'A generator and amps, and an electric guitar, and a PA system. Thought it might come in handy.'

'That's awesome,' Manish said. 'You saved the music, dude. Let's set it up!'

'Hi Vir,' I said, having finally caught up to them.

He had changed into jeans and a button-down shirt.

'Mini, I want you to meet someone,' he said to me. 'This is Koyal Khanna.'

The petite girl with him, in jeans and a t-shirt and four-inch heels, smiled and waved her hand shyly as if unsure of her welcome. But it was her—it really and truly was THE Koyal Khanna! I have to say she looked very different in real life. Smaller somehow, though still extremely pretty.

'Hi,' I said.

Vir had gone all the way to Logan in the pouring rain to pick her up?

'You're so pretty!' she said. 'Vir said you were!'

This from the person voted Most Beautiful Face in India.

Yes, I had been reading more Bollywood gossip columns than were good for me.

'Thank you,' I said. 'Would you like to have a drink? Lunch is still warm, and we also have dessert ...'

'Later,' she said. 'I have to talk to you first.'

'Ookaay,' I said.

'I heard that you guys had a big misunderstanding because of me,' Koyal said, immediately getting to the meat of the matter. 'I got stuck in Boston but I wanted to tell you in person. There was nothing between Vir and me! We're just friends! Vir helped me and Tipu meet up in spite of our parents. That was all.'

'Tipu?' I asked.

'Yeah,' she said, smiling shyly. 'You know how Vir saw you one time only and he was a goner?'

'He was?' I asked.

'Of course he was,' she said. 'He told me all about it. It was like that when I saw Tipu too. But my parents don't like him because he isn't rich, or a big director, or Hindu.'

'Oh,' I said. 'He isn't?'

'No he's not,' she said. 'But he's very handsome. More handsome than Vir even, or at least more big and strong.'

I imagined a Mr Universe type like Arnold Schwarzenegger—only Indian. The mind boggled.

Koyal was still speaking. 'And he's Vir's senior from Mayo College so Vir helped us meet up while he was in Mumbai working with his dad and going to all these parties. Because my parents thought I was seeing Vir, they were OK, because you know, Vir *is* rich. But really it was Tipu and me all the time. And then even the media got it wrong. But Vir just thought it was funny and didn't care because he wasn't serious about anyone else, and it kept all the girls off his back if they thought he was serious about me.'

'Go on,' I said, drinking in this fascinating glimpse into Vir's life.

'But now that I see you I can tell why he wasn't interested in those stupid girls,' she said. 'Because you were over here waiting, and he had to come find you.'

Koyal Khanna clearly had very romantic notions of love and dating. But talking to her had taken a huge load off me. If I jumped on the spot right now I might even float off of the ground. I knew Vir enough to see that Koyal was not at all his type. She would drive him crazy in no time.

'Oh, please hold that dog,' Koyal shrieked suddenly. 'A dog bit my brother once, and I'm so scared of them!'

'I've got him,' I said. 'And he's friendly, see. Yogi, give paw!'

Yogi held out a paw, and tilted his head adorably, but Koyal was not going to touch him with a ten-foot pole.

'Koyal really likes homemade laddoos too,' Vir said. 'And her mom's not here to make sure she sticks to her diet. So, you want to go get some, Koyal?'

'Yes,' Koyal said, scanning the tent hungrily until she spotted the tiers of laddoos. 'I'm so going to get some.'

Vir had been talking with Ernie Uncle who looked smug about the fact that we were friends. He gave me a told-ya look before walking off and leaving me with Vir.

'You talked to Koyal,' Vir said.

'Yes,' I said.

Happy now? His eyes asked.

I smiled back at him—because, yes, I was.

'That is Koyal Khanna, Mini?' someone whispered in my ear. One of Beeji's friends with eagle eyes had recognized Koyal even in her jeans and t-shirt.

'Aunty, you can't tell anyone, you can't take photographs, you can't ask for autographs,' I said. Koyal was a guest in our house and I wasn't going to let anyone ogle her.

'Good luck with that,' Vir said.

***

The house glowed with the string lights strung around our trees.

The last group pictures had been taken, the last gift envelopes stashed safely away, and last autographs signed, and the last picture with Koyal Khanna taken (We won't show anybody the photos, beta, *no* one!). Koyal herself had eaten her fill of Beeji's laddoos, to Beeji's eternal pride.

Outside Avi and Ari and Rahul floated paper boats in the rain, water overflowing from the gutter.

In the garage Manish and his friends played the most amazing music. I sat beside Vir, Yogi curled up at my feet and listened to them play. I had no idea that they could sound like that.

And then Manish's friend Samar took centerstage. Samar was a Punjabi from Pakistan and he sang so beautifully that Beeji wept.

'How he sings, that Samar,' Beeji cried. 'That's what you call real singing, Mini, real singing!'

'Can we go to sleep, Mummy?' Avi asked Masi. The boys had had enough of the rain and were latched onto Masi from either side, literally dropping where they sat.

'I'll be back,' Masi said. 'What about you, Rahul? You want to rest too?'

'I'll rest inside with Avi and Ari from Mumbai,' Rahul said.

'They can lie down in Vinnie's old room,' I said. 'Is that OK, Preet?'

Preet was another one with tears in her eyes, and Jackie, who did not even understand a word of Punjabi. Upstairs the kids fell asleep, and outside it still rained. Then Manish sang one last song for Vinnie—one he had written especially for her. And that's when it hit me—the thing that dealing with the crisis had kept at bay all day long. Vinnie was leaving—for good. Things would never be the same again.

'Hey,' Vir said, and squeezed both my hands between his. 'You OK?'

I managed a teary smile—not all change was bad, after all.

Masi and Beeji brought out the rice for Vinnie to fling back over her head as she left the house. Beeji cried openly but I kept it together for a cheerful hug and wave—none of the traditional weeping or crying as they drove away down the street.

But I *so* got why people did that now. I totally got it.

Almost everyone else left then too, Preet and Rahul, Rachel and Amy, Jackie and Sue—even Koyal—Chintu had gallantly offered to drop her to her hotel before the storm got worse.

There was clean-up, of course. Alan and Ritchie had taken down the tent and scraped off all the china and rinsed it off with the garden hose and stacked it back into the Taylor Rental containers. Ditto the silverware, the napkins, and the stemware. Everything counted and stacked and piled, ready to be taken away on Monday. There would be no massive clean-up needed after all. The guys were definitely in the wrong business.

***

We regrouped inside after Beeji, Bauji and Bade Bauji left. Vir was still around, and no one complained about it. Avi and Ari had fallen asleep on the couch and had to be carried up into Vinnie's old room. Dad was in the kitchen making hot chocolate for Masi, Nanaji and himself—and the television was tuned to the weather channel for the latest update on the hurricane. The reporters were leaning against the wind in dripping rain slickers, and talking earnestly into the camera about how bad it was getting in New York. And it was *bad*.

I looked out the window—the rain here had slowed to a drizzle.

'The flowers!' I said. 'They're still outside!'

'Nothing will happen to them,' Masi said. 'It's just rain.'

'It's just rain now,' I said. 'Tomorrow it'll be a hurricane.'

'Vir, help her get them, will you?' Masi said. 'I'm going to try and talk to Vinod. Now that Vinnie's married, someone has to open his mind to the possibility of a career in design—for Mini.'

'You're definitely the best person for that job,' Vir said. 'Good luck!'

It was dark outside except for the light spilling from the windows of the house.

The tent was gone, the people, the tables, the dishes, the food.

But for the flowers it may have never been.

Vir and I gathered up the mums—raindrops glistening on their petals—and carried them indoors. They filled the living room with scent and color—a living reminder of Mom, and now, of Vir too.

Three armloads of flowers done, we went back outside to check the lawn for any remaining mums. There were none.

'What will you do with them?' Vir asked.

'Plant them in the window boxes,' I said. 'It's kind of a tradition.'

'Can I help?' Vir said.

'If you don't mind getting mud under your fingernails,' I said. 'And if I can help you move to your MIT dorm.'

'Deal!' Vir said.

I put a hand on his arm—I had something to say before the night ended—and I needed to say it now.

'Vir, I'm so sorry I didn't believe you, didn't even talk to you before assuming that you were ...'

'Stop, Mini,' he said.

'No, I won't,' I insisted. 'It really was my fault and I should have ...'

But then I did stop.

Because he pulled me to him and kissed me.

When we came up for air, he smiled down at me.

'Actually,' he said. 'It was my fault. I should never have pretended to date Koyal. It was stupid. And then I should have told you, and then ...'

He was *totally* ruining the moment.

I stepped in closer.

'Stop, Vir,' I said, and kissed him.

The string lights in the trees turned on suddenly, twinkling like starlight under the gloomy sky.

'Look at that,' I said in wonder. 'That wasn't us, was it?'

'Don't ask me,' Vir said. 'I've been seeing fairy lights ever since your dog chased my cat up that hill and ...'

'Oh, hi!' It was Kristan, the photographer. 'I just turned them on so I could take some final mood shots before I left.'

'What a good idea,' I said, trying to extricate myself from Vir's arms—except he didn't seem interested in letting go.

'I don't think I got a picture of you two together,' she said. 'This would make a nice composition too. You *are* together, aren't you?'

'Yes,' Vir said. 'Yes, we are.'

So we posed for the last picture she took on Vinnie's wedding day.

We took many pictures together afterwards, but that's the picture of us that Vir still carries in his wallet.

Me smiling radiantly in Vir's arms, string lights sparkling all around us.

I'm wearing Mom's earrings, and Masi's lehenga—and Vir's first kiss is still fresh on my lips.